"The Breakup Doctor series is getting better and better [with] each book..."

—Ai Love Books

"Phoebe Fox has given us characters that are lovably fallible, funny, and frazzled."

—Elisa Lorello,
bestselling author of Faking It *and* Why I Love Singlehood

"Multidimensional and full of life...a great series, and hard to put down."

—Comfy Reading

"One of the great things about this series is the growth and change we see in each of the characters. The books are not just the same old, same old where the characters aren't learning from their mistakes. They actually move forward with their lives and relationships change."

—Susan the Book Bag

"Right up with the great chick lit writers of all time."

—Hello, Chick Lit

The Breakup Doctor (#1)

"A heartwarming and funny story about friendship, romance, and the heart-wrenching reality of breakups—while busting out some spot-on dating advice along the way."

– *Liz Tuccillo*, Executive story editor of HBO's *Sex and the City*

"A pleasure from beginning to end. The Breakup Doctor is as wise as it is funny."

—Sherry Thomas, Bestselling Author of *The Luckiest Lady in London*

"Well-paced, entertaining and easy to get into...a thoroughly enjoyable, light chick lit read; perfect to pick up when you're going through a breakup or some relationship trouble yourself, because this story will undoubtedly put a smile on your face."

—A Spoonful of Happy Endings

"Humor, romance, and wonderful breakup advice...I was expecting a lighthearted chick lit story, which it is, but it is also so much more...delightful...sharp, snarky, funny, and fast-paced."

—Fresh Fiction

"Fascinating, funny and sometimes heartbreaking...Brilliantly written (and with some cracking advice if you find yourself experiencing relationship problems of your own...), this is a warm, witty, light and hugely enjoyable read."

—Bookaholic Confessions

"A charming and funny novel that you won't be able to put down."

—*Austin Woman* Magazine

"Fox doesn't just know how to write clearly and powerfully...she has real insight into relationships...It's a laugh-out-loud read and

Praise for *Heart Conditions*

"Relationship advice doesn't get much better than from the Breakup Doctor.... the best so far"

—Storeybook Reviews

"Delightful, witty, and chock-full of warmth—I loved every page."

—Amy FitzHenry, author of Cold Feet

"Fox really has gained her place in my favorite authors spot! There is just so much charm, humor, honesty about love, breakups, friendships and living life within the pages of *Heart Conditions.*"

—Mrs. Mommy Booknerd

"Many laugh out loud moments...I would heartily recommend a dose of this when you're feeling blue."

—The Book Magnet

"Chick lit that's well written, smart, and fun."

—Polished and Bubbly

"A fun filled, heartwarming, romantic novel."

—Kraftireader

"An amusing, snarky look at love in the 21st century."

—For the Love of Books

"A beautiful woman's fiction novel...so moving and compelling...This will pull your heartstrings"

—Kristen's Book Jungle

"Completely engaging...the perfect blend of lighthearted fun and poignant observations on the intersection self-worth, friendship, and love."

—Books and Brews

"Just when I thought I'd never see another perfect book in my lifetime, here comes Phoebe Fox! ... Phoebe Fox's writing is smooth and eminently readable... Fast-paced, witty, fun-lighthearted read."

—Ms. Bird Lady reviews

Praise for The Breakup Doctor series

"Phoebe Fox's books are like a box of fine chocolates. Not to be eaten quickly but to be savored and enjoyed."

—Fresh Fiction

"Fun and addicting...you will love this series! [Phoebe Fox is] right up with the great chick lit writers of all time."

—Hello, Chick Lit

"A book series you don't want to miss...not your typical chick lit...will make you laugh out loud... Fox's books are charming and funny, but they still manage to give us dating advice we can actually use."

—DatingAdvice.com

"On the whole, the series is funny, poignant, witty, smart, and memorable. Certainly an outstanding set of books to have and keep on your home library shelves."

—*Girl with Book Lungs*

likely will seem to speak directly to women of all ages—the love troubles mentioned here run from A to Z. Fox has a real winner here."

—*Scene* Magazine

"I was expecting a cute quick read; what I got was much more. Brook's character is great. She is well-rounded and her path to self-discovery through her breakup was realistic and at times heartwarming."

—Chick Lit Books

Bedside Manners (#2)

"As heartwarming as they are humorous—Fox's books offer more than the usual chick lit fare, with a lot of heart and a smart, relatable heroine in Breakup Doctor Brook Ogden."

—Sarah Bird, Author of The Boyfriend School and The Gap Year

"Love this humorous chick lit that highlights how our own adversities and challenges can create opportunities and passion for helping others—I so related to the Breakup Doctor!"

– Kimberly Seltzer, Dating Expert and former therapist

"Phoebe Fox has given us characters that are lovably fallible, funny, and frazzled, and has proven that when it comes to love and relationships of any kind, even the sanest of us get a little crazy."

– Elisa Lorello,
Bestselling Author of *Faking It* and *Why I Love Singlehood*

The Breakup Doctor Series

The Breakup Doctor (#1)
Bedside Manners (#2)
Heart Conditions (#3)
Out of Practice (#4)

Other Books by Phoebe Fox

A Little Bit of Grace
(Berkley Publishing)

The Way We Weren't
(coming November 2021 from Berkley Publishing)

Phoebe Fox

Author Phoebe Fox has been a contributor and regular columnist for a number of national, regional, and local publications, including the Huffington Post, Elite Daily, and SheKnows. A former actor on stage and screen, Phoebe has been suspended from wires as a mall fairy; was accidentally concussed by a blank gun; and hosted a short-lived game show. She has been a relationship columnist; a movie, theater, and book reviewer; and a radio personality, and is a close observer of relationships in the wild.

In addition to the Breakup Doctor series (*The Breakup Doctor, Bedside Manners, Heart Conditions, Out of Practice*), she's also the author of standalone novels *A Little Bit of Grace* and *The Way We Weren't* (Berkley Penguin), and—as Tiffany Yates Martin—of the bestselling *Intuitive Editing: A Creative and Practical Guide for Revising Your Writing*. She currently lives in Austin, Texas, with her husband and two excellent dogs. Visit her at **phoebefoxauthor.com**.

Heart Conditions

Phoebe Fox

Chapter One

"Grab that mousetrap for me, Rae Ann, would you?" I asked my first client Monday morning as we sat opposite each other in my home office. Before she'd arrived I'd spring-loaded the trap and left it by the chaise where she sat.

She eyeballed the thing uneasily, the mousetrap primed to snap at the slightest movement. "Can you hand me a pencil or something to set it off first?"

"Just pass it over, okay?"

Rae Ann Wilson had been coming to me for several months now, after her ex had broken up with her, but Rae Ann wasn't letting herself begin to move on at all. Even after almost six months she couldn't stop contacting him and obsessing over his every move on social media as he dated seemingly half of Cape Coral.

She chewed her lip, looking around the office. "Do you have some gloves?"

"No. Can't you please just get it for me? I want it." I held out a hand.

To my surprise, Rae Ann took a deep breath and then reached for it, and for just a moment I second-guessed my little gambit.

And then at the last second she reared away.

"No, Brook, I can't. It'll snap shut on my fingers. I'm really sorry," she said.

I let out the breath I'd been holding. "So you know better than to reach out for something that is clearly set up to hurt you."

She looked bewildered for a moment, and then her expression cleared. "Paul."

I nodded, then leaned over and tapped the trap with my pen, and it snapped shut so fast and hard we both startled.

I lifted it, still dangling from my pen, and handed it to her. "Next time you pick up the phone or get onto your computer to call or monitor Paul, I want you to look at this mousetrap. Keeping tabs on Paul is only hurting yourself, and you're too smart to keep doing that."

"Well, now you make it just seem foolish."

"Never foolish." I shook my head. "You feel the way you feel, and you love him still—it's natural to want to know what he's doing."

"God, yes."

"But just because you feel this way doesn't mean he still does," I said as gently as I could. "It's one of the hardest truths, the most difficult part of breakups—he's moving on. You've got to accept that and let him go, so you can do the same—and be whole on your own. So you'll be ready when the *right* guy shows up."

The words caught in my throat, but Rae Ann didn't notice. She swallowed hard against the tears I could see in her eyes.

"He *was* the right guy. There isn't anyone else out there for me."

"Oh, Rae Ann...Of course there is, honey." The endearment slipped out, but I no longer worried about little therapeutic breaches like that. The Breakup Doctor practice wasn't like my old practice. It wasn't like any mental health practice I ever imagined I'd have, actually, but it turned out I had a knack for helping people through bad breakups. Maybe because I'd had a few spectacularly bad ones of my own.

She shook her head adamantly. "No. I was single for four *years* before I met Paul. Do you know how hard it is to meet people in this town?"

Oh, yes. I did. As a retirement, snowbird, and tourist hotspot, Fort Myers made dating challenging if you were older than twenty-one and younger than seventy-five. "I'll admit this is a tougher town than some to find a relationship. But it's not impossible. You met Paul, right? That proves it can happen."

"We were working together! And now I work at home! How am I supposed to meet anyone sitting at my desk all day in my robe and slippers with my *cat?*"

I lifted my eyebrows. "Well, for starters, we need to get you out of your pajamas."

"What's the point?" she said dully.

"The point is how you feel about yourself, Rae Ann. No one feels their best sitting around all day like they just rolled out of bed. When you worked at an office, why did you get up and shower every day and get dressed and put on makeup?"

Rae Ann shrugged. "I had coworkers. I wouldn't want other people to see me looking all sloppy."

I feigned bewilderment. "Why not?"

She shot me an incredulous stare. "Because it hardly looks professional, does it? If I don't look like I take care of myself, why would anyone take me seriously?"

I leaned forward in my chair. "So why isn't your opinion of yourself, how *you* feel, every bit as important as your colleagues'?"

Rae Ann opened her mouth, and then shut it again.

"Do you feel confident in your robe, Rae Ann?" I asked. "Do you feel put-together? Competent? Pretty?"

After a moment she shook her head.

"I have a little bit of homework for you, okay?" I went on. "This week I want you to pretend you're going into work every day. Take a shower, do your hair, wear a nice outfit—whatever you used to do when you were based out of an office."

"Okay," she said slowly. "I guess I can do that."

"I also want you to meet someone. One person—I don't care if it's your bank teller or the grocery store clerk or the UPS deliveryperson. But I want you to find out just a little something about that person—their name, why they came here, a hobby, their favorite food—I don't care. Can you do that?"

She looked doubtful. "You mean like a man? You want me to hit on a bag boy?"

"I don't want you to hit on anyone, necessarily. And no, I don't care if it's male or female or otherwise. We're just going to get you back into the habit of engaging with people. It's so easy when you work at home to fall into the rabbit hole. Some people don't even leave the house till they're desperate for groceries."

For the first time all morning a tiny grin touched her lips. "Well, I'll be honest—sometimes I think if I didn't have Mr. Theodore, I could go days without ever speaking aloud."

I smiled back. "We're going to see if we can get you into the habit of talking to more than your cat, okay? I know you love Paul, but he's moved on. It's time you start to, too."

My own advice echoed uncomfortably in my ears.

"Yeah," she said in a small voice. "I know." Her eyes filled up again, but her spine straightened, and for the first time since I'd met her she looked a little less beaten and wounded.

When Rae Ann let herself out—tucking the sprung mousetrap into her purse as a reminder—I leaned back in my chair, a breath escaping me like steam hissing from a kettle.

Breakthroughs like this were the best part of what I did, but Rae Ann's session had left me feeling like a hypocrite. How could I advise her to let go of her ex when I was having so much trouble doing the same with mine?

Six months ago I screwed up a budding relationship with Ben Garrett, a genuinely good man I was coming to care about, because I was too afraid to trust my feelings. I hurt Ben badly enough that I'd been afraid he'd never want to see me again. And for a long time he hadn't.

But then little by little we'd started to stitch together a fragile sort of friendship—he'd even started trusting me to watch Jake again, his hundred-pound Great Pyrenees I'd fallen in love with while we were dating, on Ben's frequent trips to out-of-town construction sites for the buildings he designed. I was starting to believe we might get a second chance.

And then came Perfect Pamela.

Ben's new girlfriend was the kind of woman you never, ever want the ex you still have very complicated feelings for—despite the fact that it was you who torpedoed the relationship—to date. The perfect height—an inch or two above average, but not so tall that men were threatened by her. Long red hair with a slight curl. Vivid green eyes and teeth so perfect you'd ask for the name of her orthodontist, except that you already know that she never wore braces a day in her life.

You know this only because you actually *did* ask for the name of her orthodontist the first time you met her, because your blabbering tongue wouldn't stay in your mouth with your nervousness upon meeting the perfect specimen who replaced you, and you vomited out a number of inane comments like this, and she answered with a disarming smile so appealing that you yourself felt a little stirring of attraction to her, despite the fact that you are solidly heterosexual, and she said with charming self-deprecation, "Believe it or not, I never had braces—my parents have these ridiculously straight teeth they passed on to all us kids."

Oh—and it turns out she's *a brain surgeon*. For real. On kids. A pediatric brain surgeon with a supermodel's body and the soul of Mother Teresa.

And you liked her. Despite how much you desperately, desperately wanted to hate her.

Once Perfect Pamela came into the picture, logic and my own eyes told me that my shot at a second chance with Ben had fizzled—a conclusion cemented when he'd dropped Jake off again last night en route to a romantic getaway weekend with her in New York City. And yet I couldn't let go of a stubborn shred of hope.

Was I any different from Rae Ann?

My phone intercom buzzed and I heard Jake's call-and-response bark echoing from the other side of the house. Often he sat in on sessions with clients, but Rae Ann was a cat person.

"Delivery here for you," my intern's voice announced. "Also, your next client is running late."

Grateful for the distraction from my thoughts, I let myself into the adjoining waiting room—formerly known as the front guest bedroom before my home renovations—to see an enormous beribboned potted plant perched on the reception desk.

"Paige?"

"This just came for you," said a voice from behind the plant. A blond head poked around the side. "It's very big."

I'd hired Intern Paige early in the fall, when the logistics of managing my growing Breakup Doctor practice, with private consultations, my weekly newspaper column, twice-weekly radio appearances on KXAR, and the support groups I ran, was becoming more than I could handle alone. A grad student in psychology at nearby FGCU, Paige had easily assuaged my initial fears about letting go of total control over the logistics of my practice with her competence, drive, focus, and intelligence. But she'd been working with me long enough now that I knew not to fire off my knee-jerk response to her observation (*Is it? I hadn't noticed*). Comedic sarcasm flew right by my serious-minded assistant.

"Yes, I see that," I said instead, coming closer to look for a tag. There was none, but it wouldn't be the first time a former client had dropped off a thank-you gift. "Who's it from?"

Paige stood and handed me a card. "He said to give this to you directly."

I recognized the familiar handwriting immediately, and my heart flipped.

I looked up at Paige, my mouth dry. "He brought this himself? It wasn't a deliveryman?"

"I don't know. He wasn't wearing a uniform. Should I not have accepted it?"

"No, it's fine." I looked again at the envelope in my hand and noticed the edges of it were trembling. I cleared my throat. "What, um...what did the man look like?"

Paige closed her eyes and began reciting as if he were painted on the back of her eyelids: "Tall—about six-one—average build, but on the thin side, brown hair, cut short—maybe a couple of inches—but longer in front. Green eyes. Really green." She opened her eyes again. "Sorry I can't be more specific."

I barely registered her star-witness description. The main reason I'd second-guessed my relationship with Ben had been standing out in my waiting room minutes ago, feet away from me.

Michael. The man I hadn't seen since he'd dumped me by phone two years ago.

A month before we made it to the altar.

"Thanks," was all I said, and dropped the envelope back on her desk as if it were coated in anthrax. "I'll read this later. How late did Mr. Westmoreland say he'd be?"

"Five minutes, but he was calling from College and Cleveland, so I think it'll be more like nine to eleven."

"Thanks, Paige," I said. "I'll be in my office." I stopped in the doorway and turned to see she had disappeared behind the plant again. "How about if I help you move this onto the floor?" I offered, coming back over to the desk.

She popped back up. "I wasn't sure if you wanted me to leave it here."

Any other time I'd have had to hide a smile, but as I bent my head to help lift the plant the sick feeling in my stomach overrode any amusement.

...

Later that afternoon, once Intern Paige had left for the day and the door had closed behind my last client, I came back out into the waiting room.

I'd managed to push away thoughts of Michael for most of the day, the way my problems almost always spiraled into their own compartments while I worked with my clients on theirs. But now the envelope balanced on the corner of the desk drew me to it like a mesmerizing fire I couldn't help inching closer to, a cream-colored tongue sticking out at me.

Michael had moved away shortly after we broke up—I didn't want to know where, just that he was gone. The last time I'd seen him was two years ago May. May 4, to be exact—a date I could never forget because of Michael's stupid repeated joke: "May the fourth be with you." At 7:43 a.m. That was when I'd left his apartment—the one I thought I'd be living in with him weeks later—with a frustrated admonition for him to *please* not forget our cake tasting that afternoon.

He'd been tangled up in the sheets, logy with sleep and lovemaking, after a late-night gig at the Buddha Bar the night before with his band, the Dogs of Society. He'd blinked sleepy green eyes at me. "Okay."

I stopped in the doorway of the bedroom with a huffing sigh, hands on hips like a fishwife. "I'm *serious*, Michael. Don't space this out, okay? I'm not asking you to do much for this wedding—just *please* be there. Okay? Michael?"

He started awake from a doze. "Okay, Brook. Bakery. Four o'clock. Cake. I get it."

Those would have been the last words we'd ever spoken, except for the phone call I got from him eight hours later, en route to the Sweet Dreams Bakery.

"Brook, I'm sorry. I can't do this."

An annoyed sigh had torn out of me. "Oh, for God's sake, Michael—it's cake. Surely you can do cake, at least?"

There was a long silence, and then: "No, not the cake. All of it. Any of it. I can't go through with this."

Ice had seemed to crystallize in every cell of my body. "Okay. That's fine," my mouth said. And I hung up.

That was the epilogue on our two-year relationship. The way I dealt with adversity back then was to push it way down deep and carry on, which I did: I went on to the cake tasting, though I don't remember actually tasting any of the expensive pastries I put in my mouth. The next day I called all the vendors to cancel their services, and had blindly put a down payment on a house within two weeks.

This house. Where the man it had taken me two years, two shattered relationships, and a near nervous breakdown to get over had walked in out of the blue today and left a funeral plant and whatever he'd written in his letter.

I picked up the envelope and traced my fingertips over my name in his bold scrawl, almost as familiar as my own. Holding it to my nose, I imagined I could smell Michael's distinctive sandalwood scent on it.

In a sudden movement I flipped it over and slid a finger into the gap at the edge, yanking it along the seal—and then retracting my hand with a hiss. Paper cut.

Figured.

Holding the bleeding finger away, I gingerly opened the envelope and pulled out the note inside, a business card fluttering to the floor that I ignored.

A forlorn-looking big-eyed LOL cat. Inside the printed message read, *I is sowwy.*

I grimaced, sucking on my finger, fury at the offensive "apology" warring with a strange kind of relief. Michael didn't know me at all anymore if he thought this card could breach the Great Wall of China of my resentment.

But then I read his handwritten note:

There's no card adequate for this kind of apology, so instead I went with the worst one I could find. Might as well continue my run of bad judgment.

Flowers start out beautiful and then they die, and that seemed like pretty horrible symbolism after what I did, so this is a peace lily. Unlike me, it doesn't need much attention and will happily thrive on its own. And I like the name. I'm hoping for some peace between us, Brook. You were the best thing that ever happened to me, and you didn't deserve what I did.

—M

I swallowed hard and lowered the card in cold fingers.

If he'd sent some kind of justification for his actions I'd have been enraged. If he'd begged me for another chance I'd have thrown away the card he gave me and ignored all further contact.

Instead his note was perfect—just the right amount of mea culpa, asking for nothing, and making me laugh.

He knew me through and through.

I leaned down to retrieve the card that had fallen.

MICHAEL COOPER, PROMOTIONS

Below the name and meaningless job title was a phone number with an area code I didn't recognize, and an email address. On the back was a note in his familiar block handwriting:

Anytime you say, I'll meet you anywhere. All I ask is that you listen.

I needed to stop this right now—before, like Rae Ann, I reached for something I knew was going to hurt me. Opening up Pandora's box with someone who'd betrayed me completely wasn't going to lead to anything healthy. The best thing to do now was leave it alone.

But my situation wasn't the same as Rae Ann's, a voice inside reminded me. I wasn't obsessing over Michael (or I hadn't been, until today). And I wasn't in danger of opening up that wound—I was simply considering an opportunity for the closure that might lessen an old pain. My brain had already done the work of healing, but my heart still needed it—and lately I'd started listening when that long-neglected organ weighed in.

I picked up my cell phone and dialed.

Chapter Two

I did not call Michael.

I called Sasha. Of course.

My best friend answered on the first ring, and I was talking before she said a word:

"Michael's back."

"What?!"

I took a shaky breath. "He dropped off a plant this morning."

"He was *at your house*? Did you see him? What did he say? How are you? Are you okay? Why the hell did he bring you a plant—you kill everything. Is he still there? We're coming over."

"No! I mean not Stu. I can't talk about this with him yet. He still wants to kill Michael."

My brother had always had a protective streak, but since he'd started dating Sasha this past year, it had ballooned into something a bit volatile where she and I were concerned. Last summer he'd sustained cracked ribs and a sprained ankle after he tried to intervene when Chip Santana—my greatest mistake—had launched himself at us in a blind rage on my back porch.

"Then *I'm* coming. I'll be there in seven minutes. Don't move."

True enough, exactly seven minutes later I heard my friend, who could have given Lewis Hamilton a run for his money behind the wheel, screech her car into my driveway, and within seconds the front door crashed open. Sasha stood there spraddle-legged, eyes blazing, and somehow she'd procured a Taser that she wielded in her right hand.

"Where is that son of a bitch?" she bit out, and frankly if I'd been Michael and I were standing in front of this Valkyrie, I'd have wet my pants.

"I'm so glad you're here," I managed.

And then the tears came. Hard.

By the time it was over we were sitting on my sofa, Sasha's arm around me, Jake lying calmly at our feet after Sasha commanded him to "Go lie down, buddy." My eyes were swollen like puffer fish...but I felt weirdly lighter.

"Well, *that* was a long time coming," Sasha said as my sobs tapered off. "Feel better?"

"Yeah," I said, surprised. "I do."

She nodded once. "Okay. Now that you got that out . . . what's next?"

"I don't know, Sash. Do I see him? No—what would be the point? But why does he even want to? Guilt, I guess. Do I even want to see him? I don't know. But should I? I don't think 'should' really means much in this situation."

She was leaning back against the sofa, arms crossed, watching me. "Did you need me here, or are you having a perfectly adequate therapy session with yourself?"

"Sorry," I said. "I'm just trying to work through my feelings."

She slapped a hand to her heart. "Oh, padawan. I'm so proud."

Since my spectacular breakdown last winter after my rebound boyfriend, Kendall, dumped me via text message, Sasha had taken a deeply vested interest in my awakening emotional side. Meanwhile *I* was still trying to deal with what felt like an out-of-control elevator jerking up and down the shaft. "I don't know what to do, Sash," I said finally. "What do I do?"

"You see him, of course."

"What?" It was the last thing I expected her to say.

"Honey, two years ago the most impactful relationship you've ever had imploded into a black hole. Now you have the chance to find out why. You're a therapist: You have to analyze everything—and you need answers. So go get some."

"But what about reopening old wounds? Mining a spent quarry? Going into the crack den when you know you're a crack addict?"

Sasha lifted one eyebrow. "Do you think maybe you get too into the metaphors sometimes?" I glared at her. "I'm just saying, you can toss out every tried-and-true aphorism in your arsenal, but you know from your own practice that every person is different—every situation is unique. And for you, with Michael, I think you need to find out what happened."

"So...what? I should call him? Meet up?"

Sasha shot me a skeptical glance. "Not looking like that, you shouldn't."

I reached my fingers up to press under my swollen eyes. "Well, obviously I'll fix the damage—I'm not a total idiot."

"It's going to take a bit more than a splash of water and some concealer."

"No. We are not doing a makeover montage. This is not reality TV."

"It's better. It's reality. Starring you. Hosted by me. You lucky dog."

"No, Sash."

She frowned at my face. "Honey, no offense, but he caught you...well, not the way you want to run into an ex. This"—she waved a hand up and down my body—"does not say, 'Eat your heart out.'"

I threw up my hands. "Fine. You win. Come on—you can pick something out of my closet." I stood and Jake scrambled to my side, thrusting his skull under my hand so I could put it to good use.

"Oh, no. This requires a bit more than that."

"You mean—"

"Get your purse. We're going shopping."

...

Four hours later, I had shopping bags dripping from my arms—the whole shebang: new clothes, shoes, even underwear. Sasha insisted that confidence came from the inside out, and by "inside" she apparently meant "the crack of my ass." The lacy little thongs she'd insisted I buy bisected my buttocks, but I had to admit they made me feel sexier than the bikini briefs I usually wore.

She'd also engineered a stop at the MAC counter, where she bustled her usual makeup artist over to me—a gorgeous six-foot-three woman named Trixie—with instructions to give me a "fierce daytime look that will make her ex's tongue fall out but look totally natural."

"Oh, sugar, I've been there," Trixie said with an exaggerated roll of her eyes. "Sit yourself down, honey, and let Trixie fix you up."

Trixie was a bit of a magician herself—when she was finished I looked like I'd stepped out of the pages of *Glamour* magazine, but no matter how closely I examined my face, I couldn't quite detect what product had given me such an elegant, polished look. I didn't look made up so much as I looked like the best possible me.

I bought everything she'd used on me, reflecting that a year ago I wouldn't have been able to swing even a fancy lipstick. My Breakup Doctor practice had changed my life in more ways than one.

"You come back and see Trixie if you need a little refresher on how to paint all that on, sugar," the woman said, blowing us a kiss as we left the counter.

Back at my house we did a test run of the whole thing: makeup, hair (Sasha trimmed my bangs and smoothed them into a side part that skimmed my right eye in a really sexy little swoop I wouldn't have thought my usual frizzy waves could pull off), and the outfit: faded skinny jeans with some fraying here and there that actually looked worn-in, instead of intentional; a royal blue knit tank over my new professionally fitted Freya bra that made my modest boobs look truly impressive; and a fitted hot-pink jacket that nipped my waist into nothing. "Bold colors indicate confidence, and they really make your complexion glow," was Sasha's verdict.

She had insisted on nude five-inch pumps, which I'd tried to veto, but they were surprisingly comfortable with their one-inch platform, and I had to admit they took the whole ensemble up a few notches. "Plus they'll make you an inch or two taller than he is, and that will make him feel literally and metaphorically small," she said with a satisfied smirk. She finished the look with a plain silver chain that dipped below the tank top's neckline, a chunky pink watch, and a wide blue leather bracelet.

I would never have put any of it together, but it looked...spectacular. I felt like a Hollywood star, effortlessly stylish while out picking up my kids from day care and trying to avoid the paps.

"How in the hell did you do that?" I said, staring at my image wonderingly in my full-length mirror. "I look amazing. But casual amazing."

Sasha preened as she made a minute adjustment of my pushed-up jacket sleeves. "You have your forte; I have mine. *Now* you can call that jackass and arrange to meet."

She was dead right—since I'd learned to stop running from my feelings, stop pushing them down and pretending everything was okay, I knew I needed to see Michael to finally close that chapter of my life. And *this* was the image I wanted to present to the man who'd left me devastated: this confident, polished, poised woman in the mirror. The woman, in fact, that I hoped I was well on my way to actually becoming.

I turned away from my reflection to face her. "Thanks, Sash. I'm sorry I dragged you away from Stu all evening."

Sasha's hair cascaded over her face as she bent her head to closely examine my shoes. "No big deal."

Something about her tone was odd. "Everything okay with you two?" Although I'd come to admit the two made a bizarrely excellent (if sex-crazed) couple, since they'd gotten together I lived in constant low-grade terror of what would happen if they ever broke up. My brother and my best friend were the two people closest to me in the world—halves of my heart. I couldn't imagine being divided between them.

"No, we're good. The two of us are just fine."

Something niggled at me in the way she said it, but she had raised her face up to meet my gaze, and her expression was placid.

"You realize you've been Breakup Doctoring me all day long," I said.

She gave me a wink. "Where do you think I learned it?"

"So...you think I should call him now? While I look like this?"

"I think"—Sasha took me by the shoulders and turned me to face my reflection, meeting my eyes in the mirror as she stood beside me— "that you can look like this anytime you want to. If you'd just put a little effort into it once in a while." I stepped on her toe with one of my platforms, and she smacked my arm, then squeezed it. "And that you should call him whenever you feel ready to face him and get the answers you deserve."

I nodded, wrapping an arm around her waist and giving her a one-armed hug. "Thanks, pal," I whispered, my throat tight. "I will."

One side of Sasha's mouth lifted in a sadistic smile. "But take your time. First you should make that bastard squirm and let him see what it's like to live in limbo for a while."

Chapter Three

Mental unrest was no excuse for missing Sunday-night dinner at my parents' house. Actually, there *was* no excuse short of death, so although I suggested that Sasha hang out and we'd drive over together later, she left shortly after I removed all my new finery.

"Stu and I have some stuff to get done today," she said, retrieving her Brahmin bag from my entry table.

"Oh—well, why don't I come help?"

"No, that's okay. This isn't fun stuff."

"I don't mind," I said, grabbing my own purse. "You spent your whole day firefighting my problems; let me at least return the favor."

But she tugged my purse out of my hands and set it gently back on my hall table. "Brook, really—it's couple stuff, okay?"

"Oh." Every now and then these little reminders that Stu and Sasha now had a special relationship that no longer included me still stung. I masked it with a wink. "I get it. It's sexytime, right? You've only done it twice so far today?" Sasha loved grossing me out with tales of her and my brother's busy, acrobatic sex life, but I'd started beating her to the punch.

She gave a thin smile. "Something like that."

She was out the door before I could investigate any further, waving over her shoulder and saying she'd see me at my folks' house in a few hours.

•••

I was a few minutes late—a cardinal sin, according my punctilious mom. She was tearing lettuce into a colander when I came into the kitchen.

"Hey, Ma. What can I do?"

She didn't pause. "Well, I needed some help with the salad, but I went ahead and did it since you and Stu weren't here."

No mention of Sasha being late too. She could never do wrong in my mom's eyes.

I didn't react to the small poke, though. Mom and I had been forging a much healthier relationship lately—sometimes I even actually felt we were getting close—and part of the reason was that I had learned to be less oversensitive to minor provocations. Mom was who she was.

"Sorry—I just lost track of the time. Can I finish it up for you?"

Mollified, she shook her head. "That's okay—but setting the table would be a help."

"You got it."

While I laid out place mats, cloth napkins, and silverware in the adjacent dining room, I asked about her latest production at the Neapolitan Theatre, where she'd regularly been performing since returning to her lifelong love of acting about a year ago. Predictably, her face lit up.

"We open this show March twenty-fourth," she said, "so make sure you keep the night free. I'd like you and your brother and Sasha to come to the cast party afterward."

"And what about Dad?" I said lightly. This time last year Mom had unexpectedly walked out on him—on our family, as far as us kids were concerned at the time—from some long-suppressed desire she'd had to be on her own. After the run of her first show she'd come back, but only for half the week, the rest of the time living in theater housing in Naples. Since then she and Dad seemed solid, but I was scared to think she might be gradually moving out on us for good.

"Of course your father," Mom said. "Don't be dense."

I breathed out. "Okay. Sounds great." And that reminded me—I went out to the front hall where I'd left my purse on the purse shelf (yes, such a thing existed in Mom's house, along with the key bowl, the coat hooks, and the shoe caddy) and retrieved the little figurine I'd found in a local boutique: a magnificent bird in orange-tinted glass, with widespread wings and a long graceful neck.

"I got you something, Ma," I said, coming back into the kitchen. She looked up from chopping carrots and I held the figurine up into the light from the overhead fixture so she could see its warm glow. "It's a phoenix. Because you brought your theater career back from the ashes, and you're spreading your wings onstage."

Mom stopped chopping, staring at the little glass figure.

"Because you're doing *Glass Menagerie*," I explained into her silence. "You know...how Amanda has the glass animal collection...?" I felt stupid standing there holding it up for her, like a little kid with a straight-A report card desperate for Mommy's approval.

Finally Mom nodded, blinking. "I know. Yes. Brook, that's..." She put the knife down and carefully wiped her hands on a towel, then reached for the figurine. Her fingers ran over its smooth neck, across its wings, rubbing the tiny intricate feathers indented into the glass. "It's beautiful," she murmured after a moment. "Thank you." She reached up with the hand not clutching the bird and briefly touched my chin, then leaned in to plant a quick peck on my cheek.

From Mom, that was the equivalent of a sloppy hug. I reached up and gave her arm a quick squeeze. "It was my pleasure, Mom. I'm proud of you."

It was such an unusual moment of connection, I almost blurted out what was still preying on me: that I'd seen Michael. One of my mom's palliative "oh, honeys" would go a long way toward healing the wound his appearance had picked the scab off of. But things were getting uncomfortably mushy for the Ogden household, so I volunteered to go to the garage fridge for the drinks and let Dad know dinner was imminent.

I found him in his usual state: bent over a woodworking project, safety goggles over his eyes outlined by flecks of wood chips and sawdust clinging to his skin. When he heard the door shut behind me he looked up from the long, thin piece of wood he was turning and switched off his lathe.

"Doll!" he cried, a smile stretching his face. With the goggles on and his sweat-shined scalp shining from beneath thinning hair, he looked like nothing so much as a Minion.

"Hi, Daddy," I said, going over to him. "What are you working on?"

"Oh, a rocking chair. What do you think?" He held up a perfectly rounded spindle, gesturing with it to a line of them carefully aligned on a towel on his workbench.

"They're beautiful. I love the darker wood." I didn't say what popped to my mind: *Why are you making another rocking chair when you never sit in the ones you have?* My father was always making something in his shop, and nine times out of ten it was something for Mom. But years ago he'd labored for months over two perfect, intricately wrought wooden rocking chairs and presented them to her at Christmas, bubbling with excitement as he told her they were for the two of them to sit and relax and enjoy the life they'd created together.

For all that he adored my mom more than anything on earth, even I knew that she wasn't the sit-and-rock type.

But my mother exclaimed over the workmanship, the beauty of the chairs, and my father's thoughtfulness. She'd had him carry them immediately to their front porch, where she settled into one and insisted he join her in the other. While we kids watched, they rocked for a few moments, sharing the kind of smile I remembered feeling uncomfortable over as a child. Dad knew her best after all.

But that was the last time Mom had ever sat in them, to my knowledge. They still resided on the porch, but as décor more than anything else. I don't think any of us ever even really saw them anymore, like old familiar wallpaper.

I ran my fingers over the perfectly smooth length of the spindle my dad held. "I think Mom's pretty happy with the ones you made her last time, Daddy. I don't know if she'd want to replace them."

My father pushed the goggles to his forehead, sending wisps of hair up over them in crazy directions, enjoyment sparking in his eyes. "Sometimes people don't really know what they need until you give it to them, sweetheart."

"Okay, Daddy." There was no deterring him once he'd started a project.

"Dinner ready?" he asked.

"Almost. Stu and Sasha aren't here yet. I came out to grab drinks." If it was tempting to tell Mom about Michael, it was almost impossible not to blurt it out to my dad. He'd always been my listening ear, the one who let me talk things out with no judgment, no commentary at all really, just a receptive, loving sounding board for me to figure out my own feelings about something. But Mom was sun of his universe, Dad her happily orbiting moon. Even if I could trust him not to say anything about it, I didn't want to burden him with keeping something from her—and there were too many hot buttons with my mom around Michael and the canceled wedding (and my parents' lost deposits) for me to want to open that Pandora's box.

"I'll get cleaned up, sweetheart. Let your mom know." He took off the goggles and the lab coat he wore to protect his clothing and headed back to the utility sink he'd installed years ago in the garage to keep from mussing "your mom's nice clean floors."

By the time I came back through the foyer with my arms full of bottles and cans, Sasha was sitting on the hall bench, bent over her shoes.

"Hey," I said. I heard my brother in the kitchen talking to Mom. "You're lucky you're you—I bet Stu's getting an earful right now for being late."

"Yeah." She didn't look up from slowly untying her other shoe, glacially prying it off.

"I didn't call Michael yet," I said sotto voce. "I'm going to let him dangle—as long as I can, anyway. I have a feeling curiosity's going to get the better of me before I—" Sasha finally eked her shoes off and raised her head, and I stopped cold. She looked...absent, her eyes faraway, and her face was so pale her makeup looked like splotches of color on her skin.

"Sash! What's wrong?"

She shook her head. "Nothing."

"Don't give me that. What's the matter?"

"Shh!" she hissed, making a chopping gesture with her hand. "It's fine."

She stood and propelled herself past me, disappearing into the kitchen. When I followed, I found her leaning on the counter looking unconcerned, Stu ribbing Mom about something she'd said, one arm around her, and his usual easy grin on his face.

"What up, suck-up," he said when he caught sight of me. "I see you did our job to get on Mom's good side." He pointed his chin toward the table I'd set earlier.

"Someone had to, since you were *late*," I retorted automatically, but the tension in my belly refused to uncoil—even when Stu pulled me in for his usual greeting noogies.

We all filed noisily into the dining room, and as we passed the dishes and served ourselves, Mom went around the table in her customary grilling of each of us on our weeks. Sasha chirped out something about the paper and some story she was working on. Mom smiled and nodded, always a rapt audience for my best friend, while Stu and Dad dug obliviously into the spaghetti and meatballs.

But I knew my best friend. Despite her perky delivery, her eyes remained unsettlingly blank—and yet somehow I was the only one who seemed to notice.

...

After dinner we three kids washed the dishes, per tradition, while Mom put away the leftovers and wiped every surface to clinical sterility. Dad, who used to wander back out to his workshop after family dinner, or sit outside on their screened lanai beside the pool and read the paper, was clearly trying to change his habits. But he wound up instead lurking like a beneficent ghost around the kitchen, uselessly prodding at tasks he didn't quite know how to finish, like gathering the place mats, only to stand holding them in confusion, not knowing where they went.

I tried throughout the rest of the evening to corral Sasha alone, but I finally gave up. It wasn't going to happen while we were held snug to the bosom of my family. But when she and Stu made motions to leave, I grabbed my purse and was right behind them. Mom and Dad walked us to the door to say good-night, and while Dad followed his usual fierce hug around my waist with ones for Stu and Sasha, my mom surprised me by leaning in to give one to me.

"Good night, honey," she said. "Thank you for the phoenix. I love it."

I patted her shoulder awkwardly, pleased but disconcerted by her warm words. "I'm glad, Mom. You're welcome."

Outside I tried to snag Sasha before she got into the car, but she stuck to Stu as if she'd been glued there. He let her in on the passenger side of his Jeep and shut her door. She waved goodbye but didn't lower the window; it was like trying to have an intimate conversation with a bank teller at the drive-through.

"Everything all right?" I asked Stu casually as he walked around the car. " You guys okay?"

"Yeah. Why?"

Eh. Asking Stu emotion questions was like asking a chimp about chess. "Just asking. We didn't get to talk much tonight."

Stu looked at me as if I'd turned into a vacuum cleaner. "We talked all night long."

I sighed. "Night, Stuvie." Sasha was staring straight ahead out the windshield. "Night, Sash. I'll call you," I said, making stupid phone fingers before I caught myself.

She gave a pallid smile as Stu backed them out of the driveway and his headlights faded down my parents' street.

Chapter Four

Waiting to call Michael was like putting off doing your taxes: You know you probably have to do it or it's going to create more trouble down the line, but you dread it. And the longer you push it off, the larger the specter looms before you.

After Michael walked out on me I went through every Kubler-Ross stage of grief—some of them twice (denial ain't just a polluted waterway in Egypt, friends). I'd tried to bury my grief and pain in new relationships—all of which ended disastrously, in every case largely thanks to me: first with my breakup breakdown after Kendall dumped me, then by ill-advisedly getting involved with Chip Santana, a former client with an anger-management problem it turned out he hadn't quite licked yet. That one had cost Stu his cracked ribs, and me my dignity—and Ben, the one healthy relationship I'd managed since Michael's jilting, and then ruined because I still hadn't been able to get past it.

I reached down and scratched Jake's furry ruff where he lay patiently at my feet in my office late Monday afternoon. Jake, the sweetest dog alive, the best therapy there was, and my last tenuous link to Ben. I tried not to let the shard of hope it provided be overtaken by the more practical explanation: Not many people were willing to take his willful, hundred-pound, rampantly shedding Pyrenees into their homes while he was away on his frequent building jobs out of town.

What could Michael possibly have to say that I wanted to hear? That would offer me any kind of explanation that would make sense of my last two years of moving through the fossilized amber of my hurt? I couldn't imagine. I needed to know. I was afraid to hear.

The stasis of my conflicting emotions and other people's problems kept me from a decision about what to do for most of Monday, between my morning radio show and my private clients. By the time I was finishing up with my last client that afternoon I wasn't even thinking about Michael at all.

This session demanded even more focus than my usual clients.

Priya had thought she and her girlfriend, Misha, were "on a break" because Misha worried they were moving too fast, only to discover her ex had quickly gotten serious with someone new. When Priya had heard the news—from a mutual friend—she was blindsided, devastated…and furious.

The problem was, Misha was also a client of mine. A fact neither of them knew, and that I hadn't found out until I'd started seeing both women. I felt a little unsure about the ethics of the situation, but terminating treatment with either or both before they were ready seemed worse. So I walked a tightrope in each of their sessions to make sure I rigidly guarded their privacy, revealing nothing the other had told me—or let slip to either one that I was seeing her ex as well.

On the other hand, the social experiment of hearing the same breakup story from both sides was doing wonders for deepening my understanding of relationship psychology.

"I wish you could've heard what she told me," Priya was saying now. "She said she was developing such strong feelings for me so fast it was scaring her. That because she and Rani had so recently broken up after such a long relationship she wanted to slow things down, take a little time to process it all so we could really build ours on a solid foundation."

Rani was Misha's ex-wife, with whom she'd been together for nearly twenty years, and the relationship had been fairly volatile and unhealthy. I knew this from both Misha's and Priya's accounts, and Misha was indeed working through the emotional legacy of that relationship and its breakup. I knew what Misha had said when she and Priya broke up from the seven previous times Priya had related almost these exact words. Priya felt angry, confused, and misled.

The problem was, Misha thought she'd said something else entirely. In her mind she'd worried Priya was moving things along too fast and Misha just wasn't feeling it. She didn't want to lead Priya on, so she gently let her know she wasn't ready to get serious.

I had no idea what the actual truth was, and honestly, it didn't matter. The "truth" to each woman was the way she perceived it, but reality was the same for both: The relationship ended, and Misha had moved on.

Priya, however, hadn't—and as long as she kept trying to pick apart what she thought she'd heard, parse out Misha's motivations, and let herself stew in the injustice of what was done to her, she wouldn't.

No one could force someone to accept something they weren't yet able to accept, or to move on before they were ready. The best you can hope for is to point them toward the path that will lead them to that destination. So for the rest of our fifty minutes I let Priya wrestle with the exact same ouroboros she'd been wrapped up in during all our sessions so far, and tried to gently hold the mirror up to her words so she could come to see for herself what anyone else could see so clearly, even if they didn't have the advantage of hearing Misha's side of the story: Priya and Misha were over.

Until Priya was ready to accept that, she couldn't move past it.

"She got scared," Priya said. "I get that. I wasn't pushing for anything. I told her I'd wait as long as it took."

"Wait for what?" I asked, knowing the answer from previous sessions.

"Until she worked through her divorce. Until she was ready."

"What do you mean by 'ready'?"

Priya threw her hands out in a *come on!* gesture. "You know— emotionally ready. Ready to be in a new relationship. And I know what you're going to say," she added, holding up a finger. "That even that could have felt like an expectation on her."

That wasn't actually what I was going to say. Priya was still trying to dissect Misha's psyche, which was a futile effort in any relationship between humans—and it didn't matter. Misha's mind-set wasn't the one we needed to address. But Priya was still talking.

"But I didn't *say* that. I just said I'd be there. That I was in. I wanted her to know there was no rush—I'd be waiting. I let her know she could count on me no matter what, so I wasn't putting any pressure on her at all."

I let her statement sit between us for a moment. Sometimes in the silence we're able to hear the truth in our own words. But I never let silence fall for too long—people sharing their deepest vulnerabilities didn't need them met with an impenetrable, expressionless wall. Most of them were already feeling rejected or unimportant or invisible.

After a moment I asked, "So what did 'waiting' look like for you after that conversation?"

"I didn't put my life on hold or anything, if that's what you're thinking." Priya loved to dissect what I might be thinking too. I was seeing a pattern in her behavior: She spent so much time worrying about what might be in others' minds she didn't tune into what was going on in hers. "I went to work, went out with my friends, kept doing my cooking club every Tuesday night, my pottery classes on Saturdays. I wasn't just pining away till Misha was ready to resume things with us. I'm not one of those women who thinks she has to be in a relationship. I had a rich, full life before Misha and I started dating, and I kept that rich, full life while she was doing her emotional work. Or so I *thought*," she added angrily.

I nodded. "Those sound like rewarding interests. What made you keep all that up?"

She gave me a look of "duh." "Why would I give up something that I enjoy, that's important to me?"

I shrugged. "I don't know—it sounds like you've been dealing with some challenging stuff, emotionally."

"I get a lot out of all those pursuits. Of course I keep them in my life, no matter what's going on. *Especially* when hard stuff is going on—why would I give up something that really matters to me and makes me happy?"

Aha. "That makes sense." I nodded.

Priya frowned, laser-eyeballing me as if trying to x-ray my head. "You're thinking that if I really mattered to Misha, she'd have wanted to be with me not just despite everything she's dealing with, but partly because of it. Because it made her happy."

For once Priya got her mind-reading pretty right. But... "It doesn't matter what I think, Priya. What are *you* thinking?"

This time I let the silence lie, and Jake raised his head as if making sure everyone was okay. He inched across the floor to Priya's feet and she bent over to rub his ears.

After a little while she looked up, and I could see in her face that something was beginning to hit home. "I guess time's up for this week?"

Normally I didn't like to end sessions in the middle of what might be a budding realization, but I could tell that Priya needed some time to mull over whatever was going on inside her head, now that we were moving the focus from everything Misha might have been thinking. She might not be ready yet to face the full reality of what had happened between her and the person she'd loved so intensely.

But, I suddenly realized, I was.

...

For some reason, as I drove toward Fort Myers Beach to meet my ex-fiancé, I couldn't stop thinking about the day he proposed.

It had been our one-year anniversary, and Michael and the band had found themselves with a rare free four days off when a gig fell through at the last minute. It was too unusual a chance to resist—I'd rescheduled my patients from my shared practice at the clinic on Cleveland, and we threw the basics into my Accord (the last thing we wanted was to break down on Alligator Alley in his battered Jeep) and headed down to Key Largo.

I'd heard of Christ of the Abyss, the eight-foot statue of Jesus submerged near Dry Rocks, but had never done a dive at Pennekamp Park. More than once Michael had heard me talk about the oddity of the thing—a replica of an identical statue in the Mediterranean Sea off the coast of Genoa, cast from the same mold and brought to the Florida keys, where it was donated to the first underwater park in the country and sunk twenty-five feet deep.

It had been startling to come upon the weathered bronze Christ on our dive amid the park's coral reef, wondrous and moving in its incongruous placement below the waves. But I couldn't help reflecting that with his head thrown back and hands raised toward the surface, the son of God seemed to be doing nothing so much as asking someone to please throw him down a line and pull him up.

We hovered before the holy figure silently offering us his blessing. In the shaft of sunlight that filtered down and lit up the weathered and pitted yellow face of Jesus, Michael's hair seemed to glow amber as it floated around him. Bright yellow fish flitted past our faces, and spotted eagle rays fluffed the sand surrounding the thick concrete pedestal anchoring Jesus's feet, the white geometric markings on their black backs looking like lace against the pale sand. I swam down, mesmerized by the balletic flapping of their wings, the tiny clouds they stirred up.

Michael touched my shoulder and pointed to the algae-laced Jesus, as if I were somehow missing seeing the statue towering over me, but I couldn't drag my gaze from the graceful rays.

He reached for me again, this time a firmer hold, and I gazed up with a silent, impatient *What?*

He pointed to Jesus, and I nodded. *Yes, I see the statue. It's amazing. Now leave me alone for a sec.*

He was flipping his fins to stay close beside me, pulling at me, still pointing at Christ with an insistent finger, and finally I followed its trajectory up the statue's arms.

Where something glittering and bright contrasted starkly with the dulled gray and yellow of the barnacled metal—something hanging from the tip of Jesus's middle finger.

I felt my eyebrows bunch in confusion as I pushed up from the bottom and glided over to the hand to investigate, Michael close behind me.

It was a ring.

My wide eyes flew over to Michael's, which were now squinted behind his mask with the smile that stretched so wide his lips gapped around his mouthpiece, and he nodded a confirmation.

My heart slammed into my ribs, and bubbles erupted from my mouth as I squealed, the high-pitched sound probably confusing whales for miles. I reached for the ring—gold, with a center diamond flanked by smaller ones, brilliant and sparkling in the light, even underwater.

His hand reached for mine and he took the ring from me, then swam away, back toward Jesus's huge feet. As I watched, he paddled with his hands until he rested on the sand, one leg bent behind him, the other kneeling on the sea floor. He held the ring up in an echo of Christ's position, raising his shoulders in a questioning shrug.

I nodded furiously, tears steaming my mask and collecting in the bottom of it.

A wet tongue on my cheek from the passenger seat yanked me out of the memory I'd avoided for years, and I wiped away a trail of Jake slime. "Thanks, buddy," I said, tangling my fingers in the ruff of fur at his neck. I hadn't wanted to face Michael alone.

Calling him—hearing his voice—had felt impossible. Instead I'd sent a terse text—just a location and a time. His reply had come back immediately:

I'll be there.

This was the exact wrong time to be thinking of his proposal, I thought as we drove toward Bowditch Point on Fort Myers Beach. I didn't need to be feeling vulnerable when I was about to see the man I'd agreed to marry two years after he catastrophically changed his mind. But like trying not to think of a pink elephant, the harder I worked to avoid the memory, the more it took over my thoughts.

Still floating in front of underwater Jesus, I'd eagerly held out my left hand, and Michael reached to drop the ring onto my third finger—only to fumble it.

As it tumbled in graceful slow motion he reached for it, but his hand closed only on water. He flipped to follow its path downward, the ring visible only in flashes as it glinted each time it turned over and caught the light. He spun in a panicked circle, searching the water around and below him for the ring, but from where I floated above him I could see where it landed and came to rest at Jesus's feet.

I finned slowly down to the base of the statue to retrieve it, laying a hand on Michael's arm as I passed to signal that I had it. But he was thrashing around so frantically his adrenaline-fueled kicks created powerful eddies in the water.

One of which caught the ring and swept it off the pedestal and down to the sand below.

Bubbles funneled up from my mouthpiece again as I shouted, but it was too late—the ring had disappeared.

There ensued a good panicked fifteen-minute session of the two of us combing every inch of sand around the pedestal, patting it, sifting through it, sending so many particles of it flowering up around us that the water seemed viscous and dull.

Until finally Michael held his arm up in triumph, the ring clutched so firmly in his clawed hand that I could see his whitened knuckles.

For months afterward he'd loved to tell the story of our underwater engagement, making a joke of the near loss of the ring and his heroic treasure hunt for it—all part of the lore of us that he created.

I always smiled along as he regaled everyone he met with the tale, and never revealed my interpretation of the true moral of the story: Despite his good intentions, Michael never thought things all the way through—case in point, a four-thousand-dollar engagement ring nearly lost at sea in his ill-thought-out romantic gesture.

Or his asking me to marry him when he clearly hadn't been ready for that.

Or, I thought, my anger rekindling as my tires crunched into the Bowditch Point parking lot and I caught sight of his achingly familiar figure, his coming back here and opening up a can of worms I'd long since sealed. My heart started pounding.

Michael stood from the picnic table he'd been slouched over and waved as soon as I stepped out of my car, but I didn't bother to wave back. I went around and opened the passenger door for Jake, my hands shaking.

Why had Michael come back here, anyway? I brooded, stalling by letting Jake pee on every weed in the gravel lot at the tip of Estero Island. To clear his conscience? And what could he possibly say that would make me feel any better about the worst thing I'd ever experienced? *I'm sorry, I freaked out?* That seemed obvious. *I'd met someone else?* My heart twisted at that one—it had entered my mind more than once that maybe Michael had been cheating on me. But I'd made peace even with that. There was nothing I could do about that if it had happened, and it said more about Michael than it did about me.

It wasn't you; it was me?

That one caused a bigger pang in my chest, but not because of Michael. Those were the words I'd said to Ben after I'd stupidly slept with Chip Santana.

I'd meant them—I hadn't been ready for what Ben had been offering me at the time. But I could see now how hollow and useless they must have sounded to him.

Ben had been all the things I'd ever hoped for in a partner...and I hadn't been ready for it because of what the man still standing beside the picnic table, hands by his sides and patiently waiting, had done to me two years ago.

No, there was nothing that Michael could say that I needed to hear anymore. And I wasn't going to help him salve his conscience by letting him apologize and wheedle and excuse his actions. All I needed, I realized as Jake took a really impressive poo in the grass bordering Estero Boulevard, was to tell Michael how I felt. What I thought of him and what he had done. Like Priya, I needed to stop trying to figure out why Michael had done what he'd done, and simply focus on moving on.

I unrolled a baggie from the holder on Jake's leash and leaned over with it to pick up his mess. The most eloquent possible statement of my feelings would be to bring it over to Michael's table and leave it in his lap.

But my days of unbalanced broad gestures—another grim legacy of the Michael fallout—were finally behind me. I'd simply say what I needed to say and leave.

Jake didn't seem to pick up on my state of mind, nearly pulling my arm from the socket as we neared Michael in his efforts to offer him his most unreserved affection.

"Hey, big guy!" Michael said, car-washing the dog's huge head as Jake buried it in the vee of his legs. "What's your name?"

"Spike," I lied, pulling Jake back harder than I needed to. *Traitor.*

And then Michael looked up at me and I couldn't move. I'm pretty sure I forgot to breathe, judging by the way my lungs started to burn and I suddenly took in a huge gasp of air.

He looked so...normal. So familiar standing in front of me with those grass-green eyes peeking out from under the unruly lock of dark hair that fell over his right eye the way it always did. I had to stop myself from reaching out to push it back, out of habit. He was dressed the way I'd always seen him, in slim-fitting faded jeans and a battered black concert T-shirt, this one from a David Bowie show that had to have happened long before he was born. I could almost let myself believe no time had passed since I saw him last—except for the uncertain expression he wore, instead of the slightly cocky grin I'd been used to.

"Brook," he finally said.

My mouth was so dry I couldn't have formed words even if my flatlined brain had provided any. Which it did not.

"Thank you for coming." He kept talking, speaking in a slow, soothing cadence as if he was afraid I might bolt any second. Which I was considering. "It's more than I deserve."

"I'm not staying." My voice came out breathy and uncertain, and I put some diaphragm into it. "I just came to tell you some things."

"None of it can be worse than what I've said to myself. But first will you let me tell you one thing?" he asked. "Not because I need it for my own peace of mind...although I do. But because you deserve to hear it. Please?"

I had loved this man so deeply that there were times it actually physically hurt my chest. He stood in front of me now with a nakedly pleading expression, those verdant eyes I knew so well meeting mine directly, intensely. Whatever had happened between us at the end, what we once shared was real.

"Fine," I clipped out. "I'll listen." I took a seat on the bench across the nicked wooden table from him, pulling Jake in close beside me, and Michael settled onto his bench.

We sat in silence for a long moment. I watched Jake. Michael watched me—I felt his gaze even without needing to look up and confirm it, but I wouldn't meet it. I couldn't.

Finally he cleared his throat, and then he spoke.

"Walking out on you was the best thing I ever did."

Chapter Five

For a moment I sat there, sure I'd misheard him.

But within a flash the words sank in, and brought up a surge of rage so strong and long-held I shook with it. He'd conned me into letting him talk first so he could *gloat*? I shot to my feet.

"You son of a bitch," I said, my voice trembling. "How *dare* you say that to me." I shoved my way out from where I was sandwiched between the table and bench, Jake scrambling out of my path, and rounded the end to stand over Michael like an avenging Fury. "I may not have been perfect, and I may have done a lot of things wrong. But I *loved* you. I gave you everything I could, and maybe it wasn't enough for you, but that was the best I had at the time. And you weren't perfect either, you selfish piece of garbage."

Michael was leaning back from my unmasked venom, his eyes stricken, but the words were fountaining out of me like pea soup out of Linda Blair, and I couldn't stop.

"But I loved you for who you were, imperfections and all, because people are *flawed*," I bit out. "We're messy, and we can be assholes, but you know what? We *grow*. And love means growing *with* someone, encouraging every little seedling and *nurturing* that and cheering it on, not stomping out the first tendrils because they aren't perfectly formed. Love is a *living* thing, not stagnant. And you were a shallow child who couldn't see that, wasn't willing to trust it—and didn't have the courage to tell me that you couldn't handle it."

My chest felt as if it were on fire, and I didn't realize I was starved for oxygen until I finally sucked in a breath.

"So you come here," I said, fury still throbbing under the words, "and make all this effort to talk to me not even as some kind of bandage to your conscience—but to let me know how *unaffected* you are by what you did to me—to us? How *grateful* you are for it?" I pinned him with a gaze I hoped was filled with all the contempt I could muster. Michael's hands clutched the lip of the table so hard the skin had whitened, but he made no move to leave or to defend himself. One tiny point in his favor.

"You may have hurt me, Michael," I went on. "You broke my heart so badly I didn't think I'd ever get over it. But I have. And you did me a favor, because I'm *glad* I felt all of that for you—even if it was a lie. It taught me that I'm alive, and I'm human, and I can be vulnerable. And I *wasn't* foolish to love you, even though everything about your love was phony. It taught me how to really love someone, and someday I'll find someone worthy of that." My heartbeat stuttered as a picture of Ben flitted into my head, but I pushed it away. "I feel nothing for you anymore but pity. You'll never even know what love is."

I had nothing left to say to him. Jake's warm head pressed into my thigh as if in solidarity. My rage was gone, evaporated as if it had never been, except for an exhaustion left behind, and an inexplicable lightness so complete I thought I might just float up and away from him and be gone.

As if a burden I hadn't realized I was still carrying had lifted.

"Goodbye, Michael," I said, and somehow the words felt almost tender. I turned to go.

"Walking out was the best thing I ever did because it woke me up to what a dipshit I was," he called out behind me.

I stopped, then turned around, my eyes narrowed. "Say more about that."

He stood, watching me. "It's true. Leaving...being away from you...it showed me exactly what I'd left behind."

"And yet you stayed gone."

"I did," he agreed. "Because I didn't know how to undo it."

"There was no way to undo what you did," I said in a chilly voice.

"Yeah, I knew that. Which was why I..." He stopped, stepped out from behind the picnic table, running a hand through his brown hair in a frustrated gesture I knew well. "Can we talk this out a little closer than half a football field away?" His self-mocking grin tipped one side of his lips up as he held a hand toward me, palm up. "And if you're through with them, can I please have my balls back? That was some speech."

"Totally deserved," I said, fighting a traitorous quirk of my lips.

"No argument."

I could try to convince myself all I wanted that I didn't need to know his explanation for what he did, but the truth was, now that I was right on the verge of hearing it, it would kill me not to.

Not that I was going to let him know that. I raised one shoulder in an unconcerned shrug. "Fine. If it makes you feel better to tell me. Whatever." I swanned back over to the picnic table as if I were disinterestedly checking out the four-dollar lunch buffet at Golden Corral, Benedict Jake trotting amiably over to Michael.

I sat back down across the table from him as he sank onto the other bench. And then, for the first time since he'd come back, I really let myself look at him.

Familiarity hit me with a jolt. The arch of his eyebrows, a shade darker than his ashy brown hair, fanning out at the outside edges into little individual hairs I used to smooth down with my thumb. The raised freckle on his right cheekbone I'd run my fingers over a hundred times. The shape of his earlobes—I could still remember the feel of them on my fingertips, unexpectedly tender and soft. There were new creases beside the eyes I'd always loved to look at, making him look a little bit older, but not in the bad way I might have wished for. Instead they lent him a hint of depth, a gravitas he hadn't had before.

He was watching me too, examining my face with the same intentness I was no doubt training on him. I wondered what he saw, how the last two years had etched themselves into my face.

"It's so good to see you again," he said quietly, and I had to steel my softening heart.

"You said you wanted me to hear you out. So talk."

He nodded. "Right. Okay. Brook..." He looked down at the table, then back up at me, shook his head. "The truth is, I panicked."

"No kidding."

"You were...you are...so..." He gestured in the air, as if he thought he could pluck the right word out of it, and I waited with shameful anticipation, wanting to hear his compliments, his contrition, his words of flattery and regret.

"Mature."

I sat back, crossing my arms over my chest. "Gee, thanks, Petrarch."

The indentations beside his eyes deepened as he offered a sheepish smile. "Yeah, I know—I suck at words; you know that from the band."

It was true. It had been one of the things that always frustrated him—Michael could write music that plucked at the deepest chords of a listener's soul, but he was unable to finish a song without his bandmate Chris, who penned the lyrics—his words the Cyrano to the beautiful but literally dumb Christian of Michael's melodies.

"What I wanted to say..." he went on. "You're a grown-up and you always were. And I was...well, a musician. You had it all together, and you always knew what needed to be done—and then you got it done. It made me feel like a kid, a stupid, irresponsible kid just drifting aimlessly through life."

Something panged behind my ribs—a flutter of recognition...and guilt. That was how I'd thought of Michael, wasn't it? A beautiful boy with his wild artist's heart, and me, his island in a storm, his safe harbor, the anchor that grounded him.

Not the indispensable rock I thought I'd been for his flighty creative soul, but in the end, I'd bitterly admitted after his abandonment, the millstone that held him back, held him down.

Looking back I could see now how over and over I'd nagged—haranguing him about the bills, his late nights long after his gigs had ended as he jammed and rehearsed and partied with the band, finding a "safety net" job he'd never wanted to consider...

...Showing up on time for our cake tasting. The final straw that had sent Michael fleeing town—and fleeing me.

Shame rose up hot in my throat. "I never meant to make you feel like that," I muttered. And I *hadn't* meant to. But I knew now—knew all along, if I were honest—that I had done it anyway.

"It wasn't your fault. You were an adult wanting to have a relationship with another adult. And I wasn't ready to grow up yet."

"I didn't let you be yourself." I wasn't sure how I'd gone from righteous rage to apologizing. "I tried to...to shunt you into a mold that wasn't right for you. To change you."

"You tried to help me, Brook. I just wasn't ready to admit I needed it."

His gaze was steady on mine, the corners of the lips whose curve I'd known almost better than my own lifting slightly in a gentle smile. "I was an idiot. I freaked out and ran away like a kid because seeing how together you were all the time just made me feel like the mess I was. I hurt you...the person I loved more than anything...because I was a coward."

I was straining so hard to hear his quiet words I'd stopped breathing.

"And I'm sorry for that," he said, the smile chased off his face. "Sorrier for that than anything I've ever done."

The words undid me.

A strangled noise rose out of my throat, and when Michael stood and came around to sit beside me, to wrap me in his arms, I didn't even try to stop him. I clung on to him like a piece of floating flotsam after a shipwreck.

For the first time in two years I felt at peace.

...

It was dark by the time I drove back home, Jake curled into an impossibly tight ball on my passenger seat, his head wedged at an unnatural angle up the passenger door and his paws poking straight out almost to the dash.

Michael and I had talked for hours, sitting side by side on a rickety swing set rusted at the joints that groaned out a protest as we swayed gently back and forth, overlooking the placid gulf at low tide. We stayed away from the immediate aftermath of our broken engagement—it was still too tender a wound—but we caught each other up on the last two years of our lives, words pouring out of us. Making our peace together felt as though a part of me that had shriveled up was regenerating, tender spring leaves shooting from a withered brown branch. It was healing and comforting and soothing—but I didn't know what it all meant.

I knew who would help me figure it out, though.

I was dialing Sasha before I even waved goodbye to Michael as I pulled out of my parking space, but the call went to voicemail. Did she have a late interview today? I couldn't remember.

"Sasha...call me. I need to talk to you," I said to her recording.

When I pulled into my garage I had to coax Jake inside the house—he seemed perfectly content to sleep where he was all night if only I'd agree to stay there with him, worn out from a taxing evening of trotting back and forth as we'd sat on the swing, trying to keep his head beneath our hands. When he saw me get out and open his door, though, he pulled himself wearily up and lumbered out his side of the car.

I tried Sasha again, rolling into voicemail. "Sash, where are you? Call me as soon as you get this."

I fed Jake and myself, and as we both ate—him from his bowl beside the sliding door to the patio, me at the kitchen island beside him—my phone finally rang.

"Hi, Brook," came the familiar voice, and my heart thumped involuntarily in my chest.

"Ben," I said, and then promptly choked on the food I hadn't bothered to swallow.

After a hacking fit that lasted at least close to thirty embarrassing seconds, during which my watering eyes didn't allow me to find the "mute" button on my phone, I brought it back to my ear from where I'd tried to muffle it under my armpit. "Hey...how's New York?" I said, as though there'd been no interruption.

"Are you okay?"

"Oh, fine," I replied breezily. "Just a...a frog." Ben was calling me on his romantic getaway with Perfect Pamela? Things couldn't be all *that* romantic if he was thinking of me. "It's really good to hear from you," I said.

"I just wanted to make sure everything's going okay with Jake. He being a good boy?"

"Oh...Yes, of course—wonderful. I love having him ba—having him here," I corrected myself. "Are you guys having just the best time *ever*?"

"Well, I guess," Ben said after a moment, seemingly taken aback at my overcompensation. "It's not really all fun and games, of course."

"It's not?"

"Well, she's been prepping for the interview, which is tomorrow, so we've pretty much stayed close to the hotel. But hopefully we'll get out and see some of the sights after that."

"The interview?" Was Pamela up for a job in New York? Was she moving away?

A shard of ice slid into my chest. Was Ben planning to move *with* her?

"Well, yeah," he said. "That's why we came. For Doctors Without Borders?"

I didn't know which was worse—the idea that Ben might have been moving away with Perfect Pamela, or that she wasn't just perfect...she was saintly.

"Wow, well, that's...Wow. Well, good luck to her. And to you. I mean, you're not interviewing, of course. I just mean...Um, that's...quite impressive, isn't it? She's...amazing..." I trailed off miserably.

"How are you doing, Brook?" Ben said into my self-pitying silence. "I mean with Jake?"

"I'm fine," I said. "Jake's fine—I'm taking good care of him, and you have nothing to worry about. I promise."

"I never worry about him when he's with you."

I blinked at his words. "Thanks," I said quietly. After everything that had happened between us, I was floored that Ben could say he trusted me again.

"So we'll be back Thursday," he went on. "How about we meet somewhere dog-friendly, and I can buy you dinner that night to thank you?"

The idea of sitting through dinner with Ben and Pamela to hear all about their trip and her attempts to save the world practically triggered my gag reflex. "Why don't I just swing him by your house when you two get back? I'm sure you'll want to...you know...um, get unpacked." I winced at how ungracious I'd sounded.

"Oh. All right. Thanks."

"It's a really nice offer, but not necessary," I tacked on. "I'm happy to have Jake. Anytime—really. I've missed him."

"He misses you too, Brook."

I listened to him breathing for a moment, unsure what to say, unwilling to hang up.

"Say hello from me!" Perfect Pamela's silken voice in the background cut through my stupor. I wished she'd sounded snarky or controlling or jealous, but no. She just seemed sincere.

"Hi to Pamela!" I said brightly. "Please wish her big, big luck from me!"

"Will do. Take care, Brook."

"You too, Ben. Bye."

I set the phone down, the quiet of my house feeling even more acute. Sasha still hadn't called back. Ben was gallivanting through the Big Apple with Saint Pamela. Michael was...well, I didn't know what Michael was. I needed someone to figure that out with.

Jake had finished his dinner and was lying contentedly at the base of my stool, head resting between his paws. "Hey, buddy," I said. "Come here. Come here and talk to me."

His eyes blinked open and he gazed up at me, but made no move to get up.

"Jake," I said. "Hey, Jakie! Come here, boy. Come here! You want some love?" I infused my voice with great excitement, but Jake only closed his eyes, let out a sleepy groan, and farted.

I sighed.

Chapter Six

Sasha finally called me back late the next morning. I was with a client, so I missed her call, but when I returned it I got her voicemail. "Call me back!" I said insistently.

And she did—later that afternoon. Again my return call went to voicemail. The cycle happened one more time that day, and I finally realized she was deliberately calling in the first fifty minutes of an hour, when she knew I would be in a consultation with a client.

My best friend was avoiding me.

I remembered how strangely she'd been acting at dinner at my parents' Sunday night—the last time I'd talked to her directly. Something was bugging her, and there was only one problem she could have that she might feel she couldn't talk to me about.

Stu.

My stomach tightened—was my brother reverting to his old commitment-phobic ways?

That would devastate Sasha. She really cared about him—and she was herself with Stu in a way I'd never seen her with anyone else: relaxed, comfortable, goofy and...happy. I'd been certain he felt same way about her, but I couldn't think of any other reason Sasha would be avoiding me like the clap.

Her final message said she was meeting with her trainer that evening for an extra-long workout at the gym, and wouldn't be able to talk. Clever girl. She knew I would never set foot in there.

Intercepting her at her place wouldn't have done any good—she and Stu had lived together, for all intents and purposes, practically since they'd started dating, and this wasn't something I could talk about with her in front of him.

That meant I had to get creative.

The one thing Sasha cannot resist (besides, up until the recent development of my baby brother, a completely unsuitable man) is a cry for help. So after work the next day I baited a Sasha trap.

"Hey," I said to her voicemail on the umpteenth time she ignored my call. "I slept with Michael." And I hung up.

Her return call took exactly thirty-seven seconds.

"What the hell, Brook!"

"Hey, Sash."

"What happened? Why did you do it? Are you okay? Did that bastard hurt you again?"

I was lounging on the sofa in my living room, contentedly filing my nails, Jake stretched out on the floor beside me. But I produced a few sniffles and a shaky sigh. "I don't know what to do, Sash...I'm a mess."

"I'm on my way over."

I almost felt guilty about how easy it was.

...

I was waiting for her in the living room when she got there, an open bottle of wine on the cocktail table, two glasses already poured.

"Okay," she said, barely stopping to drop her purse and keys on my entry table. "What do we need here—damage control, pep talk, or confidence building?"

I pushed one of the glasses into her hand and came clean: "None of the above. I didn't sleep with Michael—but I had to do something to make you stop avoiding me."

Sash set her glass down on my coffee table so hard I thought she'd snap the stem. "Seriously? What are we, twelve?"

"You tell me," I countered. "You've been playing 'dodge-call' with me for three days."

"I've been busy."

"You've been cagey. What's going on, Sasha?"

Her face shuttered in a way I'd never seen; Sasha was always an open book—to me and anyone else.

"Is it Stu?" I pressed.

"No, it's not Stu."

"Sash." I folded my arms and gave her my best "quit bullshitting me" expression. I ought to have mastered it, having been on the receiving end of my mom's for thirty-plus years.

"It's not, Brook," she insisted. When I just kept my stare fixed on her, she sighed. "Your brother and I are fine. We're great, actually. In fact your call interrupted a really nice blowie I was giving him, and—"

My hands shot up to my ears. "Lalalalala! Okay! Geez, I was just asking."

Sasha gave a dry laugh, but there wasn't much humor in it.

I frowned. "So what is it that's bugging you? Work?"

"You know, a smart therapist I know taught me that when there are things people don't want to talk about, they deflect the attention onto someone else."

"No fair therapizing me."

"Then quit stalling. What happened with Michael? Did you have sex with him?"

"Hell, no! He wanted to talk, and I...Like you said, I needed the closure."

"Did you wear the outfit we bought you?"

"Oh...I totally forgot."

"Brook! I put a lot of effort into that." She looked so put-out I had to laugh.

"I know—I'm sorry. I'll wear it. I just...I hadn't planned to see him. It was sort of an impulse, and I just...went. I left from work, though," I added, "so I looked nice."

She tipped her head slightly, offering me a skeptical look. "Okay," she said, sinking onto the sofa beside me. "Tell me everything."

So I did, from the peace plant being delivered all the way through our hours-long conversation. Sasha listened, rapt, until I finally wound down.

"So he moved to *Seattle* after he left you?"

I nodded. "He said he had to get as far away from the memories as he could. But he hated it. Hated himself."

"Rightly so."

"He never left his apartment. When he realized that he'd spent an entire week without seeing another human face or speaking a single word out loud, he finally moved to Portland."

"Where he joined another band." She was sorting out the facts to keep them straight in her mind.

I nodded again. "Except he hated that too."

"So now he's a band promoter."

"Well, he was. He got them signed to a label, and he got cut out of the deal."

"Too bad. So sad."

"Sash. He's not bitter about it. He's happy for them. You know, he's not an awful person. You liked him once."

"That was before he broke your heart in the worst way anyone can. That's unforgivable."

"Well, I have," I said.

She narrowed her eyes. "You have *what*?"

"Forgiven him," I said simply.

"When did *that* happen?"

I shrugged. "Sometime between him telling me why he left, and sitting and talking to him. Little by little...I don't know. It was like a weight I didn't know I was carrying lifted off me. I've been hating him for so long—even after I convinced myself I was over it—that it's colored everything I've done since—and not in a good way."

"That's not true," Sasha protested. "Look at your Breakup Doctor stuff. You're doing amazing things for people, helping them in ways you never would have before."

"Maybe. But I've been so angry, so determined never to let myself get hurt that way again, I haven't really been open to anything new, have I? I mean...look at Ben." I stopped, my throat closing up.

Sasha held up a hand. "Oh, no. You will not beat yourself up over that. You were right to take some time to figure out what you wanted before you two got serious."

Her words would have made a lot more sense if I hadn't filled that time with my disastrous hookup with Chip Santana.

"I just wonder, if I'd been able to let go of everything with Michael sooner, would I have been ready for what Ben was offering? And now…it's too late."

As if sensing my upset, Jake, who until now had been sitting quietly at Sasha's feet like a huge, hairy white angel, pushed himself up and padded over to me, resting his head on my lap and gazing at me with his big liquid brown eyes. I stroked his head, a wave of tenderness for him crashing over me.

"Is it?" I heard Sasha say, and looked over to see her eyeing us with an assessing expression.

"Well." I sighed. "He's got Perfect Pamela."

"And you have his dog."

Jake broke into a grin as if to agree, but I didn't have the heart to remind my best friend—or myself—that no matter how much I loved him, the Great Pyrenees was only a consolation prize.

•••

After Sasha left I cleaned up our glasses—she'd been so laser-focused on me she'd hardly touched her wine—and I realized I never got back around to asking what was bothering her. She'd gotten me completely distracted.

I straightened, frowning. She'd accused me of deflecting…had she masterfully done it to me without my even noticing?

What was Sasha avoiding telling me?

•••

With Michael in mind, I sat down later that night to write my weekly Breakup Doctor column for the *Tropic Times*.

"Putting Down the Weight You Didn't Know You Were Carrying"

Somebody broke your heart.

I don't have to know you to know that's true—if you're alive and you interact with people, then chances are you've had your heart broken.

No matter what kind of heartbreak you've suffered—romantic or otherwise—it's the worst kind of wound. Unlike a physical wound, emotional ones don't heal straightforwardly. They get ripped back open over and over. They fester. They refuse to heal, handicapping everything you do, every new connection you try to make. It's not that you were hurt once and you fear being hurt the same way again—it's that you were hurt once and you are still hurting in that same place, the gash in your heart as tender as if it were new, making you overcautious, overprotective...fearful.

Faced with the choice between a broken leg and a broken heart, most of us who have experienced the latter will choose the leg—as painful as it is—because we know this truth: that physical wounds heal more easily.

But it's only when we realize our happiness rests, at least partially, in someone else's hands that we truly understand what it is to love them— and to lose them. When you have nothing, you have nothing to lose—it's only by understanding what's at stake that we can appreciate the glorious risk that love is. And that it is a risk worth taking.

So be grateful to those who broke your heart. Yes, it hurt. Yes, loving someone deeply means mourning their loss just as deeply. And that's okay. Like a personal trainer, they have pushed you farther than you thought you could go, and in the process they helped make you stronger. And when the next love comes around, thanks to the one that didn't work out you'll recognize it. You'll be ready for it. You'll be open to it.

But first you have to let go of the injury, let it heal—and get back in the game.

Chapter Seven

Come to office. 911.

The text came in at eight a.m. the next morning, a good half hour before I usually headed to the office area of my house. When I unlocked the door from the back hallway to my waiting room, Intern Paige was standing outside my office door, her ear pressed to it, knocking urgently.

"I am so sorry," she said, hastening over to me as I opened the connecting door. "She just pushed past me and went in there and locked the door. I told her you weren't in yet. I've been trying to pick the lock since she went in, but that's much harder than it looks on TV. I didn't know what to do." She was in an unprecedented dither, her hands flying out as she talked and her usual tight twist mussed from where she'd clearly pulled the pins out of it, presumably to try them in the lock.

"Okay, it's okay," I said soothingly. "Who's in there?"

"Lisa Albrecht."

Ah. Lisa, my editor at the *Tropic Times*, was never known for her tact or diplomacy. She'd started out as a client—my first as the Breakup Doctor, actually—when her husband, whom she'd supported financially for years, walked out on her and her two sons with no notice. For a *much* younger woman. Lisa, to say the least, had not handled it well, but lately she seemed to have finally gotten past her hurt and rage. This new explosion of fury couldn't be good.

I needed to know just what I was dealing with before I went in there. Lisa was a tough customer on a *good* day. And technically she was also my boss.

"Did she say anything when she came in?" I asked Paige.

She nodded. "Yes. She said, 'Where's Brook?' and when I said you weren't in the office yet, she said, 'Then *get* her in here.' I asked her to wait while I called you, but she was in your office and slammed the door before I could get out from behind the desk. I'm sorry, Brook." She looked crushed.

I put a hand on her shoulder, and she froze, blinking up at me like a cornered fox. "It's not your fault. You did everything right. Lisa is...well, she has her own way of approaching people. Sometimes there's not much you can do about it." I didn't want her beating herself up over Lisa Albrecht's sense of entitlement, but clearly physical contact was not the way to comfort Paige. I dropped my hand and she visibly relaxed.

She took a breath and nodded. "I just feel terrible. She's in so much pain."

I stopped halfway to my office door and turned back around. "That's what's bothering you? Not that she's in my office?"

"Well, yes, I mean, I know that's bad, and I should have stopped her. But she's obviously upset and uncomfortable feeling all that pain, and it's making her react aggressively."

I couldn't help the smile that drew up the corners of my mouth. "You're going to be a good therapist, Paige."

Her bemused expression was the last thing I saw before I turned back around and knocked lightly on my own door. "Lisa, it's Brook. I'm coming in." I put my key in the doorknob and pushed open the door.

Lisa was lounging on my chaise, one leg tented up, her arms crossed behind her head, looking for all the world as if I were late to a cozy girls' tête-à-tête.

"I thought about lighting up a cigarette, but you don't have any ashtrays," she said.

"I prefer no smoking in here. And you don't smoke anyway, Lisa." I calmly walked past her and took my usual seat across from the chaise, waiting for her to explain. Rising to Lisa's provocation only resulted in heightened dramatics.

"Yes, but I'm thinking of starting. I mean, why not? My lungs will forgive me, right? It doesn't matter how bad anything I do is—apparently all I have to do is let it go and magically it's all okay. At least, that's what I just read."

Ah. Lisa was unhappy about the column I'd turned in last night.

"Forgiveness is about emotions, Lisa. Our psychological well-being. It doesn't really affect physical ailments."

She shot upright, sudden fury pulsing from her so strongly I could almost feel waves of it hitting me. "It doesn't work for *any* 'ailments,' Deepak Chopra," she spat. "What, so people can do whatever they want to you, and all you have to do is forgive it and it's like it never happened? A big get-out-of-jail-free card? A license to hurt anyone, in any way, and poof! All is forgiven? That's *crap.* I don't pay you for that kind of New Age bullshit. And I'm not running it."

I nodded. "Okay. If you didn't like the column, all you had to do was call me. I'm happy to rewrite it."

"I don't want you to rewrite it. I want you to trash it. It's irresponsible! It's quackery!"

I frowned. "I'm not sure I see—"

"You want to give people carte blanche for bad behavior! You want me to publish something that's going to make anyone who's ever been angry over what someone did to hurt them—*rightfully* angry—feel bad about themselves because they can't just wave their magic wand and feel better and say, 'No problem that you stomped on me...I *forgive* you.'" She said the word as if it were coated in slime.

Paige was right: Lisa was uncomfortable with anything that made her feel vulnerable. Her first reaction was to strike back—but what was underneath was simply raw, naked pain that terrified her.

"Lisa," I said gently, "that article was inspired by something in my own life. I needed to be able to forgive someone—my ex-fiancé who jilted me, actually"—I thought it might help if I let her have a glimpse into my own embarrassing past—"so I could finally be able to move on. But that doesn't mean I think what he did was okay."

"That's sure as hell what it sounded like."

I didn't actually think so, but I considered the possibility that Lisa was right. "What part sounded like I was absolving people who hurt others?"

But she didn't seem to hear me. "What if my asshole ex sees it? What if my kids see it? Then I'm the jerk who can't forgive their dad, and he's the angel, right? I'm raising *sons*, Brook. *Men.* What am I supposed to teach them—that it's okay to do anything they want to a woman, because ultimately there's *forgiveness*?"

Lisa was usually so fiercely defensive and dedicated to her own point of view, she didn't have a lot of concern for anyone else. But now I realized what was troubling her—she was personally offended, yes. But mostly she didn't want to raise her sons to do to some woman what their father did to her. What Michael had done to me.

And that was downright...compassionate.

I let out a long breath. "I see your point. Let's not run this column, and I'll get you a replacement by end of day."

But Lisa didn't jump up with a vindicated smirk, as I'd half expected. Instead she sat back against the cushion, her brows pulled together.

"When did you get jilted?" she asked.

It took me a beat to answer—conversations with Lisa tended to be exclusively one-way. "Two years ago," I said. "A month before the wedding."

She winced. "And this jerk, he asked you to forgive him for that?"

"He didn't ask outright. Actually, I never saw him again after the breakup—he left town. But I realized when he came back and wanted to see me recently that I needed to forgive what he did or I'd never move past it." I chewed on my lip, thinking. Why *did* Michael come back?

"And you did? You just let it all go?"

I pulled my attention back to Lisa. "I don't know. Probably not entirely, but yeah, mostly I guess I did. Holding on to it has caused me a lot of...issues." I had no intention of telling Lisa about my meltdown after breaking up with my rebound boyfriend after Michael, or the mortifying evening in jail that followed, let alone about Ben. It was foolish to show my throat to the lion.

She grunted and pushed up off the chaise. "I have to get to work." Our little moment of connection was over, apparently. "I'll let you know by lunchtime if I need another column from you."

The door had closed behind her before I could even react to the unprecedented act of Lisa actually softening a position.

...

I was antsy for the rest of the day, a low-grade static buzz that left me feeling anxious, especially in between clients, when I couldn't distract myself by focusing on someone else. I thought perhaps my nerves were about waiting for Lisa to let me know whether my article would be buried and I'd have to throw together another one last-minute, but Intern Paige left after my one-o'clock client checked in—she had late classes on Tuesdays and Thursdays—and Lisa still hadn't called.

Was it about Michael? Lisa's interrogation had me questioning what I hadn't before: Michael's motives in coming back to Fort Myers, seeking me out. He couldn't be moving back now that he was working as a band promoter, given that our local music scene was mostly made up of workmanlike musicians doing Jimmy Buffett covers for the tourists.

Was it just to get my forgiveness, as Lisa had suggested? He'd specifically said he wasn't asking for that, but I wasn't putting total trust in his word anymore, for obvious reasons. Maybe he just wanted to clear his conscience, or—like me—finally put closure on our unfinished last chapter. But it would have been easier to do that via a heartfelt letter or e-mail, especially since he had no reason to expect that I'd have anything to do with him if he did make face-to-face contact.

A new suspicion bloomed in my mind, simultaneously filling my belly with ice and my chest with heat.

Did Michael come back to rekindle something between us?

He had to know that that wasn't a remote possibility. I could forgive, yes, but I would never forget a betrayal as thorough and foundational as his. How could I ever trust again that he'd stick around?

Even if he did seem to have changed.

And anyway, if that were a possible motive, Sasha would have jumped all over it—she wouldn't cut Michael one inch of slack as far as his intentions went, and she'd have lit into me about being on guard. I'd call her tonight, though, and ask her directly.

Tonight. Ben was coming home from New York, and I would see him tonight when I dropped off Jake.

The sudden fizzing feeling in my belly told me I'd finally lit directly on what had been making me so jumpy all day long. I was going to see Ben. Hearing him and Perfect Pamela tell me all about their trip wasn't exactly top of my list for anticipatory events.

The light on my wall that signaled an arriving client lit up, saving me from further useless ruminating, and I moved to the door to invite my next appointment inside, grateful for the chance to get out of my own head and into someone else's.

...

By way of being a dog, Jake got to act out the reaction I had to stifle when Ben opened his door and the two of us first caught sight of him: The dog let out one loud yip of excitement before his tail started wagging so hard it blurred. Two bunny hops and a lot of whining followed, and then Jake charged him like a bull, Ben putting his hands out in a futile effort to slow the oncoming train before the big white dog hurled himself full-length into him on his hind legs, wrapping his big shaggy paws around his shoulders and licking his face.

Lucky dog.

"Should I leave you two alone?" I joked.

"Okay, buddy, no jumping," Ben said soothingly, easing the dog's paws back to the floor before grasping Jake's head in his hands and assiduously rubbing his ears. "How's my boy? How's my Jake?"

Jake was excellent, he wanted Ben to know as he pressed his entire body against his master, but had clearly been starved for attention.

"As you can see, I've spoiled him rotten and there's been utterly no discipline at my house," I said. "Sorry about that."

"That's okay—it was a vacation for you too, right, Jake?" Ben straightened to face me and did a double take. "You look nice."

"Oh…I just threw on some old jeans." I brushed an indifferent hand over the outfit Sasha had carefully curated last weekend. I felt a little foolish standing on his front porch holding a bag of dog food and wearing sky-high pumps, but I couldn't take the idea of facing Ben and Pamela without putting a little more effort than usual into things.

"Let me get that for you. Has he eaten?" he asked, tipping his head toward Jake as he reached to take the dog food from me, his fingers brushing the skin of my arm.

I shook my head. "Not yet."

"Come on back," he said, and disappeared toward the kitchen, Jake scrambling after him.

I froze for a beat at the unexpected invitation, then took a deep breath and followed, planting a welcoming smile across my face for Perfect Pamela. But Ben was pouring food into Jake's bowl while the dog sat patiently at his feet, and there was no sign of her.

"Where's Pamela?" I ventured, broadening my smile so wide I could actually see my cheeks. "I'd love to hear how her interview went." Almost as much as I'd love to stick egg beaters in my eyes and whisk.

"Dropped her off at home on the way from the airport. She's got an early surgery tomorrow," Ben said.

Of course. "Oh," I said eloquently. "So, is she off to save the world?" I heard the pettiness at the edge of the words as soon as I said them, but Ben didn't seem to notice.

"She won't know right away. You'd be amazed how particular Doctors Without Borders is about their volunteers—they only take the best of the best."

"Well...I'm *sure* she'll be chosen then," I gushed. My overcompensation thudded into the silence that fell after it, and Ben just looked at me for a moment, as if I were a particularly obscure passage of building code.

"Do you know about the High Line on the West Side?" he asked finally.

I stared for a moment, trying to make sense of his question. "You mean the pedestrian park in New York that used to be an elevated train track?"

He nodded. "That thing's amazing. I walked it from one end to the other while I had time on my hands. It's transformed that area by the Hudson docks—it's all planted up and beautiful—and it's added really needed public space to that area. Plus they're reusing what were idle resources, and avoiding the waste of having to demolish the old track infrastructure."

I loved listening to Ben talk about architecture and green building. His passion for what he did was part of what had initially attracted me to him, and his enthusiasm was contagious. While we were dating I'd started to see my surroundings through his eyes—the beauty and potential in places people had forgotten about: abandoned homes, old warehouses, stretches of land or beachfront where hurricane-damaged buildings still littered the landscape. He always saw the hidden value in things other people had written off.

"You think there's a way to do something like that here?" I guessed, knowing the way his mind worked.

He nodded. "Those old defunct Seaboard Railway tracks? They'd make a fantastic hiking and biking trail, and the parts that run through town could be turned into a similar kind of park. They did something like that in Tampa, and—"

Jake's bark cut him off. The dog had finished his dinner and brushed past me on the way to the back door—he always had to poop immediately after eating—and I automatically reached to unlock it and let him out into the yard.

"Thanks," Ben said, but the easy rhythm of our conversation had been broken. We stood there in silence for a few moments, until it grew awkward. There was no reason for me to stay longer—I knew that—but standing here in Ben's home, alone with him, I was reluctant to go.

I couldn't put off the inevitable. I pushed myself away from the counter.

"Hey, did...Does everything seem okay to you?" Ben asked, peering at me.

I stopped. "How do you mean?" I asked cautiously, my heartbeat seeming to pick up force and hammer at my ribs.

"With Jake. Did you happen to notice if he's acting weird?"

I blew out the breath I'd been holding. "Weirder than normal, you mean?"

Ben gave a half smile. "Yeah. Does he seem lethargic to you, or...well, depressed?"

I leaned back again, grateful for the momentary reprieve. "Jake?" Looking out the kitchen window to the backyard, I could clearly see the dog running in frenzied circles around the majestic live oak in Ben's backyard, his gaze fixed upward, barking excitedly at either something in the uppermost branches, or God. "I wouldn't say depressed, no," I said wryly. "Why?"

He shrugged. "I don't know. I sort of thought he was acting strange the week before I left. He'd just lie around, and he looked...this sounds dumb, I know...but he looked sad." Ben looked a bit sheepish himself at the words, but my heart swelled at the tenderness he showed the dog.

"I wasn't watching for anything like that, but he was with me pretty much nonstop," I said. "I probably would have noticed if he was acting so different from his usual manic-manic disorder."

Ben gave an embarrassed laugh. "Right. Helicopter parent—sorry."

Don't apologize. It's adorable. But I didn't say it out loud. "If you're worried about him, I could take him to the vet for you," I blurted. "I mean...if you're too busy with work."

"Really? I hate to ask, but if you have time..."

"Of course I will."

When he moved close beside me to share Jake's vet info on his phone, I breathed in his scent—cedar and citrus. We transferred the contact info to my phone, and Ben said he'd call the front desk tomorrow to let them know I was authorized to get treatment for the dog. Too soon he stepped away, and again I pushed myself away from the counter.

"I'll leave a key hidden outside for you, so you can pick Jake up and drop him off at your convenience," Ben said.

"Sure," I said nonchalantly, but I was fighting the urge to smile. It wasn't quite giving me a key to his house, but it still felt...I didn't know. Like *something*.

He opened the back door to let Jake back inside, and I bent to ruffle the dog's fur and kiss him goodbye on top of his nose. I managed to control my giddy impulse to do the same for Ben, but after we said goodbye I waltzed out to my car with an undeniable bounce.

Ben had asked me to watch his dog while he was out of town. He'd welcomed me inside tonight, purposefully made conversation, seemed reluctant to let me go, and now he was asking me to take more responsibility for Jake. Well, agreeing, anyway. Granted, his mom was out of town and Perfect Pamela was probably too busy doing brain surgery on sick kids to worry about taking care of his dog for him, but still...

This was what we in the mental health field called *inroads*. For the first time since our breakup, I thought there might actually be a crack in the door I thought had closed for good.

Perfect Pamela aside.

(Details, details...)

Chapter Eight

"I loved your article."

I could tell as soon as I answered his call that Michael knew my column that had run in this morning's paper was about him. About us. No surprise—once upon a time I thought he'd known me better than anyone.

Lisa had ended up running it verbatim—a startling testament to the new Lisa, I thought; the one who heard other people's points of view and actually considered them instead of bulling through with an autocratic dictate. I wasn't sure I'd ever actually *like* Lisa, but I was coming to respect her.

"Thanks," I said, balancing the phone in the crook of my neck as I swiped on mascara. "And also...thanks. I'm glad you came back and we finally talked."

"Me too. I didn't actually think you'd let me within throwing distance." I knew him well enough to hear the smile in his voice.

"Neither did I."

There was a moment's silence, not uncomfortable, and then: "There's something I wanted to talk to you about," Michael said, serious now.

"Yeah?" I said lightly. "I'm surprised there's anything we missed in our marathon conversation." My heart had sped up and I put a hand on it, not liking my reaction. I didn't want Michael to want anything from me. Did I? I finally had peace from everything that had happened, and I'd moved forward. If Michael was hoping to renew something between us...wasn't that moving backward?

Maybe it's just going home, an unwelcome voice whispered in my head.

"Are you free later today? Tonight?"

"I'm working all day," I hedged. "And I have my radio show later." I'd deliberately arranged my twice-weekly radio schedule for Monday mornings and Friday afternoons, because callers tended to need to talk to someone about their breakups most either right before a lonely weekend, or right after one.

"Okay. Tonight, then. Oh...Unless you have plans..." He deliberately left that hanging. Friday night—of course a single woman had plans.

Except that I didn't. And Dating 101 said that you never, ever accepted a last-minute date—especially on a weekend.

But this was not a date.

"Brook?"

I realized I'd let a lengthy silence fall. "I can't do tonight, actually."

"Oh." He sounded disappointed. "Right."

"But I can meet for a drink or coffee right after my radio show," I found myself saying. "Just for an hour."

As Michael's tone brightened and we planned where and when to meet, I hoped my change of heart was motivated only by curiosity.

...

My last caller on the Kelly Garrett show took up more time than the perky, pretty deejay and I usually allotted, but the woman's situation was complicated—and one I thought a lot of listeners might relate to. Nina had been with her boyfriend, Greg, for more than five years when she finally laid down the line: He came up with a ring or she was gone.

No ring was forthcoming, and Nina literally walked her talk and left him, moving out of their St. Pete apartment and relocating to Fort Myers to start over. But she was still deeply grieving the loss of her lover, best friend, and partner, and worried that she'd taken a perfectly healthy, happy relationship and thrown it away. She was working a mindless new job in retail that she hated, had made no friends here, and was still living in the barren furnished apartment she'd rented, surrounded by unpacked boxes.

This was a lot more than we could tackle in a three- to five-minute phone call—the radio call-in sweet spot, I'd learned in the last year on air.

"That's a hard situation, Nina," I said into the mike. "How long since things ended and you moved here?"

"Four months."

"That's a long time."

"A *long* time," she said, and her voice started to wobble.

"Without knowing more, it's hard to get to the bottom of what happened, how you might address things as far as you and Greg and your relationship. It sounds like it might help you to talk to someone to work through that. But meanwhile it's important that you not live in limbo because your relationship ended."

"What do you mean?"

"You were a 'we' for a long time, and you created a life as a couple, it sounds like. But since then it seems you've been living in a vacuum—not seeking out meaningful work or friends or even making a home for yourself. Regardless of what may happen between the two of you—or not—you still *exist*, and you have to treat yourself with the importance you gave to the two of you as a couple. It sounds like although you backed up your ultimatum to Greg and moved away, you're still waiting for him to recant—not creating anything you wouldn't want to walk away from here because you're still hoping he'll change his mind and call."

"Well, of *course* that's what I'm hoping for!" Nina exploded. "We've been together so long, and we shared everything—even bank accounts. For all intents and purposes it was a marriage, so how does a piece of paper change anything? If I stay gone long enough, he's going to see that."

Kelly looked up from the mixing board and caught my gaze, and her usually smiling brown eyes were drawn down in a mix of sympathy and disapproval.

Nina hadn't truly backed up her bluff—she was just playing the long game. There was clearly a lot of backstory here that couldn't be neatly tied up in our quick and very public phone call, but I wanted to leave her with at least something to work on in the short term.

"Maybe so, Nina. But maybe not. I don't want to counsel you on what to do about Greg without knowing more, but I can tell you this: If you don't figure out who you are on your own, then you're going to live the rest of your life as a satellite, orbiting around Greg or someone else and your couplehood with them, and you're never going to truly feel at home in your own skin."

There was a beat of silence and then: "I don't know what you mean."

"You gave Greg an ultimatum—"

"I *hate* that word. What a stupid cliché!"

"Call it what you want—you drew your line in the sand, and Greg didn't step over it. Okay, there are a lot of ways to address that—but meanwhile you're still living Greg's life, not your own. You're on hold while you try to force his hand into doing what you want. Four months have gone by, and you say you're trying to move on, but are you? You're working a job that requires nothing of you, you've created no attachments of your own, and you haven't even unpacked your own things into the place you're living. You're not living *your* life—you're still trying to make Greg live the life you think you want. You want to work things out with him, and maybe you can, but right now what is it you think he'll be drawn back to?"

"What do you...I mean, *us*. What we had," she said heatedly.

"That's gone. Live in the present."

In the pause that followed I heard a shaky breath and a sniffle. "I don't know how to do that."

For the first time she sounded vulnerable instead of defensive, and now we could do some productive work. "Start small. Unpack a box. Then another one. This is your home—at least for now. Live in it. Find a job that fits your experience, that fulfills you on some level if this one doesn't. *Talk* to people. Make a friend. Treat yourself as though *you* matter—until you do, neither Greg nor anyone else is going to think so."

"That sounds so...permanent. I don't know if I want to settle in here. St. Pete is home—I *had* all that there."

"Then stop playing games and go back—and do all those things on your own in St. Pete. You're more than Greg's girlfriend, Nina—but that doesn't necessarily mean becoming Greg's *wife*. Be Nina first. You won't know what you really want until you do."

...

Michael was waiting in a corner booth at the Hot Pot when I got there after the show. He was leaning against the wall, one leg bent up onto the banquette, reading a newspaper, and for one second time moved backward. I'd seen him exactly like this dozens of times on lazy Sunday afternoons when we rolled out of bed late because of his Saturday-night gigs and took our rumpled, unshowered selves to brunch at some nearby restaurant.

He looked up and time caught up with itself. A pressed button-down replaced his usual wrinkled concert T-shirt, and his hair was combed and neat, threads of gray reminding me that he wasn't the same Michael from my memories.

But I couldn't help a smile. It was still good to see him without having to hate him. I slid into the booth.

"Am I late?" I asked.

He sat up, lowering his leg back under the table so quickly it slammed into the edge, and he winced before loosing his familiar crooked smile on me. "I'm early. How about *that*?"

One of our ongoing spats while we'd been together was Michael's chronic inability to arrive anywhere at an appointed time, as if structure were for other people, but didn't apply to him. It was what precipitated our final argument, in fact.

"That *is* unexpected," I said. "I debated telling you we were meeting at six, just to get you here on time."

"I didn't want to keep you waiting." He tapped his fingers in an erratic drumbeat on the menu on the table. "I was going to order you a dirty martini, but I didn't know if that was still your drink."

"I'll just have a beer, actually." Partly I wanted to make sure I kept my wits about me, and dirty martinis went down far too easily. But some perverse part of me ordered something different because I didn't want Michael to still think he knew me so well. Or that I hadn't changed.

He raised his eyebrows and smirked, and I knew he'd understood my motivation as clearly as if I'd said it aloud. "Let's get the lady a beer, then. PBR?"

"God, no. Busch, please."

He laughed and caught our server's eye, motioning her over. The girl, leaning against a counter, arms crossed, stared uninterestedly at us for a moment before pushing herself upright with visible effort and trudging over. "You need something?"

Michael eyed our empty table, then me, and I could read his expression like a headline: *You think?* I smothered a chuckle.

"We'll have two Anchor Steams, please. No mugs."

"Yeah." She ambled off.

Michael was a beer snob, and had turned me into one while we'd been together. He knew there was no question that any brew found at a NASCAR race would cross my lips.

It was so easy to fall back into our usual banter. Too easy. I schooled the smile off my face. "So...you had something you wanted to talk about?"

He straightened. "Oh. Yeah, I do. It's about your work. The Breakup Doctor."

"My...work?" Of all the scenarios I'd pictured for Michael's return, having him retain my services wasn't even on the map. Did he want to hire me to get him past a breakup?

Oh, good lord. Did he want to hire me to get him past *our* breakup? He'd told me at length what bad shape he'd been in after he jilted me. Was Michael still not over it?

Or was this just a way to try to get me back?

Not that long ago I'd sat here with another man—Chip Santana, a former client I'd been certain was about to ask me to go out with him. Instead he told me he wanted to hire my Breakup Doctor services, and I'd felt like a vain fool—at least, until Chip disastrously confessed that hiring me was indeed just a ruse to get close.

I wasn't going to make either mistake again.

"Michael, I don't have to tell you that working with me is a bad idea. You know better than that. And if this is just a way to try to start something between us, that's not—"

"No, no—I don't want to hire you, Brook. I want to help you."

"You...What?"

Our ennui-filled server showed up with two bottles of Anchor Steam gripped in her left hand. In her right were a pair of cardboard coasters; she flung one down in front of each of us as if she were dealing cards. "Two Anchors, no mugs." She set the beers in front of each of us. "You want food?"

"Can we have a few minutes?" Michael said.

She shrugged. "It's your stomach."

After she shuffled away, Michael put his arms on the table, leaning in and ignoring his beer. "Brook, what you're doing...it's so unique. Your column, the radio show, all your clients—you're obviously good at this, and there's obviously a market for it, judging by how fast you've turned this into a business. But you can reach, what, a handful of people you actually counsel one-on-one? Maybe you can do some group therapy or something, but outside of that and these local media outlets, it doesn't scale up, am I right?"

He was startlingly right. My attempts to see more people than my office hours could allow had led to my starting group therapy sessions for the recently bereaved (of love) that I ran every Saturday. And it still bothered me when I was too busy to fit people in who needed acute help—like Nina Edelburg this morning, who'd called back after the show went off the air and asked about scheduling a series of sessions with me. My first available slot wasn't until more than two weeks away—an eternity in the acute stages of a breakup. Michael's quick insight into the limitations of my business model was impressive—and disconcerting.

"Yes," I said cautiously.

He nodded once, fingers once again tapping out a complicated Morse code on the table. "And I know you—you're probably working way too many hours and having trouble making sure you keep a work-life balance. And still feeling guilty that you aren't able to do enough for people."

I felt blood surge to my face. "Maybe," I said, rather stiffly.

"I don't think you have to push yourself so hard to reach all the people you probably want to reach. All you have to do is work smarter."

I narrowed my gaze on him and framed my words carefully. "Look, I appreciate that you've obviously given a lot of thought to this, but this is my business. It's not really any of yours." I didn't mean to sound harsh, but I was uncomfortable with his avid interest in my career. And, if I were honest, with how thoroughly my ex-fiancé still seemed to know me—and at how little I'd apparently changed.

He released that grin I knew so well, and I felt walls slam up into place. "Don't get defensive. You're right—it's not my business. But promotion is. And I'm good at it, Brook—seriously good at it. *No* promoter gets a band signed the first time up at bat—no one. But I did—partly because I *am* good at this, but a lot of it had to do with them. They were damn talented. And so are you. That column in this morning's paper? And I've read your other ones. It's good advice—and you get a ton of comments posted every week, which tells me you know how to hit a cultural nerve. You're a natural on the radio. You're too good to be lost here in some rinky-dink beach town when you could be reaching a bigger audience. A much bigger audience. I'm talking about newspaper syndication. Magazines. Radio syndication. TV."

Something inside me leaped at the picture Michael was painting. I'd long been thinking how to expand my Breakup Doctor practice, but always ran up against the wall that it wasn't exactly something I could hire help for, or farm out to others. My business could grow only to the point that I could sustain my current pace, and I had resigned myself to being maxed out where I was.

If I could do more, reach more people...The idea held massive appeal.

But any enthusiasm I felt was overshadowed by anger—and hurt. Michael hadn't come back here to ask my forgiveness, or tie up our badly frayed loose ends, or even to try to get me back, as I'd narcissistically convinced myself.

He'd simply seen a business opportunity.

"No," I said flatly, forcing myself to stay planted in my seat and taking a casual swig of my beer. Leaving in a wounded huff would only show Michael that he could still affect me—and I wasn't going to give him the satisfaction.

Michael blinked. "No? Just no?" He stared at me intently, eyebrows bunched together, and then shifted his gaze down to the table. "Oh. This is because of me, isn't it," he said quietly. "Because of what I did."

I gave a humorless laugh. "Believe it or not, Michael, it isn't. My practice is quite different from what I used to do as a therapist when you knew me. I don't know how to explain it to you in a way you'll understand. It's about personal connections. Heart. It's not something I'm willing to turn into a Jerry Springer sideshow or some reality-TV garbage. Yes, I'm sure you could pimp the idea out and reach more people—but minus the soul of what I do."

One corner of his mouth turned up in a rueful grin. "I deserved that. I didn't mean to come on like a bulldozer. I guess...I'm just nervous."

"Nervous about what?"

That half grin ghosted away. "About you, Brook. What else?"

The words sent an odd jolt through my chest—the intimacy of the way he said "you." The way he spoke my name.

"Nervous about *what*," I repeated, but this time my voice was thready.

He didn't look up, shredding the ragged edge of his coaster with a fingernail, and I realized I'd been so distracted I'd missed his "tells"—fidgeting, breaking eye contact, the anxious busywork of his hands. I could see his Adam's apple lift and fall as he swallowed and then finally answered.

"I really do admire what you're doing, Brook. For the reason you said—it's personal, it has real heart. And I think there's so much opportunity to widen your reach, give more people the chance to take advantage of what you're offering. But that's not why I'm here." He looked up, and the impact of his green eyes shooting directly into mine stopped my heart for a flash of a second. "I'm here for *you*. Because it took me much too long, and I'm scared as hell I'm way too late. But if I don't try I'll never be able to live with that."

Every drop of saliva seemed to leave my mouth like a tide retreating before an oncoming tsunami.

"Try...what?" I croaked out after the long silence had grown suffocating.

"Us."

For a second I forgot to breathe. It was exactly what I'd feared...and exactly what I'd once wanted most.

The most universally cherished breakup fantasy is this: that one day the person who dumped you will come crawling back, professing that he made a mistake, begging you to give him a second chance.

But now that that fantasy was here, I didn't feel like crowing my triumph and rubbing Michael's nose in all he'd thrown away. Nor did my pain magically feel erased. If anything, a supernova of sorrow exploded in my chest at his single, chest-quaking word. This felt almost...worse. Michael loved me. He wanted me back. The last two world-shattering years didn't ever have to happen.

I ached with it.

But none of this exited my mouth in the form of words; I just sat staring, my head shaking side to side as if of its own accord.

"I'm not so stupid that I think we can pick back up where we left off," Michael went on, oblivious to the whirlwind of thoughts crowding my head. "I blew that. But maybe...maybe we can start over? Slowly—I'm not pushing you. Let me date you. Let me know you again. Get to know *me* now, Brook—I've changed."

I knew he had. Or I desperately wanted to believe it from what I'd seen since he came back. I'd changed too. For the better, I thought.

Was there a possibility that all we'd needed was time to grow up a little more?

He didn't wait for me to come up with a reply, but reached across the table and took my cold hand in his, my fingers curling into his through sheer subconscious muscle memory.

"There's still something here, Brook," he said, his warm thumb stroking the back of my hand. "Please give me—us—another chance. I swear to God, I will not screw it up this time."

It was hard to breathe, and Michael's face had grown blurry where tears had clouded my vision.

The two years with this man had contained some of the best moments of my life. The two years since had encompassed some of the worst, after everything I'd thought was certain had been yanked out from beneath me. Because of Michael I'd hit lower than any rock-bottom I'd ever known before. I'd turned into someone half-crazed I barely recognized, frozen in place in my relationships to the point where I'd finally had to step completely away from them.

Wasn't it just last night my heart was leaping at the thought of Ben and me getting back on track? How could I be thinking of Michael in the same way?

He was right, though. There had been something real between us. Something rare.

I wasn't willing to completely shut that door.

But I wasn't ready to throw it wide-open, either.

I eased my hand out of his grasp and reached into my purse to lay a ten on the table. Michael's expression clouded.

"It..." My voice faltered, and I swallowed and started over. "It took me a long time to survive getting over you, Michael. I'm scared to risk having to do it again."

"I can understand that," he began. "But—"

"No—don't say anything yet." I pushed myself up out of the booth and stood looking down at his painfully, achingly dear face.

"I *am* willing to try for a friendship," I said. "If you were serious about working with me to expand the Breakup Doctor practice we can try it. *Slowly*," I added quickly when his face brightened. "And I have final approval on anything you do. Don't give me your answer yet," I said, holding up a hand when he opened his mouth to speak. "You have to swear you won't try to win me over in the meantime. I'm too vulnerable where you're concerned, and I have to know that I can let you back into my life a little bit without being frightened that you'll take me over." I looked down, blinking away moisture, and then met his eye again. "Give me some time to think about this. To get used to it. I can't promise you I'll be able to...to try again."

His eyebrows drew together, and a wounded look crept into his eyes—only to clear like a passing storm at my next words:

"But I can't promise you that I won't."

Chapter Nine

I did not call Sasha.

I had to actually physically stop myself from doing it—by hiding my cell phone from myself just as I would after a breakup—but I already knew her feelings about Michael. I needed a little space to figure out mine. And yet after lying awake long into the night thinking about what he'd said, I still had no idea what I wanted.

At group therapy the next morning, I felt a little bit like a hypocrite.

Chrissie Tomas finished sharing and set the claw—the garden cultivator I'd brought in when I'd first started the group sessions to signify that whoever was holding it had the floor and was not to be interrupted—back in the center of the circle. She had been telling us for the last ten minutes why she was still constantly calling her boyfriend who'd dumped her two weeks ago—because he was also her best friend and she needed him to help her get through the breakup.

"You can't be friends with your ex," slipped automatically out of my mouth, and a few heads around the room nodded. It was one of my most strongly held tenets of breakups—trying to be pals with an ex while the breach was still fresh was like trying to heal a cut while you were still holding the razor to it.

"That's insane," Chrissie shot back hotly. "Are you supposed to just suddenly chop someone you care about out of your life forever? We're not in high school. *Adults* can still be friends."

I heard this a lot from clients unwilling to completely close the door. "Yes," I said. "Ideally you're right—maybe you can be friends again one day, if you're both willing. But he can't be your breakup buddy when your pain is the most raw. You're asking Mark to help you get over *Mark*. He can't wear both hats, Chrissie. The man who decided he doesn't want to be with you anymore and broke your heart is the same Mark who you want to console you about it. Do you see the impossibility of that?"

Chrissie's eyes filled with tears. "I still can't believe it," she said in an unsteady voice. "I know he loves me—half the time he's the one calling me. Why doesn't he want to be with me anymore?"

These were some of the worst kinds of breakups—when two people genuinely cared about each other, but the romance just didn't work out. Losing a lover, a partner, a mate was bad enough. Losing your best friend on top of that, just when you needed one the most, was almost unbearable.

If I hadn't had Sasha after Michael and I had broken up, I would have been exactly in Chrissie's situation.

But Mark was making it even worse on Chrissie by staying in contact—and she was making it worse on *herself*. Although Michael's disappearance after our broken engagement had shattered me, it was actually a kindness. It forced me to let the wound start to heal. Poor Chrissie was just having it ripped repeatedly back open.

"I don't know," I said gently. "I wish I did—sometimes it feels like at least having an answer will make things easier to bear."

Chrissie nodded, not looking up. I leaned over to pluck a few tissues from the box I always kept at hand, offering them to her.

"It doesn't, though," I went on. "When someone has decided we're not what they want anymore, it doesn't help for them to explain exactly why. How about you guys—thoughts?" I asked the group.

Brett Rorbach, a stylish lady in her early thirties whose middle-aged boyfriend left her for a much older woman, raised a hand, and I nodded. "You can't be friends with someone who deliberately hurt you," she said. "That's not what friends do."

"Amen," said Kiki LeKerr, whose last relationship ended when her boyfriend, who'd been separated, got back together with his wife. "You cut that son of a bitch out of your life like a cancer."

"Hold on—you can't just start hating someone you loved," Victor Underwood said. He'd left his girlfriend for an old flame, only to find out quickly that there was a reason it had burned out before. But the woman he broke up with refused to give him a second chance, and Victor had been suffering for it ever since. "That's childish, like Chrissie said. Can't we act like grown-ups? If you liked someone well enough to want to be with them in a relationship, hopefully you liked them enough to be friends. Right?"

One of the benefits of group therapy, I'd learned over the last months, was that often having everyone talk out issues among themselves let them find their own way to an answer. Even in one-on-one therapy, getting a client to see the truth for themselves was a lot more impactful than my spoon-feeding it to them, but it always went faster in a group round table.

"I think you guys are all right, to a degree."

Brett grinned. "You always say that."

"Maybe," I said with an acknowledging smile. "But it's usually true. Nothing's black-and-white, and you all present various facets of all the issues that come up in here." I turned to Chrissie, whose tears had dried as she'd followed the discussion intently. "I'd like to think we could be friends with the people we've cared deeply about...even if we choose not to be with them romantically." I was thinking of Michael, but fresh on the heels of that an image of Ben flitted across my mind, and I added, "Or if we *can't.* But maintaining a connection with them while the pain is still so fresh only makes it harder for us to move past it. It's like asking the guy who just shot you to please help you take out the bullet."

A watery laugh erupted from Chrissie, and a few chuckles echoed around the room.

I leaned forward in my chair. "All I'm suggesting is that you give yourself some room from that pain. Don't tell yourself you have to cut Mark out of your life forever—that hurts even worse, doesn't it?" She nodded furiously. "Okay. So think of this as just for right now.

Sometimes getting over a breakup is like any other substance addiction. We can take a page from AA: One day at a time."

"That's right," Victor spoke up. "If I told myself I could never have another glass of Scotch, I promise you guys I'd be sitting here tanked out of my gourd right now. But *today* I won't have that glass. That I can do."

I looked at Victor, who'd never confessed to us before that he'd had a drinking issue. "Thanks for sharing that, Victor."

On the other side of him, Chrissie bobbed her head and echoed, "Yeah, thanks."

I returned my gaze to her. "So tell yourself that just for today, you won't call Mark. If he calls you, you'll ask him to give you some space—just for a while. When you break your leg you know you're going to need crutches for a little while to get back on your feet, right?"

"Right," she said quietly.

"Okay. So for now, some distance from Mark is your crutches. Once that leg heals you won't need them anymore—and that's when you can try for a friendship again, if you still want one."

"And how long will that take?" she asked me, a vulnerable, pleading expression on her face.

I offered her a rueful smile. "I wish I knew," I said honestly, wondering whether I'd tossed my own crutches away too soon where Michael—and Ben—were concerned.

...

I knew I couldn't put off telling Sasha about Michael any longer—I always told her everything, and the truth was, I needed her as a sounding board to figure out what I wanted to do.

But once again I rolled into voicemail. Sasha's phone was attached to her hand almost as securely as her fingers were; there was no way she missed my call.

She was still dodging me. And it was past time I figured out why.

As soon as I left the Fort Myers Yacht Club conference room where we held the group sessions, I dialed my brother.

"Hey, sis," he answered, and I waited for his usual follow-up—something childish like "'Sup?" or "What's shakin'?" or "How's it hangin'?" But that was all he said.

"Hey, Stuvie." I registered the buzzing sound in the background. "Where are you?"

"Dad and I are headed out fishing."

"Oh. Where's Sash?"

"She wanted me to get out of her hair for the day."

I frowned. "Everything okay with you two?"

I heard a loud rustling, as if he'd shifted position into the wind, and then after a moment it settled.

"Why do you ask?" His voice was low, and he sounded cagey.

"She seemed weird the other night. And she's avoiding my calls. Is she all right?"

Another long silence filled only with the sporadic sounds of the boat motor, as our connection got spotty. He and Dad tended to go out on the gulf pretty far. "I don't know."

I frowned. "What's going on?"

After a moment I made out, "...can't...have to ask..."

"Stu." I used the tone that always made my little brother confess any transgression to me when we were kids. "Are you fooling around on her?"

"What?" he yelped. "No! I can't bel..."—the connection faltered—"...ask me that, Brook!"

His horrified tone was too genuine for me to doubt him. "Then what's going on?"

"...can't hear you. Just ask..."

"Stuvie—"

"...you later—" The connection dropped.

I stood on the asphalt holding the phone, staring at the line of royal palms bordering the yacht club's parking lot as they rustled in the breeze. It seemed like the problem wasn't on Stu's end—at least, not as far as he knew. And I hadn't done anything to upset Sasha that I could think of.

So if she was afraid to tell me something, I thought with dawning horror, that left only one logical thing I could think of.

Sasha was about to break my brother's heart.

...

I'm not proud of the fact that I ambushed her, but I really didn't see any other choice. When I called Sasha she once again let me roll into voicemail.

So thirty minutes after I hung up with Stu, I was standing on the concrete walkway outside her apartment, and I came bearing gifts (okay, bribes): a cardboard tray with two lattes in one hand, and a bag of fresh, still-warm cinnamon rolls from Merritt's bakery in the other. Even health-obsessed Sasha couldn't resist their cream cheese frosting.

"Knock, knock!" I hollered cheerfully. No answer.

Her car was parked right outside, though, so I balanced on one leg and kicked the door with my foot—perhaps slightly less delicately than I meant to. "Hey, rise and shine, lazybones. I have cinnamon rolls from Merritt's and I'm going to eat them all unless—"

The door swung open and I almost kicked my best friend in the shin.

"Will you please stop shouting like a crazy person!"

It took me a moment to get my tongue working. Sasha—who could wake up from a two-day bender looking like she'd just walked off a magazine cover shoot—looked horrible. Her eyelids were puffy and raw, as if she'd moisturized with poison oak, the skin underneath sunken and dark. Her hair had clearly been untroubled by a brush today, and her face was free of makeup, just a sheet crease that shot down her left cheek like a lightning bolt. Most alarming of all, she was wearing a faded and worn pair of baggy pajama bottoms of some kind of flannel—a material I'd have sworn up and down would never touch her body—and a shapeless oversize green hoodie that said PANAMA

CITY, SPRING BREAK across the chest, a twin of mine from our sophomore year that I'd long since trashed.

"What *happened*?" I asked, aghast.

She frowned, still planted in the wedge of open door with her hand firmly around the edge of it. "I'm not feeling great, Brook. I just need to sleep, okay?" She started to shut the door, but I quickly shoved one Birkenstock against it, coffee sloshing across my fingers.

I winced, ignoring the burn. "Then I'll nurse you," I insisted. "What was Stu thinking, leaving you to go fishing? He should be here taking care of you."

"No!" she barked, and then blinked, as if surprised by her own sharp tone. "No, I told him to go. It's okay, Brook, really. Thanks for coming by. I'll call you lat—"

"No," I said, not budging. I dropped all my false cheer. "Don't insult me, Sash," I said quietly. "If you don't want to talk to me about it, you don't have to. But please don't pretend I'm going to buy that you're sick. That's not what's going on. Is it."

Her tangle of blond hair fell forward, obscuring her face as she stared down at the floor. A dark round spot appeared on the terracotta tile in the entryway—and then another one—and then I realized my best friend was crying.

I all but dropped the coffees and bakery bag to the concrete walkway and took her in my arms. "Sash..." I said helplessly. "Sash...What is it? What's wrong?"

She was clutching onto me like a life raft, and now she was sobbing—I could feel her body heave, but she still made no sound, and that was the most awful part of all. Histrionics from my dramatic best friend I could handle—I was used to it. This silent, racking grief felt too deep for me to know how to reach.

I led her inside and onto her red velvet sofa and held her for a long time, saying nothing, just gripping her tight and stroking her shoulder, her back, her hair, the pit in my stomach yawing wider.

Finally she grew still and her breathing evened out, and I relaxed my hold on her enough to pull away and look her in the face. Or try. Her head was still bent down, her gaze on the carpet.

"Tell me, Sash," I said, bracing myself for the worst. "We'll get through it—whatever it is. I swear to you." I reached up to wipe her face, but she didn't even seem to register my touch.

"I'm pregnant," she said dully.

For a second I literally couldn't find the breath to speak.

"What?" I finally wheezed out.

"Yeah."

"You...and Stu?"

Sasha's brow crinkled. "Yes, me and Stu—jeez, Brook. Who else?"

"No, that's not what I..." I scooted closer and put my hand on her leg. "When are you going to tell him? Do you need me to be there?"

Sasha looked at me as if I'd grown a second head. "I already told Stu, Brook. I tell him everything."

I goggled at her. She told him *everything*? Sasha, who kept so many threads of what she wanted a man to know running at the same time, I suspected she had to use a spreadsheet?

"You do?"

She gave a one-shouldered shrug and looked away. "He's my best friend. Next to you."

If I'd ever had one second of doubt about the two of them, Sasha had just casually blown it away like the fluff of a mimosa bloom.

"Sash...I know my brother—he might seem like a total goofball, but there's no way he'll bail on you. He's crazy about you. I promise he'll be on board with this," I reassured her. He'd *better*.

"I know he is. He's already talking about buying a house, getting married, and I—"

"Stu wants to get married?!" I didn't realize I had shouted the words until I heard the ringing echo in the room.

"Take a breath, crazy," Sasha said flatly, eyeballing me.

I obeyed, but I couldn't get my mind around it—my brother, jumping on board the good ship *Commitment* of his own free will? I never thought I'd see it.

"But then…" I began slowly, puzzling through the facts as I spoke, "what's the matter? Isn't all of this what you want?" I finished, meeting Sasha's gaze in bewilderment.

Sasha sighed and her eyes filled up. "I don't know. I don't *know*, Brook."

I'd always expected that when the day came that commitment-craving Sasha shared news like this with me, it would be an all-out bacchanalia of celebration, *Girls Gone Wild* but with a ring and babies instead of a fling and boobies. I'd never foreseen this reaction.

I took a long, deep breath in and schooled my face into a neutral expression. "Okay. All right. So let's talk it out. What part are you unsure of?"

Sasha looked at me incredulously. "It's scaring the *shit* out of me."

"Oh, Sash, of *course* it is," I said. "It's terrifying." Fear I understood. Fear I could deal with. "Stay here—I'll be right back," I said. "Let me get the rolls and coffee I left outside and we can sit and talk."

My words prompted a fresh torrent of sobbing, and I stopped midway to the front door, at a loss. "Sash?"

"Coffee!" she wailed. "Oh, God, coffee!"

I stared at her for a moment, trying to figure it out, and then: "Because coffee?" I asked hesitantly.

Sasha nodded, still crying, and I nodded too. Coffee, because a pregnant woman couldn't have caffeine. And because Sasha sucked down coffee like an SUV sucked gas.

"How about some juice?" I asked carefully.

Juice was okay, apparently, because Sasha gave a tearful nod, and I went into the kitchen instead—I didn't want to risk even carrying the coffee cups past her to toss them out—and poured us both some OJ. When I came back her face was dry, if still pinched. I handed her one of the glasses and she took a long gulp, draining nearly half.

"Thanks," she gasped when she finished, setting the glass on the cocktail table. I sat beside her and waited.

"Okay," she started, gripping her thighs with the palms of her hands as if bracing herself. "First off, I..." She stopped, took a deep breath. "I'm sorry I didn't tell you about...all of this. I didn't mean to keep it from you," she went on, not looking at me. "It was just..." I saw her eyes fill again, and she blinked. "I needed to think about it without the filter of you."

I must have blanched, because her gaze shot to me. "I don't mean that the way it sounded, Brook." Tears slipped past her lashes again—we were like a Nicholas Sparks movie—and she reached for my hand. "You were the only person I wanted to talk it out with," she said sadly. "And I couldn't—because it was your brother."

I wanted to argue, but I couldn't. Things were a little different with us now. They had to be, because whereas once Sasha and I were each other's number one confidante and ally, now her deepest loyalties were to Stu. And she was right—this wasn't a situation I could be completely objective about, I was realizing as I fought not to try to convince her to be happy about it.

And after all...wasn't that the same reason I hadn't called her about Michael? So I could think it through without the filter of her?

"It's okay," I said. "I get it."

"We don't have to talk about this if you...if it's too hard to hear."

I thought about all the times my best friend had listened to me working something out ad nauseam, serving as a nonjudgmental, supportive sounding board. "Of course we do. Tell me what you need."

"I don't know. Why aren't I happy about this?" She shot me an apologetic look with the words, but I just squeezed her fingers. "I need to figure out what I'm feeling."

"Okay," I said, turning to face her fully. "Then let's talk it out. Do you love Stu?"

"*Yes.*"

Her immediate, emphatic answer lifted a weight off my chest, but I determinedly kept digging. "I mean more than like a brother? Like, does he still seem the right 'fit' for you, everything else aside?"

"Of *course* he does."

"All right." I nodded, breathing a little bit easier. "It always seemed to me that that was what you *wanted*—someone who loves you completely, who you love. Someone who wants you more than anything."

"It was...It *is*." She frowned. "But buying a house, getting married— that all sounds like someone else's life to me. I don't know if I can handle that."

"Of course you can," I said automatically.

But Sasha went on as if I hadn't spoken. "And adding a kid to all that..." She looked down at her lap, her face bunching. "Maybe I'm just not maternal," she said in a trembling voice, and at her words her tears spilled over again, dotting her ratty sweatpants.

My heart tore at her miserable expression, and my brain rebelled against the notion. Sasha would make an awesome mom—she brimmed with genuine, unrestrained emotion she lavished on the people she loved. She was crazy enough to be playful and fun, but at her core she knew about responsibility and discipline. Frankly I always thought she'd be a far better mom than I would—I was afraid I'd wind up too much the product of my own mother, setting the bar for a child impossibly high and never letting her feel she was meeting it.

I took hold of Sasha's limp hands. "I don't know if any new mom magically feels maternal, Sash. How can anyone think they're ready for something so huge? Even for people who were *trying* to get pregnant, I have to think that once it actually happens, all that responsibility can be awfully scary."

She looked up, meeting my eyes, and the dark sadness in hers was terrible to see. "I don't know if I'm ready for this, Brook," she whispered.

There was nothing much to say to that. We sat, silent, simply looking at each other, for a long, heartbreaking moment.

Finally she blinked, and looked away. "I'm so messed up. I should want this. I so *want* to want this."

Her words kindled a spark of hope in my chest, but I held it at bay. The worst thing a therapist could do was to push someone in the direction she thought they should go.

"I used to see this sometimes in my old practice," I said gently. "When people finally get everything they ever wanted, a lot of times it scares them to death and they run away from it."

She bit the inside of her lips—a habit she'd had since we were kids whenever she was unsure. "Do you think that's what this is?"

I shrugged. "Maybe. Do you?"

She rolled her eyes. "You're therapizing me."

"Sorry."

"Help me, Brook," she said quietly. "I don't want to screw this up by not knowing what the hell I'm doing. What I want. You have to *fix* this—that's what you do. Help me be ready for all of it. *Please.*"

I took in another deep breath and nodded, meeting her eyes with an encouraging smile. "I will, Sash. We're going to make everything okay."

She practically hurled herself into my arms, gripping me with a strength that nearly whooshed the breath out of me.

But as I gently rubbed her back, staring over her shoulder, I had no idea how I was going to live up to that promise.

Chapter Ten

By the next morning I still had no plan of attack for Sasha, but I was too frazzled to keep working on it—I was due for the Sunday-morning get-together with Ben that had become our new routine, and my stomach was fluttering.

When we'd started trying to rebuild some kind of friendship from the ashes of our torched relationship, we'd began slowly, on neutral ground. The first time I'd met him and Jake at Dog Beach was a Sunday a little over a month ago, and I'd been sizzling with a nauseating mix of emotions then too: excitement at seeing him again after so long; apprehension over how he'd act, what we'd say, whether things would be awkward and painful; and a breathless giddiness.

That day I'd brought a ball, thinking not only to throw it for Jake to chase, but to occupy my attention and distract myself from the nerves that were shuddering through me.

But Jake, it turned out, was not a "fetch" kind of dog. He'd been happy enough to see the red rubber ball when I brought it out of my bag, and mouth it, lick it, and otherwise demonstrate a certain affection for it. But as soon I hurled the ball down the beach, Jake looked mournfully after it, then back at me with a wounded expression like, *We were having such a nice time…why'd you throw that toy away?* I kept trying, with equal lack of success, until I realized that Jake was just as happy to wander and sniff and wrestle with the other dogs—and I was just as happy to sit and slowly, ever so gradually, make conversation with Ben.

Today, as I pulled on shorts and brushed on more makeup than was strictly necessary for Dog Beach, my pinballing emotions had a lot to do with Sasha—I was still digesting the news, still struggling with her deep-seated doubts and what it might mean for her and my brother, my family. I was desperate to talk it out with someone, and Ben had always been a wonderful listener.

But of course I couldn't talk about this with him—with anyone. Sasha had sworn me to secrecy. And the weight of keeping such an enormous secret pressed almost as heavily on me as Sasha's ambivalence.

But my stomach also churned about Ben. Was I really sensing a door opening lately, or was that just wishful thinking on my part? And if I was...what about Perfect Pamela?

So I'd once again brought something to occupy my hands and my attention—a silly Beanie Baby frog I'd bought on a whim at a checkout counter—and Jake's circuits lit right up at the sight of it.

"Nice of you to bring him a toy," Ben said as I dropped my bag to the sand beside his things.

He wore cargo shorts, his legs below them tanned and peppered with dark hair, white sand already coating the sides of his feet and ankles. I swallowed and dragged my eyes up to his face.

"I figured he might like this better than the ball." I leaned over to show Jake the frog.

As he had with the ball, the dog made sweet love to it with his mouth—until I tossed it a few feet away. Jake barely needed to move to go get it—three steps in that direction would have yielded the jackpot—yet he simply stared at the castaway toy with a sad sense of acceptance. *Very well. We have discarded the frog.*

I tried a few more times, with similar results. Finally, resigned, I walked over to pick up the toy from the sand, angling a look back at Ben, who'd been watching with a sly grin. "I guess fetch is simply not in the cards," I said, and tossed him the animal.

At which point Jake went wild, tearing over to Ben, panting and slavering like a feral creature, doing his bunny-hop thing and barking madly.

I blinked. "Well. Maybe he only wants to play with you," I said, trying not to take it personally. "Throw it for him."

Ben obliged, tossing the stuffed animal ten feet or so across the sand.

At which point Jake sank into a pose of dejected ennui.

"What the hell, dog?" Ben asked him, and a laugh bubbled out of me, some of my tension beginning to unwind. "Go get it."

Jake let out a pained sigh.

We spent far too long trying to encourage, cajole, and coerce the dog to go pick up the frog he'd wanted so desperately mere minutes ago, but Jake was inconsolable at its loss. Finally Ben went to retrieve it—"Well, it was a sweet thought, anyway—thanks," he said—and tossed it over to me.

And Jake again went nuts.

Finally Ben and I figured out that any dispensation of the frog was a grave disappointment to Jake—but the act of throwing the toy between us made him delirious with happiness. And thus ensued a game of Pickle with Jake in the middle, joyfully hopping between us as we threw the Beanie Baby back and forth, but never once trying to actually intercept it.

"Weird dog you have there," I said after ten minutes of this, with no sign of Jake's interest flagging.

Ben tossed the toy to me, Jake following it like a comet's tail. "He's his own man. You gotta like that."

I tossed it back, and Jake went sailing after it, screeching to a halt at Ben's feet. I grinned. "Like father, like son?"

Ben's answering smile warmed me more than the bright sun heating the top of my head and my shoulders and the sand under my bare feet. "You oughta know."

His answer—even with dozens of people milling around with their dogs, twenty feet of open air between us—felt shockingly intimate, and pleasure jolted through me as I lobbed the stuffed toy back.

Ben made a show of letting the Beanie Baby plop into his cupped hand. "You throw like a girl," he teased as he arced it back in an exaggerated parabola, Jake scrambling over in my direction.

I plucked it from the air. "I *am* a girl. And I thought this was about taunting your dog, not proving our pitching skills." I drilled the beanbag frog straight at him, and watched him hustle to get his hands up to catch it.

"Nice!" he said admiringly.

"I didn't grow up with a brother for nothing."

We were grinning across the sand at each other, Jake looking between us, confusedly trying to figure out who was holding his beloved frog as we bantered back and forth.

This was what I'd missed so badly since Ben and I had broken up last year. This easy rapport, the sense of playfulness and fun that had always been such a part of our relationship. The feeling that I was authentically myself with Ben in a way I'd never really been with anyone else, not even Michael—who I'd managed to avoid thinking about, amid everything else.

Being with Ben had always felt oddly *familiar*, as though we'd known each other for years—even from our first ill-advised date, when I'd intended merely to use him to try to make Kendall jealous and instead found myself utterly absorbed by our conversation, drawn to him in a way I thought I couldn't be when I'd been wallowing in a morass of heartbreak and mild insanity. There was never any pretense between us, no games, just a genuine connection, a feeling that he knew me and I knew him, and we both liked the person we saw.

Unless I was totally misreading the situation—and let's remember I'm a licensed professional in the area of the human psyche—I thought he might be cracking open a door again between us.

The same way Michael was.

I knew exactly where Michael's head was—he'd told me. If I wanted to give the two of us another chance, I knew that avenue was wide-open.

But Ben changed the equation. I'd let him go because I wasn't sure what I wanted. In the seven months since, I'd figured it out—and I knew now. If it was being offered to me, I wasn't willing to let go of it again.

It might not have been fair to Michael to make my decision with him contingent on Ben. But then again, Michael hadn't exactly played fair with me in the past.

I swallowed a rising guilt. I had to find out where things stood with Ben and Pamela. No matter how much I still loved Ben, there were lines I wasn't willing to cross—and one of those was encroaching on another woman's turf.

I took a deep breath, tossing the frog back. "So you never really told me about New York," I said.

"Yeah, I did. We talked about it the night you brought Jake back."

Plop. The frog landed in my palms, Jake trotting happily after it and sitting in front of me with a toothy doggie grin. "Yeah, I...You know, I mean, like...you guys had fun?"

He shrugged. "Sure. New York is always fun."

Indirect tactics evidently weren't going to work.

"So, Pamela seems...really great."

Somehow Jake missed my throw and was still staring eagerly up at me when Ben caught the frog, so he gave a whistle and shook the toy out in front of him. The dog barreled over, and Ben tossed it to me just as he did. Jake nearly skidded out, throwing up a wave of sand as he wheeled around and came back at me.

"You think so?" he asked finally.

I wanted to drill the Beanie Baby at his chest again. Was he deliberately being obtuse?

"Do *you*?"

Ben shot his hands up to catch the frog—maybe I hurled it a little faster than our game of keep-away warranted—and held on to it. "Do you really want to talk about this, Brook?" he asked. He wasn't making any move to throw the toy back, just looking directly at me.

My mouth felt dry despite the moist, sea-scented air, and I swallowed. "Yes. I do."

After a moment he nodded shortly. "Okay. Yes. Pamela is really great," he said.

My stomach tumbled to the sand. And because I was apparently much more of a masochist than I realized, my mouth said, "Do you love her?"

He kept staring at me, so long my heart rate sped up. I felt foolish standing there, my hands idle at my sides, the pretext of the game over. Jake settled on the sand, head between his paws, and closed his eyes as if exhausted. Ben seemed to be searching my face for something, but he was too far away for me to tell.

"No," he said quietly. "I don't."

A smile I couldn't control began to creep across my lips, and only the dim recognition that it was utterly inappropriate let me bite it back. "Oh," I said foolishly. "But she seems...perfect," I said, her usual adjective flying to my lips. "Totally perfect," I added, unable this time to curb the rueful smile that tugged my mouth.

I took one hesitant step toward him, then another, Jake not even reacting as my bare foot settled an inch from his nose. "Why don't you think you can love her?" I said, breathless.

It seemed as if even the wheeling seabirds quieted and stilled as I waited for his answer, the sounds of the other dogs and their owners receding into the distance, even the gentle shushing of the gulf's soft waves growing hushed.

Ben frowned and shook his head, and the breath stuck in my throat.

"I didn't say I *couldn't*."

...

Dinner that night at my parents' house carried an extra delight of undercurrents.

I was still lost in my head about my conversation at Dog Beach with Ben. We'd been so close—everything I wanted dangling right in front of me until, like Tantalus grasping for the fat fruit at his fingertips, it was yanked away as soon as I reached for it.

His answer to my leading question had been so opposite what I'd expected—what I'd been so hungry for that I almost thought I'd already heard it—that for a moment I'd just stood gaping at him, as if I'd lost the ability to understand English. Confused, embarrassed, wanting to regain my bearings, I'd leaned over to pet Jake, as if that were what I'd intended all along. I couldn't even manufacture enough voice to reply—and wouldn't have known what to say if I could.

I'd kept my eyes on the dog as I stroked his fur, damp and crusty with sand, and finally, when I could trust myself to speak, I risked a glance up at Ben, who was still standing where he'd been, the frog dangling forgotten from one hand.

"Guess I need to get going," I'd said in a voice that sounded strange in my own ears, and snatched up my things, walking so quickly back out to the parking area to keep Ben from seeing my plastic smile start to wobble that he and Jake were only just emerging from the mangroves as I started my car. I waved as I drove by them, my eyes determinedly straight ahead.

As we fell into our usual chores before dinner at my parents', I could barely make eye contact with Sasha, because between my mental state and hers I was afraid I'd fall apart if I did. I avoided being alone with my dad, because I had a habit of blurting out everything to him—he was too easy to talk to. I couldn't even *look* at Stu, because I couldn't bear to see his fears and worries about Sasha written on his face.

At the dinner table, when my mom did her usual grilling of everyone's week, as soon as she got to Sasha my best friend opened her mouth and then seemed to freeze that way, like the Munch painting brought to life—and finally I snapped into the present.

Sasha couldn't lie. Not to my mother. But it was too soon—I knew she wasn't ready. If she blurted out the truth of her pregnancy—and worse, her mixed feelings about it—it would send a shock wave around the table, and only make things worse on Sasha.

So I did the only thing I could think of to avoid disaster: I leaped in and took one for the team.

"You'll never believe it, but I've been talking to Michael again."

Unsurprisingly, that turned every eye to me. "Oh, hon, are you okay?" came from my dad, and, "Are you *shitting* me?!" from Stu, and an exasperated, "Oh, Brook Lyn, haven't you learned?" from—who else?—my mother. There ensued a joyful interrogation that lasted the remainder of the evening and ended with this gem from Mom:

"Just don't run crying to me when he cuts your legs out from under you again."

It was everything I always hated about telling my family my personal business.

But one glance at Sasha's relieved, grateful expression made the whole inquisition worthwhile.

Chapter Eleven

"I'm not lying on that sofa."

Sasha eyeballed the chaise lounge where my clients usually sat as we stood in the doorway of my home office.

"No way," she stated vehemently. "I'm not a patient."

She'd come by after work late the next afternoon, desperate to get started on whatever plan I'd culled together to help her.

I hadn't yet culled together *any* sort of plan, although I did know where we needed to start: with her fears that were crowding out everything else.

But I had to admit it felt awkward. We always talked about our issues together, but this time it felt less bosom buddies and more patient-therapist, and neither of us seemed at ease with the new vibe.

"Fair enough." I one-eightied us out of the office and back into my living area. "Couch? Chair? Breakfast bar in the kitchen?" I asked, indicating various corners of my house. "We can go sit on my bed if you're more comfortable—seriously, Sash, I want you to feel relaxed."

"Well, since a glass of wine is off the table, how about we go sit on your lanai and you can give me a foot rub while we talk."

"Ha, ha."

She just looked at me, and I realized she wasn't kidding. "Of course, sure, sounds good," I blathered. "Go on out and get comfy and I'll bring us some refreshments."

When I came through my sliding doors carrying a pitcher of lemonade and a plate of cheese and crackers and carrot sticks (the latter in deference to Sasha), she was sitting on my wicker sofa, feet up. "Why is he still here?" she asked when she saw me, looking to where Jake sat whining outside the screen door.

"Oh, Ben needed to get him to the vet, but he can't take any time off work at the moment. I offered to take him today. I'm bringing him back home in a little while."

Sasha raised an eyebrow as I set the tray on the glass-topped table in the center of my little sitting area and poured for us. I handed her a glass and then walked over to push the screen door open for the still-whining Jake. He bolted inside and straight over to Sasha.

"I was going to let him in," she said, petting his head, "but I wasn't sure of the in-house dog policy."

"There doesn't seem to be one."

Sasha sighed. "Brook, you have to have some rules. You can't just let the dog make his own decisions. Dogs need structure, and a strong leader."

"See what good mothering instincts you have?"

Sasha rolled her eyes. "Come on, headshrink—you can do better than that." She'd stopped petting momentarily to reach for her lemonade, and Jake pawed at her arm, nearly upsetting her glass.

"Hey! Sit," she said firmly, and damned if he didn't. I bit my lips to keep from pointing out her skill at instilling discipline and boundaries.

"You really have to teach me that," I said instead.

Sasha lifted her legs so I could scooch under them on the sofa, then lowered them back to my lap. "It's all in your mind-set. Dogs will push things as far as you'll let them. They don't mean to be bad—it's just their nature to get away with whatever they think they can."

"Like furry, four-legged men," I said, and we snickered.

"So," Sasha said, leaning forward for a carrot. "Was taking Jake to the vet *your* idea, or Ben's?"

"A little bit of both, actually. Why, you think it means something?" I asked hopefully.

Her eyebrows bunched together in thought. "Depends. Why didn't he ask his girlfriend to do it?"

"She's not his girlfriend—they've only been dating a couple of months," I protested, then frowned. "Well...I don't think she is, anyway. What do you make of this?" I summarized our exchange at the Dog Beach.

She fixed an intent stare on me, tapping her lips with a finger as she thought. "That's ambiguous. Tell it to me again, step by step." I obliged—Sasha was the best listener, and never leaped to conclusions without at least a few retellings of the story, like an interrogating cop trying to tease out more information from a witness.

But, "Hmmm," was all she said when I finished the second recitation.

"What's 'hmm'? What do you think?"

"Well...there's a reason he told you he didn't love her—that wasn't an accident."

"That's what I thought!"

"But then to say he didn't mean he *couldn't*...I don't know, Brookie. It's almost like he's...baiting you or something."

I shook my head. "No. He wouldn't do that. He doesn't play games."

She lifted one shoulder. "Everyone plays games sometimes—even if we don't mean to. Especially when deep feelings are involved."

I couldn't really argue with that. I'd have sworn that I would never have resorted to that kind of artifice, but wasn't I playing games with Michael by keeping him on the hook while I tried to figure out whether there was any possibility with Ben?

"So do you mean he has deep feelings for me...or for *her*?" I didn't want to invoke Pamela's name, as though, like Beetlejuice, it would summon her.

Apparently Sasha had no such compunctions. "That depends on how serious things are with Perfect Pamela."

Warmth flared in me at my best friend's loyalty in using the nickname I'd coined. "That's what I was trying to find out," I said, flopping back against the sofa in frustration.

"Well, does she keep stuff at his house?"

I thought back to Thursday night, when I'd dropped Jake off after Ben's trip. "I can't remember. Nothing jumped out at me...and you'd think I'd have noticed."

"Oh, honey, no offense, but you're an amateur at snooping."

"No offense taken," I said sincerely. That was one of Sasha's talents I didn't envy.

"It's not just obvious stuff, like an extra toothbrush in the bathroom," she went on as if I hadn't spoken. "That could be casual—they hook up now and then. You have to look for the definitive signs of something more serious. First off, does the house smell female?"

"What do you—"

"Floral. Vanilla. Lavender, et cetera—any of the most commonly used feminine topnote scents in perfumerie."

I just stared at her. The range of Sasha's knowledge—and the extent to which she used it for nefarious purposes—often staggered me.

She continued. "Then check the food in the fridge—fruit yogurt, diet drinks, like that. Tampons under the bathroom cabinet. Conditioner in the shower, or a moisturizing soap—most guys never bother with that stuff."

"Sash, I dropped his dog off and he invited me in for a beer. It's not like I was casing the joint."

She shrugged. "You can't succeed if you don't try, Brook. You need to figure out how to catch a glimpse of those areas. Grab your own beer from the fridge next time. Ask to use his bathroom."

"He has a guest bath."

Sasha shot me the hairy eyeball. "You don't have a killer instinct."

"And you're avoiding the reason we're here."

She gave a long, whooshing sigh, and then wiggled her legs in my lap. "Fine. Rub, and then I'll talk."

"Okay." I set down my lemonade and wrapped my hands around her perfectly manicured feet, digging my fingers into her soles.

She moaned. "Oh, yeah. Sometimes I'd rather have your brother do *that* than go down on me."

"Ewww!" I dropped her feet like they'd burned me. "Ground rules! I won't try to convince you what a great mom you'll be, but you have to never, ever tell me anything like that again."

She was grinning at me around a mouthful of carrot. "Had to break the ice."

I shuddered and reached for her feet again. "Now this just feels dirty," I muttered. But she was right—things were back to normal between us. "Okay, so, top of your head—what's the scariest thing right now about having a child?"

"Babies," she answered unhesitatingly.

I nodded. "Fair point. Terrifying little creatures. What else?"

She glanced down, then hesitantly met my eye. "You won't judge me?"

"Never."

She nodded, pursing her lips, and then muttered something I couldn't make out.

"What's that?"

"My figure, okay? Like every cliché on earth, I'm worried that from here on out I'll go from this"—she ran a hand in the air over her perfect, taut body—"to stretch marks, a permanent pooch, and saggy boobs. I'm sorry," she said defensively. "Call me shallow. And God knows what's going to happen to my vagina."

"Mila Kunis. Julia Roberts. Fergie," I retorted, ignoring her last comment. "You're worried about getting out of shape—there's proof you don't have to."

"They have trainers. Personal chefs. And we have no idea of the state of their va-jay-jays. Plus, look at their careers. Downhill after kids. There's another one of my big fears—career death."

"Okay, then how about Reese Witherspoon? Kelly Ripa? And of course Angelina Jolie—she has, like, a litter of children, and she's still working, and even growing her career now as a producer/director."

"Nannies," Sasha said, sounding bored.

"At least I didn't say Gwyneth Paltrow."

"I would have gotten up and left."

I stopped rubbing long enough to reach for my glass and take a long sip of lemonade, regrouping. "Okay, you're right," I admitted. "Hollywood celebs maybe aren't the best examples. But what about my folks? You've always thought my parents had a great marriage," I said. Sasha didn't know about the affair my dad had when Stu and I were little because Mom was so absorbed by us he felt left out—no one did except him, my mother, and me. And it certainly wasn't a story that would help my case, even if I were willing to betray my dad's confidence—which I wasn't. "And Mom's pursuing her dreams, even though she's married and has kids."

Sasha raised one eyebrow. "Are you forgetting your mom *left* your dad to do that?"

"Temporarily."

"And that she had to put those dreams on hold till you guys were grown and on your own? Rub," she commanded, flippering her feet at me.

"Let's go back to babies," I said as I obeyed. "What scares you about them, specifically?"

"Poop. I'm not going to lie."

"Yeah. That's pretty nasty. But I heard it's not so bad when it's your own kid."

Sasha tipped her head down so she could laser-stare me. "Uh, really? Smelly liquid green poo sliming you and your carpet and—dear God—your clothes is okay when it's *your* kid's fecal matter? I don't think so."

"Okay, so let's agree that that's probably one of those manipulative lies parents tell other people."

"Yes," Sasha said fervently. "Along with 'You won't even remember the pain of childbirth.'"

"Hoo, boy. That's on the list, huh?"

She nodded. "And birth defects. And crib death. And never sleeping again. And puberty. And paying for college. And also *not* paying for college because my kid is a deadbeat who won't get a job and lives at home for the rest of its life. Honestly, Brook, it would be easier to list the things that *aren't* freaking me out."

"Oh! Okay, that's good—let's do that. What's not freaking you out about this?"

"Christmas," she said immediately. "Having a kid around at Christmas—with all you guys—but also...Okay, this sounds stupid, but I picture Christmases years from now—or whatever, Thanksgiving, Easter, you name it—when this kid is an adult, and he comes home to me and Stu for the holidays and...we have a family. My *own* family."

Sasha sounded forceful on that last line, and a pang shot through me. When we were kids she spent most of her time at our house, like my parents' honorary third child. But at holidays, only-child Sasha had to stay home in her silent, angry household where her parents seemed to barely tolerate each other, and when they finally—blessedly—divorced, she spent holidays shuttling back and forth between them, crushed every year at having to miss the time with me and Stu and our parents.

I squeezed her leg. "That sounds nice. Promise you'll let me come for Christmas."

"Are you kidding? You and your family *are* Christmas. That's the best thing about all this."

I smiled. "What else?"

Her face softened. "Having a teeny Stu. You remember what a cute little bastard he was when he was a kid?"

"You're half right, anyway—he was a little bastard." But my words lacked any sting. I was too happy that for the first time, the prospect of impending motherhood was putting a graceful smile on my friend's face instead of pulling it tight with fear.

"What else?" I asked.

Her smile vanished like clouds chasing away sunshine. "I don't know, Brook. That's all I've got in the plus column. Really. Why do you think I'm so scared?"

"Okay. We can work with this." I leaned forward over her legs and took another sip of my lemonade. In the silence between us I could hear birds arguing in the live oaks in my backyard, the shushing sound of passing cars on Winkler.

"That's it?" Sasha said, paddling her legs in my lap. "You're finished?"

"Sash, I've been rubbing for like fifteen minutes!"

"Not that, bonehead. My life. I thought you were going to fix it."

"Oh. Right. Let me give it some thought and figure out a plan." I set down my glass, turned to face her, and gave her my best Wise Therapist expression. "Don't worry about a thing."

...

My phone beeped with a text just as I pulled into Ben's neighborhood to return Jake: *Running a little bit late from work, but left you the key.*

Dammit. After talking things out with Sasha, I was hoping that another conversation would yield some answers about how serious things were with Perfect Pamela. I couldn't put off making a decision about Michael forever.

But as I let myself into Ben's dark house with the key I'd found just where he'd said it would be—under one of the stepping-stones to the backyard—Jake happily trotting in ahead, Sasha's words about figuring out a way to scope out the private areas of his house came back to me.

What better chance could I ask for?

Flipping on the entryway light just inside the front door, I glanced around in its modest spill of illumination. With Sasha's instructions in mind I took a long inhale through my nose. The house didn't smell "feminine" that I could tell—just of something clean, like bleach or Febreze—underneath the barely detectable scent I always associated with Ben: cedar and citrus, a fresh smell like cut grass. And the barest musk of eau de Jake.

I walked over to the lamp on a table beside Ben's sofa, clicking it on. There were no definitive clues in the living room—a single half-drunk glass of water on the cocktail table, the remote beside it. A throw blanket cast over the arm of the sofa—maybe Ben had pulled it over himself and Perfect Pamela as they snuggled in front of the TV late one night...or maybe he'd just flung it there out of the way.

Sasha's words still playing in my head, I headed into the kitchen, but the refrigerator offered no clues.

I walked over to his bedroom door and glanced inside as Jake came and sat beside me, looking into the room as if he were a spectator to some mysterious sport that would unfold before us. The bed was made, no frilly pillows or stuffed animals on it. (I did register, on some level, that I was ascribing to Perfect Pamela the habits of a prepubescent girl.) There were no women's slippers lined up at the foot of the bed beside the pile of castoff shoes that Ben always let accumulate there.

But Sasha said the bathroom would tell the real story.

As I took a step inside, Jake leaned his head into my thighs, impeding my forward movement.

And this was the point at which I once again became a rational adult.

What was I *doing*? The last time I'd snooped around someone's place was right after Kendall had summarily dumped me via text message, and I'd let myself in, determined to find proof of another woman.

I hadn't, but my rooting through his things had turned out to be the first loose rock in my avalanching sanity. And we all knew how that turned out.

I was not going to go down that road again. More than that, I wasn't going to betray Ben. He'd given me his dog to care for, a key to his house. How could I meet his renewed trust with an immediate breach of it—whether he ever knew about it or not?

As Sasha said, everything that was happening between us lately was a good sign. I'd try to have faith in that.

I bent to pet Jake, who still sat leaning into my leg in the doorway, as if anchoring me to reality. "Thanks, buddy," I said, stroking his soft head. "Thanks for saving me from myself."

Jake just wagged his tail and jabbed his nose into my eye, blissfully unconcerned with the ridiculous affairs of humans.

I fed Jake—it was nearly seven, past his usual dinnertime—and we were standing together in the backyard for his usual postprandial poop when the dog cometed over to the side of the yard, barking joyously and doing his bunny-bounce—Ben was home. My heart did the bunny-bounce too.

I coaxed the dog around to the back door, and we were waiting in the kitchen by the time Ben came in from the garage. Jake streaked over to where he stood carrying a fifty-pound bag of dog food in one hand and a paper sack in the other.

"Hi, buddy!" he said to Jake, setting the sack on the breakfast bar so he could pet Jake's bouncing head. He looked up at me. "I was hoping I'd catch you."

My heart fluttered. "Me too. I went ahead and fed him...since it's a little late."

"Thanks." He carried the dog food over to the pantry. "So what'd the vet have to say?"

I leaned back against the counter, hands braced behind me, letting myself enjoy watching the muscles in his strong, tanned arms work as he opened the bag and poured the food into the big plastic container he kept it in. I cleared my throat. "Um...Jake's lonely."

Ben straightened, facing me. "What?"

"Your codependent dog is lonely."

"That's what the vet said?"

"No—she's a vet, not a mental health professional. That's *my* analysis."

Ben cocked an eyebrow at me with a corner of his mouth lifting, then retrieved two beers from the fridge, popped the caps, and stepped closer. His green Millennium Homes shirt was smudged with something dark, and underneath his usual clean scent was the faint hint of dried sweat—musky but not unpleasant. Actually, I reflected, remembering studies of pheromones in men's sweat and how they affected women's sex hormone receptors, slightly a turn-on. Ben never simply delegated to the men on his company's build sites—he got in there with them and did the work. It was one of so many things I liked about him.

"And why do you think that, Madam Therapist?" He handed me one of the beers.

I shrugged, hoping my quickening pulse at the implied intimacy of the casual offer—one we'd played out so many times when we were dating—didn't show beneath my skin. "My guess is he was taken from his mother too soon."

He laughed. "No, I mean what makes you say that?"

"Oh...Well, the vet said his health is fine—perfect, actually. But I told her how you said he'd been acting—lethargic, low appetite. The doctor asked if anything had changed or there had been any stress in Jake's life lately, and all I could think of was that your mom is out of town and he usually stays with her during the day." And also that Ben had recently brought an interloper into their lives, and it was very likely that Jake was making his disapproval known. But I'd kept that theory to myself then, and deemed it politic to do so again now. "She said that suddenly being alone a lot could be enough with a needier dog to bring on a mild depression. And I think we can agree Jake is on the needier side."

Ben sighed, leaning back against the counter perpendicular to the one supporting me. Inches away. "I should never have gotten a dog, with my schedule. It's not fair to Jake."

"Are you kidding? Look at him. That's a happy dog." We both glanced down to where Jake was now lying between us on his back, wiggling his body this way and that like a bear scratching against a tree, his tongue lolling out almost to the floor.

Ben gave a wry smile. "That's just because he's been spending time with you."

I wanted to take that as a thinly veiled statement of Ben's own feelings, but I suspected he just meant Jake had had a warm body and available petting fingers nearby all day.

"When does your mom come back?" I asked.

Ben sighed. "Not till next Monday. Poor Jakie. Hang in there, buddy," he said, gently rubbing his belly with the side of one workbooted foot.

I took a sip of my beer, playing out the words in my head to see if it was a good idea to say them, considering that I still had no clear idea about the Pamela situation. "Well, why don't I take him during the days till Adelaide gets back?" I said before I'd actually made up my mind.

Whoops, now it was out there.

I'd expected Ben to protest that it was too much trouble, but to my surprise he seemed to be considering it. "Really?"

I gave a one-shouldered shrug. "Sure. I'd love to have him."

His face eased into that warm smile I loved. "That would be great. I can drop him off in the mornings and pick him on the way home."

I took a long sip of my beer, my heart quickening its pace. That meant we'd be seeing a lot more of each other—twice a day, for a week. "Or I can bring him to you at night. Either way."

Ben held his bottle up to mine. "You're a lifesaver, Brook—thanks."

I clinked with him, then took a long swig, trying to cool the flush of guilt heating my face.

...

When my phone rang as I was getting ready for bed, I was surprised at the way my heart lifted at Michael's name on the caller ID. I hadn't heard from him since Friday, and I'd begun to think he might have left town at my ambiguous response to his wanting something more. Michael wasn't a "let's be friends" kind of guy—it was all or nothing with him. But there was a part of me that had hoped he wouldn't give up so easily.

"Hey!" I blurted. "I wondered why you hadn't called."

"I wasn't sure if I should," he said. "You told me to wait."

"I...Yeah, well, I'm glad you did. Call, I mean."

It was the truth—but I still had no idea what to say to him. I didn't want Michael to keep trying to win me over until I knew what I actually wanted—but I also didn't want him to stop.

I kicked off my jeans and pulled on cotton boxers, my usual sleepwear, as I listened to him breathing on the other end of the line.

I wasn't used to this awkwardness between us, the weight of things left unsaid.

"So, what do you think...?" he said finally, and my breath hitched. "Do you want to get together? Sometime?" he asked, as I unhooked my bra and let it drop to the closet floor.

I crossed my arms over my bare chest at the naked earnestness in his tone, my stomach lurching like a faulty elevator.

I wanted to see him—I couldn't deny that. But that stubborn flame of hope with Ben refused to go out. It wasn't the only thing keeping me on the fence with Michael, but it was the one clamoring the loudest. Now that I'd be seeing a lot more of Ben for a while, I couldn't rule out the possibility that that door might still be open.

But even though I knew it wasn't fair of me...I wasn't ready to let this one close.

"I don't know, Michael," I said finally, wanting to offer him at least partial honesty. "I'm sorry, I...I still don't have an answer for you."

There was a beat, and then: "Okay. Well, I've been working on some ideas to show you for your business. How about if we meet to talk about them?"

Business. That was my comfort zone—I could keep things on a professional level for now with Michael while we got to know each other again...and at the same time not close off any possibilities with Ben. The best of both worlds.

I was meeting tomorrow with Sasha, so Michael and I made plans to get together Wednesday evening at a seafood restaurant we used to like near downtown, on the river.

After we hung up I lay awake in the dark for a long time, Michael's soft, "Good night, Brook," thrusting me back to the hundreds of times he'd crawled into bed beside me after a gig and murmured the same phrase sleepily in my ear before gathering me close in the night.

Chapter Twelve

Ben dropped Jake off early the next morning—he had to leave Fort Myers by six a.m. to make it to his Marco Island build site by seven. I'd offered to come pick the dog up, to save him at least a little time dropping by my house, but he said he was already inconveniencing me enough. "Although that's pretty early," he'd said last night as we discussed the logistics of the week. "If you'd rather, I can—"

"No, it's fine, actually," I said quickly. "I'm a really early riser." Not exactly a lie, as I *did* get up at four thirty a.m. to do my radio show on KXAR Monday mornings, but it wasn't like I was habitually conscious and perky at sunrise.

But damn skippy I was this morning, rising at my radio time so I could be showered, dressed, with hair and makeup carefully done by the time Ben arrived. I'd brewed extra coffee, and I met him at the door with a travel mug of it.

Ben's face brightened when he saw it. Or maybe when he saw me? Either way, I smiled back. "One sugar, no cream. Have a good day," I said, waving him off as he grinned and toasted me with the plastic mug. "See you tonight!" I called, trying (and failing) not to feel too giddy at the lovely intimacy of it all.

Jake had always been a crowd pleaser in my practice—most clients were delighted at the presence of the big friendly dog, and in some cases I swore that he helped loosen their tongues—and their emotions. Sitting and stroking his soft fur as he lolled orgiastically at their feet seemed to calm churning hearts, and it gave people something to focus on in those moments when naked vulnerability made it hard for them to meet my eye.

When my last client left at six, I quickly fed Jake and let him into the backyard to pee before heading to Sasha's. I could have dropped him off at Ben's on the way over—he said he'd be working late again—but if I left him here instead and came back for the dog afterward, I'd reasoned, I'd get face time.

I had a finite window of opportunity for it. I wasn't going to waste a second.

Time was obviously of the essence with Sasha too, but I knew I had to start slowly. Stu had agreed to stay at his own place when I suggested to Sash that we work one-on-one at her apartment for this, and tonight I was unveiling step one in what I was calling "Operation Bring It On."

While she put together a tray of appetizers for us—now wasn't the time to work on her maternity diet and address what passed for snacks to Sasha, which was generally crudité and air—I sat on her pristine red velvet sofa and opened the carry-on bag I'd packed with supplies, setting it so that the open top rested upright against the arm and concealed the bag's contents from Sasha's chair. Part of this strategy relied on the element of surprise.

But I was the one who was surprised when she came back into the living room with a tray bearing the expected raw veggies, along with sliced cheese and what looked like hummus.

I raised my eyebrows. "Wow. Calories."

She shrugged. "Protein."

The simple exchange pleased me all out of proportion. Sasha adjusting her diet was an excellent sign—but I knew better than to make an issue of it. Besides, the offerings suited my purpose admirably.

I leaned forward for a glass of orange juice she'd poured—another welcome sign. "So...I thought we'd start small," I began. "You said you were afraid of the mess of a baby. Poop, spit-up, that kind of thing."

She shuddered. "Please. I'm eating."

I ignored her. "So in behavioral therapy with phobias, there's a conditioning technique called systematic desensitization—you've probably heard of it."

"You mean like working on my fear of kids by taking me to that observation-room thingie in the hospital where they keep all the crates of babies?"

"*Cradles*," I corrected her.

She waved a hand. "Same difference."

Maybe her maternal instincts were a bit more buried than I'd thought. "We wouldn't start there—that's too much." I reached for a carrot stick and scooped up a blob of hummus. "Desensitization involves having the person with the phobia face the least anxiety-provoking stimulus related to the thing they fear. So if someone is afraid of spiders, let's say, we'd start with a picture of a spider, then when they could tolerate that, perhaps a rubber spider, and so on, up to the real thing, until the anxiety has been dealt with successfully." As I finished talking, I deliberately brought the carrot down to the seat of the sofa and, never taking my eyes off hers, smeared the glop of hummus against the velvet nap.

"What the hell are you doing!" Sasha yelped, jumping up with a handful of napkins.

I raised a hand. "We have to get you used to tolerating a mess," I said calmly.

"But that sofa cost three thousand—"

"Don't worry—I'm going to clean it. I promise."

"But it's going to ruin the velvet if it sits for—"

"Sash, you asked for my help."

She stopped trying to reach past me with the napkins, and after a moment reluctantly lowered herself back into her chair. "What happened to starting with pictures," she muttered. "Why not show me a *picture* of a ruined couch."

"It's not ruined." I reached into my bag of tricks and held up the Oxy stain remover I'd brought. "This takes out anything—trust me. It's gotten red wine stains out of several pairs of pants, and Jake vomit out of more places than I can count."

Sasha grimaced. "Ugh."

"How are you feeling?"

She glared flames into me.

"Okay, good! Let's sit with that sensation for a few minutes."

"I'll give you a sensation to sit on," she said darkly.

I tipped my juice onto the carpet.

Sasha shot up again. "Dammit, Brook—"

"Sit."

She slowly dropped her rump to the chair, but looked like she wanted to chew through the cocktail table to get at me.

I smiled. "You're really doing very well. Much better than I expected."

Sasha grated out, "There will come a day when—"

In one movement I whipped out a squirt gun from my carry-on, took aim directly at Sasha, and pulled the trigger for all I was worth.

A thick stream of water shot out straight at her head and into her hair, down her face, and across the cream-colored silk tank she wore.

Sasha didn't move. She was so still, in fact, that for a moment I worried she'd had a coronary. Finally her mouth opened, and she licked away moisture from the side of her mouth with one slow, deliberate swipe of her tongue.

"Get out," she said with zero intonation.

"Sash, this is all part of the process that you asked—"

"You need to leave."

"You have to trust—"

"Brook, if you don't leave now, I'm going to beat you up."

That got my attention. Sasha worked out like a fiend; she could inflict some damage if she was serious.

She looked very, very serious.

I straightened slowly, dropping my weapon into my bag, careful not to turn my back to her. I offered a conciliatory smile. "Maybe we call this enough for today. It's a good start. I'll just start cleaning up the—"

"Go. Now."

I'd seen that homicidal look in Sasha's eyes dozens of times after a bad breakup—but never blazing directly at me. The effect was terrifying. I flipped the top of my suitcase closed and zipped it so fast I pinched the skin of my index finger, but I didn't dare stop to assess the damage—I'd seen what she was capable of when some man had lit this fury in her eyes.

"Okay, so I'll call you later to set up our next session," I babbled, already halfway to the door. "OxyClean's there on the floor—good work today!"

I was already halfway down the walkway by the time the door swung shut behind me, and I didn't slow down until I was safely in the car.

...

Ben was already home by the time I picked up Jake and got to his house.

In fact, I saw as he opened the door to my knock, he'd had time to shower, judging from his damp hair that curled at the ends, and change into a pair of faded jeans I remembered from when we dated. A dark green t-shirt did lovely things to his hazel eyes and to the muscles the shirt clung to beneath it. For a fleeting moment I wondered whether, as I had this morning, Ben had done the male version of primping for my arrival.

I was trying not to let my heart leap to conclusions, but things like this were making it hard. So was Ben's warm greeting as he let Jake inside and invited me in for a beer.

As we had yesterday, we stood together in the kitchen, taking sips of our Cigar City Oatmeal Brown Ales in between Ben feeding Jake and letting him out while I filled him in on how the dog had seemed today (which was blissfully content). It was easy and comfortable and warm, the way we'd once sat together in the evenings telling each other about our days.

If it hadn't been for the fact that Ben was dating another woman, it would have felt utterly...domestic.

Chapter Thirteen

I needed a day to regroup and work on my game plan with Sasha, given my lack of success so far. But first I had one more rabbit in my hat—this one involving Intern Paige. At lunchtime I brought her a sandwich and carefully explained what I wanted her to do. Then, Jake at my heels, I went in to eat at my desk—something I probably did too often—and texted Sasha to call me at the office.

I could tell when the phone rang a few minutes later that it was her from Paige's loud announcement from the reception area: "Oh, *hi*, Sasha!" she shouted.

That was my cue. Silently I picked up the extension in my office, careful to press the mute button.

"You caught me in the middle of making a college loan payment," Paige was saying—rather woodenly, I had to admit.

"Oh. Cool. Hey, Brook wanted me to call her on this line. She around?"

But Intern Paige determinedly plodded ahead: "Yes, my tuition isn't really that bad because I chose an in-state school—and I'm paying it through partial scholarships, grants, and low-interest student loans."

"Uh, wow. That's terrific."

"Yes. And another thing is that my parents instilled in me the need for higher education. They helped me understand how important it is."

I rolled my eyes. I'd written down a few bullet points for Paige to bring up, but I'd hoped she'd do more than read them.

"Is that so?" Sasha's voice had taken on a predatory tone I knew well.

"That's what I said."

"That is fascinating, Paige," Sasha said. "But I call bullshit."

Dammit.

"What do you mean?" Paige said, sounding nervous.

"I have never met anyone more focused and serious about their schooling and career than you. I'm guessing you popped out of the womb with your eight-year college plan already formulated in your head."

"Well, that wouldn't be possible. Babies' thought processes aren't fully—"

"Your parents never said a word about college, did they?"

Dead panicked silence on the other end of the line told me I needed to step in and save poor Intern Paige.

I unmuted the phone. "It's okay, Paige. Just tell her."

"Um...they didn't really care one way or the other. They just wanted me to be happy. Sorry, Brook."

"My fault," I said wearily.

"I knew it!" Sasha accused me.

I thanked Paige and let her off the hook—I hadn't told her the reason I'd enlisted her for my college campaign, but one of the many excellent things about Intern Paige was that she threw herself wholeheartedly into anything I requested of her, no questions asked. She offered a hurried goodbye on a tangible wave of relief, and I braced to face Sash with a mouthful of apologies.

She made me grovel for her forgiveness before she offered it—and only after I threw in the promise of another foot rub—but when I told her about meeting Michael tonight, all was immediately forgotten.

"Really? Just the two of you, out at a restaurant alone? I don't think so. I'm coming."

I laughed. "Come on, Sash. I'll be fine. It's not like he's dangerous."

"You're too forgiving of people. It makes you gullible. I'm not letting you get tangled up with him again without vetting things for myself."

I tried to dissuade her, but when she threatened to call Stu and tell him to meet us there too, I finally relented and said she could come along. One of them I could control—but both Sasha and Stu in righteous-anger mode might be lethal for my ex.

...

I picked Sasha up after dropping Jake off at Ben's—unfortunately before he'd gotten home from work—and I kept a hawk eye on her as we walked into Flamingo Joe's.

It wasn't that I was worried about what she might do to Michael when she finally saw him in person (although to be truthful, I did have my concerns). Mostly I wanted to see her reaction to the new-and-improved version of my former party-boy-musician fiancé.

He shot to his feet as we approached his corner booth, and I saw the moment he realized who was walking beside me: His whole face blanched, but he recovered almost immediately, pushing the smile back onto his lips.

Sasha reacted to him too. He wore a neatly ironed blue-and-yellow-striped button-down and nice khaki pants, a navy sport coat pulling it all together. His jaw was smooth from a fresh shave, his usually tousled hair tamed. He looked undeniably handsome, but disorientingly unfamiliar. I darted a glance down to his feet; the navy Converse high-tops comforted me—as much as I liked the new-and-improved version of him, I was glad the old Michael hadn't completely disappeared.

I could tell she was momentarily thrown by the polished stranger in front of her who resembled my ex-fiancé, but I caught his smirk and the spark of amusement in his eyes that revealed the Michael we had known.

"Sashimi!" he said in a hearty tone. "Good to see you again."

Sasha stopped dead in front of him and shoved a finger about an inch away from his nose, a black look on her face. "No. You do not get to call me that anymore, doucheface. Sit."

Michael arced a glance to me, but to his credit he sat. Sasha loomed over him like an Amazon warrior priestess, trying to glower him into submission, but when he refused to cower away from her she finally broke off her death glare and followed me to the other side of the booth, saving me from my own internal dilemma: How did you greet your former fiancé? Did we hug? Shake hands? Slap a high five?

We sat in uncomfortable silence for a few moments, but when it became clear that neither one of them was going to speak, I fired an opening sally. "So...I brought Sasha along because she was interested in hearing about your plan for my Breakup Doctor business."

"I was *interested* in making sure you aren't jacking my friend around. *Again*," she bit out, still staring hard at Michael. "I don't trust you. And I don't like you. Brook's a better person than I am, and for some reason she's decided to acknowledge your sorry existence. But just so we're clear...I don't care what J. Crew store you raided, or how much product you glopped into your hair—if you're here to screw with her in any way, I will saw your scrotum off and shove it down your severed windpipe."

I just about choked on my own saliva, but Michael merely nodded. "That's fair. I wouldn't expect anything less of you, Sashi— Sasha."

Her finger jabbed toward him again across the table. "And don't pretend you know anything about me, or that we're still any kind of friends. You destroyed that along with your relationship with Brook." Once upon a time Michael and Sasha had been close—sometimes I thought she had been almost as hurt as I was by his sudden defection.

"I know," Michael said quietly. "I'm sorrier about that than I can tell you. About everything." All trace of his forced joviality had evaporated, and I scanned Sasha's face for any sign of softening, but her arms were knotted across her chest, her eyebrows colliding.

"What can I get you guys to drink?" The server's interruption provided a welcome distraction—at least for me—and I gratefully ordered a glass of water. Sasha followed suit, Michael ordering iced tea. Before they could resume hostilities, I tried to steer things back to safer ground.

"Why don't you show us what you have in mind for my business, Michael?" I prompted.

His gaze lingered for a moment on Sasha as if he were reluctant to take his eyes off her (I couldn't blame him—you didn't turn your back on a rabid coyote). But finally he reached over to where an open briefcase rested on the banquette beside him—a briefcase! From the man whose "business plan" for his old band had mostly involved notes scribbled on crumpled cocktail napkins—and set it on the table. He pulled open the top and tapped the keyboard, and the screen jumped to life to reveal a PowerPoint slide: an image of a broken heart with a Band-Aid patching it together, above the words "Breakup Doctor Promotional Proposal."

Sasha rolled her eyes.

"Okay...here's where you are now," he began, hitting another key to advance the slide.

He'd done some homework, based on what I'd told him, pulling up each prong of my current business and then showing its organic reach: the number of clients I could fit into an average week, considering fifty-minute sessions and a nine-hour day; my group therapy clients (about ten to twelve per six to eight weeks); the circulation of the *Tropic Times*, where my weekly column ran; and ratings for the radio station where I did my twice-weekly appearances, as well as those of the individual shows I appeared on. Seeing it all laid out like that made me realize just how much my business had grown.

The server showed back up with our drinks and we ordered food, none of us consulting the menu—the bayfront restaurant was a longtime haunt for locals, and there was only one item Michael and I had ever ordered there: their famous grouper Reuben. Sasha ordered the grouper balls. "And a sharp knife for the balls," she added to the server, but her flinty eyes were pasted on Michael.

As soon as the server left Michael resumed, pulling up a financial report, many of the spaces blank.

"You don't have to tell me exact amounts if you don't want to," he said, swiping the touch screen with his thumb and finger to blow up the empty graph. "I just want you to start thinking about what's yielding the best results, income-wise, so we can focus our game plan."

"Hold it right there," Sasha said, putting up a hand. "First off, it isn't 'our' anything. This is Brook's business—not yours. You're just a tool." She gave a mirthless smile. "Literally. Second, her financials are none of your damn business either. Is that what this is all about? Are you trying to cash in on Brook now that she's a huge success when you're such a complete and total failure?"

"Sash, he's not—"

"No, that's okay, Brook. She's right—the specifics don't have to be my business. I'd just like to try to help you maximize your potential."

"And how much do you want her to pay you for this little maximization?" she retorted inexorably.

"Nothing right now."

Sasha snorted.

I wanted to ask her to tone it down—we'd never get past the second slide at this rate—but there was a part of me that was basking in having someone tear Michael a new one on my behalf. I'd forgiven him, but I wasn't such a saint that I didn't enjoy seeing him suffer a little.

"Really?" she said, skepticism dripping from her tone like acid. "You're doing all this just out of the kindness of your shriveled heart?"

Michael sighed and looked up, as if seeking divine intervention for the termagant across the table. "No, Sasha," he said patiently. "As with any agent or manager, I will take a percentage of whatever contracts I'm able to negotiate for Brook. A standard fifteen percent," he cut her off as she opened her mouth. "And only if Brook agrees. Does that seem fair?"

She just narrowed her eyes and looked out the window at the undulating river.

"It's not really germane at the moment," I jumped in, trying to smooth our own choppy waters. "Except for my actual counseling, the rest of all that doesn't..." I trailed off. "I mean, I do charge a little something for the group sessions. And I get a stipend from the paper. But mostly those efforts are about reaching more people."

Michael raised an eyebrow, leaning back against the red vinyl booth. "Is this Big Eyes all over again?"

When I'd had my old traditional practice, I'd often operated on a sliding scale to help people who didn't have insurance or might not be able to afford therapy otherwise. Michael had always told me I slid things way too far: *I know you want to help everyone, but you can't keep slashing your rates for every pair of big sad eyes and a sob story. It devalues what you're doing.*

"No," I protested. "Well, a little," I conceded immediately. "But you have to admit it's good promotion—I get a lot of clients from the column and the shows."

He spread his hands. "Which we've just determined you have a limited capacity for. Not the best use of your resources, Brook. And besides, it really deval—"

"—devalues what I'm doing," I finished along with him. "I know, I know."

He was smiling at me with fond exasperation, like a parent watching her two-year-old come inside covered in mud. "You can't say no to anyone, can you?"

"I can say no."

"I'll bet if I offered to buy you a Joe's Chocolate Volcano after dinner, I can prove you can't say no." He wiggled his eyebrows.

"Oh, really?" Sasha cut in flatly, her sharp gaze now pinned back on Michael. "She said no to *you*."

Her harsh comment chased his grin away and served as a bucket of cold water in the face of our banter.

I didn't actually mind the reminder. It was too easy to fall into our old comfortable rapport.

Michael shrugged and offered a weak smile. "Yes. She did. So you don't have to worry, Sasha. Brook's in no danger of letting her guard down with me. She can take care of herself."

I thought she'd bristle at that, but she only growled, "Damn straight. Don't forget it."

I cleared my throat and put my hand on Sasha's leg beneath the table. She'd always been protective, but I'd never seen her in full mama-bear mode to this degree. I wondered whether it was entirely because of Michael, or had something to do with budding maternal instincts. I fervently hoped for the latter. "This is a weird transition for us," I said to them both, hoping to soothe the crackling conflict between them. "There are going to be some growing pains."

Sasha's eyes slid over to me and the taut lines around her mouth eased ever so slightly. She uncrossed her arms and dropped them to her lap, resting one hand over mine out of Michael's sightline. I squeezed my thanks.

"Okay, Michael. What do you suggest first?" I prompted.

"Well..." he said, inclining his head. "You need a Facebook page for the Breakup Doctor. You need Twitter. Maybe Instagram. But that's basic—and it's easy."

"And it's stupid," Sasha said, but her protest lacked some its earlier heat. "This is still therapy—not some kind of celebrity fan page."

He sighed and looked out over the Caloosahatchee, with its hodgepodge of watercraft bobbing on the water. "Sasha, if Brook's agreed to try letting me promote her business the way I successfully promoted the first band I represented into a major recording contract, can you at least start with the assumption that I know what I'm doing? Just a little bit?"

Her glare didn't falter, but she held her tongue. I had to hand it to him—Sasha in full-on homicidal mode was a not-unintimidating force to be reckoned with, but Michael was holding his own.

"Okay," he said after a moment. "Here're some avenues I had in mind for expansion." He pulled up a new slide with a bulleted list headed "Growth opportunities." The headings were almost the same as the ones on the first slide, delineating all the diversifications of my current practice, with a few additions that made my eyes pop: "Speaking engagements," "Magazines and Media," "Books." I saw a flare of interest in Sasha's eyes too, but it was quickly extinguished.

"This is just a long-range overview of my thoughts," Michael said, "but I'm guessing you'll be more comfortable starting slowly." He hit a few keys and the last several items disappeared. "For now, I think you're already maxed out with private clients. There's only so many you can take on, right?" I nodded, and the first bullet point sailed off the screen. "With your column, we're going to look at getting it picked up by other papers throughout Florida, with an eye to eventual syndication." The mastheads of area newspapers whose names I recognized popped up at points across the screen like fireworks.

"Fancy," Sasha said dryly.

He slid a smirk at her. "Presentation is everything."

The next bullet point wiped the screen clear: "Radio." Sasha leaned in despite herself.

"The radio plan is similar—but I think first we need to get you actually employed by the station. I assume this is another Big Eyes— I mean, a volunteer position for you?" he corrected with a quick glance to Sasha, and I nodded affirmation. "Well, no one's going to even *look* at syndicating a drop-in guest. This is the first thing I'd like to address—approaching your station and seeing about putting you on the payroll—and getting you a show of your own."

"Whoa!" I said, just as a food runner showed up with our dinner and set the plates down in front of us. "I don't know how to do all that technical stuff the deejays do."

"There are engineers for that. All you have to do is be the on-air personality—which you're already doing."

"Well, I don't think they'd be willing to pay me much, let alone offer me my own show." As I spoke I nudged half my sweet potato fries off my plate and onto a spread napkin as Michael did the same with his regular fries, and we pushed our respective piles toward each other.

"What are you two doing?" Sasha asked sharply.

I realized it apparently just as Michael did: He stared at me with a startled expression that no doubt mirrored my own.

"Oh," I said quietly.

He didn't take his eyes from mine. "Old habits die hard."

"Yeah."

"Let's all keep our own side dishes to ourselves," Sasha said flatly, and she dragged our napkins back to our respective plates.

We all started eating, as intent on our food as if we were restaurant critics. Finally Michael filled the heavy silence.

"I'll see if I can compare the station's ratings to what they were before you came on those shows. But either way, I think they know you're a commodity. I've been listening in for a few weeks"—my eyes flew to his at that news—"and the phone never stops ringing on your shows. That's listeners—and that means ad revenue. And that's our bargaining chip—similar to what we'll do with your newspaper."

Sasha had stopped chewing and was fixing him with an assessing look. "You do know what you're doing."

"You don't have to sound so surprised."

She lifted one eyebrow. "I think we can all agree you didn't used to be so..."

"Grown-up?" he asked wryly.

She shrugged, as if uninterested. "Focused."

They stared at each other for a moment, and something seemed to pass between them that I missed. Then his lips curved slightly upward. "Thanks. But you might as well hold off on the compliments until we see if I can actually put anything in motion. So, Brook...is it a go?"

"'It...'?"

He tapped the screen. "The radio show, first off. I'd like to approach the station ASAP. Do I have your permission?"

"Wait—*you're* going to do it?"

"That's what promotion is. The talent never negotiates for themselves. I'm your representative. An agent. A representative can push for things that the talent has to stay clear of."

"It's weird that you're calling me 'the talent.' Like an inanimate object."

"As far as they're concerned, Brook, that's what you are. This is business—you're the commodity."

"Or it just makes it easier to pimp people out if you can dehumanize them," Sasha grumbled, but her barb was halfhearted.

"Yes or no?" he asked me, ignoring her.

I'd told Sasha that often people freaked out when they finally achieved everything they ever wanted. Here was an unexpected chance for me to show her how to embrace new opportunities—to *not* operate from a place of fear.

Michael waited with a neutral expression and at least a good show of patience, letting me decide.

Finally I wiped my grease-streaked fingers on my napkin and reached across the table.

"Okay. Yes." We shook hands. I couldn't deny the jolt I felt at the contact.

When we let go he left his hand extended and moved it over to Sasha. I thought that took a fair amount of courage, as I was pretty certain she was as likely to take a bite out of it as she was to do anything else. But my best friend shocked me by reaching out and meeting his grasp.

"I'm not saying I'm not going to eventually punch you in the face," she told him. "But if Brook wants to give this a chance, I'm always on her side."

His sudden wince told me she'd tightened her freakishly strong grip on his hand, and Sasha smiled a shark's grin at him. *"Always."*

...

"What in the name of sweet Raptor Jesus was *that?*"

Sasha laid into me as soon as the front door of Flamingo Joe's closed behind us—after stalking backward from our booth, making a vee of her fingers and pointing them at her own eyes, then Michael's in a Mafia-movie "I'm watching you" gesture.

"What was what?"

She laid a hairy eyeball on me. "Don't give me that. You two were all cozy-cozy with the side dishes and the repartee. What's going on?"

I stopped when we reached my car, looking at her over the roof. "I...I don't know," I said. "There's so much history there...so much familiarity. It's just easy to fall into that."

"Don't let your guard down with him, Brook. No matter how much he may have changed or how sorry he is, you can't trust him. Not ever again."

The finality of that plucked at something in my chest. "I don't know, Sasha. You saw him. He's...different—don't you think?"

I couldn't read the long stare she gave me in the spotty illumination from the few parking lot lights. She made impatient clicking motions in the air with her thumb, pointing down to the car, and I hit the unlock button. As soon as we both slid in and the doors were closed she faced me head-on.

"Mike Rowan. Tyler Engel. Joe Herrera. Jude Something. Guy from that band at Sharkey's."

"What?" I asked, confused.

"All guys you told me were toxic after they dumped on me. 'You don't drink twice from a poisoned well,' you told me. In fact, you suggested I get it tattooed on my arm. A bit hypocritically, as it now turns out," she said with a glare.

I sighed, dropping the ignorant act. Sasha was a bloodhound. "I know, Sash, but this is different. We—"

"Are you seriously going to try to justify this? To me?"

I didn't say anything, looking down to avoid her eyes.

"Honey..." Her tone was gentler now. "Are you actually considering getting back together with that—" She stopped herself. "With Michael?"

Silence filled the car for a long moment. "I don't know," I said almost inaudibly to my lap.

Air gusted out of her like a blown bicycle tire. "What about Ben?"

"What about him?" I met her stare. "He has a girlfriend."

"You said she *wasn't* his girlfriend."

"I don't know!" I shouted. "I have no damned idea! I think I'm getting one message from him, and then I get something totally different. For all I know all of it's just in my head and nothing's changed with us—I still blew it and he's still moved on. But meanwhile, the man I thought I was going to spend my life with—who I loved, for *real*, let's remember—is back, and seems like a better person, a grown-up now, and he wants me, Sash. He *wants* me." I fell silent again, looking back down at my hands, which still held the key I hadn't pushed into the ignition.

"Honey…" she started, but I shrugged her hand off my shoulder.

"No. I can't talk about this with you." I tried to find a way to articulate what was churning inside me without hurting her feelings—or our friendship. "Look, you've got problems you're dealing with, and I want to help you with that. I do. I want to be a good friend and a good therapist and help you figure out what you really want. But, Sash…" Heat speared into my eyes, and I felt the prickling of oncoming tears. "Everything you're struggling with right now…that's everything I *want*. So how can you possibly know what I'm feeling?"

Silence dropped like a sandbag between us.

"Because I've been there too," she said finally, after a long moment. "Up until Stu I *lived* there—wanting so badly not to be alone, to be loved by the right guy. I get it, Brookie—I do. And I can't explain why I'm freaking out when I'm finally getting everything I ever thought I wanted. But it doesn't mean I can't relate to what you're feeling—the same way you were still a great Breakup Doctor even when you were neck-deep in the crazy after Kendall."

I gave a watery laugh. "Thanks."

"I'm serious," she said. "And you're right—you don't know what's going on with Ben yet. And I get not wanting to cut things off with Michael until you do. Just…be careful, okay? I don't want to see you get hurt. There are a *lot* of people in the mix who might get hurt."

Michael. Ben. Pamela. No matter who she was talking about, she was right.

"I know," I said softly. "I'm trying to figure this out."

"You know I've got your back whatever you decide, right?"

I nodded, smiling through blurry eyes. "Yeah. I always know that."

Finally I put the key in the ignition and started the car, backing out of the parking spot. "You were terrifying back there, by the way."

"I *was*, wasn't I?" Leaning back in the seat, she closed her eyes, smiling that creepy predator's smile. "*God*, it was good to feel normal again."

We rode home in spent stillness, like the quiet hush after a squall has passed, until we turned off Summerlin and I pulled into Sasha's apartment complex. Instead of idling in the visitor's slot, I turned off the car and turned to face her.

"What do you think about backing off on Operation Bring It On?"

She slid a narrow glance at me. "Is this some new strategy?"

"No. You said it was nice to be normal again."

"Threatening to castrate and garrote your ex…good times."

"It was," I said, grinning, and she laughed.

"Well, I won't complain if we're not all pregnancy, all the time. That's what Stu's doing and it's making me crazy," she said.

"Agreed then—brief moratorium?"

She blew out a breath as if she'd been holding it for a long time. "Agreed. Thank God." Sasha reached for her door handle, then stopped and turned back to me. "But there is a built-in time limit here, don't forget. I can't put off making a decision forever."

"We won't," I assured her, realizing that neither could I.

Chapter Fourteen

After Ben dropped off Jake on Thursday morning, his bright smile when I opened to the door doing nothing to help sort my jumbled thoughts, Rae Ann Wilson was my first appointment. I was looking forward to seeing the change in her after our conversation last week and the homework assignment I'd given her. I suspected that simply taking better care of herself, looking more polished, would have done wonders for her self-esteem. I sequestered Jake in my bedroom—Rae Ann was strictly a cat person.

But when my office door opened, it did not reveal the woman I'd expected. Rae Ann hadn't even made an attempt at grooming today, wearing the same slouchy sweats and sneakers I'd seen her in for months, no makeup, her hair pulled back in a plain, low ponytail. She galumphed into the room and slumped down into a corner of the chaise.

"It didn't work," she said flatly, before I could even offer a greeting.

"Oh?" I asked neutrally.

"Before you ask, I did it—I got up every day and got ready. And I made an effort to leave the house more—I went to the post office instead of printing the postage from home, went inside to pay for my gas instead of paying at the pump, went into the bank instead of the drive-through, blah, blah, blah." She lifted her feet onto the sofa and pushed herself back against the arm so hard I was surprised a chunk of food didn't come flying out of her mouth. "First of all, it's weird to ask someone about their hobbies while they're making change for a twenty, okay? But I did it. And at first you were right—it was kind of nice to talk to someone besides Theo. But then..." She trailed off, glaring at her sneakers as though they'd insulted her.

"Then what happened, Rae Ann?" I prompted.

She transferred her scowl to me, and I had to fight my instinct to lean away. "Someone asked me *out*, Brook!" she snapped.

I waited, but that seemed to be the extent of the egregious trespass against her. "Um...good?" I ventured.

"No!" she whined. "*Not* good! I was in the checkout line in the grocery store yesterday, and they were slammed, so I grabbed a magazine off the shelf to kill time. And then I hear this guy behind me kind of chuckle, and he holds up *his* magazine to show me that we're both reading the exact same article. 'Great minds,' he says. So like you said, I tried to talk to him, right? Instead of what I wanted to do, which was just turn around and mind my own business. So I did, and he was all *friendly* and we talked about the article for a few minutes, and he asked if we could meet for coffee later after we both unloaded our groceries at home."

As she paused for a breath, a dozen scenarios crowded my mind for what could have gone wrong.

"So I say yes, and we agree on this place and a time, and he gives me his number just in case I need it...and...and..."

I frowned in growing alarm as Rae Ann became increasingly distressed. Had the guy turned out to be some kind of predator?

"And *I never showed up*, Brook!" She hurled the words at me like an accusation. "I left this really nice guy sitting there all alone, stood up, probably feeling like there was something wrong with him, when the truth is *I'm* the one who's defective! You want me to *date*? I don't know even how to *talk* to people!"

She'd worked herself into near hysterics, breathing too hard and too fast, and swallowing air. I moved over next to her on the chaise and put an arm around her. "Okay. Okay, Rae Ann, slow down," I said soothingly, rubbing her back. "It's okay...it's not your fault. You're all right. Breathe."

"I...know it's not...my fault," she said raggedly, between hitching sobs. "It's *your* fault. Why couldn't you just help me get over Paul, like I came here for!"

I didn't want to explain my reasoning in the face of Rae Ann's very real pain. Instead I simply sat beside her, making calming circles on her back.

"You're right," I said when her tears finally stalled and her breathing evened out. "I pushed you too hard, and I'm sorry."

Rae Ann nodded sullenly, not looking at me.

"I *am* going to help you, Rae Ann. We'll do this together."

She angled a wary glance at me. "What do you mean?"

In school and training it had been deeply ingrained in me to keep a certain remove between myself and patients, not to color their thought processes with my own input, and never, ever to get directly involved their lives.

But this wasn't a theoretical scholastic exercise—this was real life. And I didn't run a typical psychological practice anymore.

"Go home and put on clothes and do your hair and makeup," I said to her. "You think you don't know how to talk to people? Fair enough. We're going out together tonight, and I'm going to help you learn."

...

I hadn't heard from Stu since Sasha had told me everything. The last time we'd talked—when he and Dad were out on the boat—he'd sounded troubled. And when my baby brother was upset, it raised a primal protective streak in me that made me want to slay his dragons.

I didn't know if there was anything I could say to reassure him right now. But I could try.

I wasn't meeting Rae Ann until later this evening, so as soon as my last client of the day left, I texted Stu: *Got time for a drink? Mickey Mack's?*

His reply came almost immediately: *Gross. Hell, yeah. See you in 30.*

When we were kids, Mickey Mack's was someplace he and I loved to go together. As soon as I got my driver's license I'd drive us to the harbor-front shrimper dive bar anytime we had things to talk about that we didn't want our parents to overhear, like planning a nighttime sneak-away with our high school friends, or TP'ing the neighbors. The place fascinated us then—splintering raw-wood picnic tables, peanut shells all over the floor, a bartender who looked like he might also moonlight as a hit man. Sitting in their battered wooden chairs, we felt dangerous and grown-up, the only kids in a group of rough-looking shrimpers off the boat after a week on the gulf, drinking up their paydays. It was a miracle we never got hurt—or contracted staph. The tumbledown shack couldn't have passed any health inspections. That was one reason I'd suggested the place—I knew we could sit with Jake out on the dockside deck. Though I doubted that the staff would stand on ceremony if I did bring him inside. Jake had probably had a more recent bath than half the clientele.

Stu was waiting for me out front when I pulled into the gravel lot, and as soon as he caught sight of Jake bounding out of the car, he dropped to his haunches and threw out his arms.

"Jakie! The Jakemeister! My main man!" he gushed as Jake practically pulled my arm out of the socket yanking on the leash to greet him.

"Jesus, Stu, I thought Sasha told you not to get him all riled up." During the time I'd kept the dog when Ben and I were dating, Sasha and I had discovered to our amusement (and her mild revulsion at their openmouthed kisses) that Stu and Jake shared the love that dare not speak its name.

"But that was a long time ago, and maybe Stu forgot!" he said, speaking directly to Jake in baby talk. "Maybe Stu missed his best buddy too much to be cool! Didn't he? Didn't he?"

Jake was basking in the attention, twisting his giant body this way and that in an apparent effort to become one with his soul mate.

"Well, you make it harder on Ben when he has to reinforce discipline every time you see the dog," I muttered.

Stu's eyebrows lifted from behind the corona of white fur now engulfing his face. "Are you two getting back together?"

I gave a half shrug. "No. Maybe. I have no idea."

Stu gave Jake a final ear flap and then stood, wearing a sympathetic expression. "Sorry, sis," he said. "I know you care about him."

Old Stu would never have picked up on my complicated feelings about Ben. He really was growing up.

That was the other part of why I'd wanted to meet with him face-to-face—despite Sasha's assurances, I needed to make sure for myself that Stu was truly ready for marriage and fatherhood.

"Come on," I said to my brother. "Let's get a table."

There was no wait service at Mickey Mack's, so I sat with Jake while Stu went in and ordered for us—I opted for just a bottled beer and a bag of chips, a snack that I knew came in a factory-sealed cellophane bag rather than the Mickey Mack kitchen. It seemed my days of blindly trusting that I wouldn't get giardia had been left in my childhood. When my brother came back out, he carried two bottles of Heineken—about as micro a brew as could be hoped for at Mickey Mack's—and a grimy laminated card with a number on it, shoved into a rusty metal stand. He set it all down and slid into the bench across from me.

For the first time ever with my brother, I put on my therapist's hat.

"So...how are things going, Stuvie? How are you?"

"Not bad," he said, never looking up from massaging Jake's head.

"You know I know, right?" I clarified.

The slightest wave of pink crept across my brother's face and he glanced up at me. "Yeah. I figured Sash wouldn't keep anything from you."

I didn't point out that in fact she had—for days. I simply nodded, reaching across to play with the glass sugar container on the table. It was sticky, the sugar inside clumped and grayish, and I set it back on the weathered wood, wiping my hands on my jeans and grimacing.

"You feeling okay about everything?" I probed. "I mean...it's a lot. And it's fast."

"I know it is. But I'm good with it."

"Dirty diapers. Spit-up. No more partying...I honestly never thought I'd see the day, bro."

"I know. Neither did I."

I narrowed my eyes as he fondled the ecstatic dog. "It's a lot of responsibility—physical, emotional, financial. And it's hard. And it's not always satisfying—some studies show that people with kids are significantly less happy overall than people without. And it's *forever*. No days off. No end date. No guarantees that your kid will turn out okay. Plus there's your relationship—a lot of times kids can really throw off the dynamic between two people."

"I'm going to be a great dad. Sasha will be an amazing mom. And we'll just work extra hard to make sure we don't lose sight of each other."

"Well, that's what a lot of couples think, until the reality hits and—"

He stopped petting Jake and abruptly turned to face me. "You think I can't handle this. That I'm going to jump ship." He sounded bemused more than hurt, but shame plucked at me anyway.

I shrugged guiltily. "It does fit your usual MO."

He stared at me for a moment, and then to my surprise nodded. "Fair enough. But Sasha's not usual," he said. "Sasha's...well..." A smile crept over his face, his eyes taking on an expression I could only call besotted. "She's Sasha. You know what I mean."

I smiled back. I did.

"If you'd asked me with anyone else if I could see myself getting married, having a kid...I'd have said no way—you know that. No time soon. But this doesn't even feel like the same thing. It's like...it's just the next part of *us*. It's just *right*. And I don't know what's going to happen, and I know we'll screw up and make mistakes. But we'll hold on till we can fix things again. I'm not letting go."

My throat ached with tenderness, but Stu cut me off before I could embarrass us both with major waterworks in the middle of the tough shrimpers' bar.

"It's Sasha who's not sure about all this. About...about *me*, I think." His smile melted away.

"Oh, Stu," I said. "She loves you. All the way. You have to know that."

"Yeah. I do. But I'm not sure she...I don't know if this is what she wants. If *I* am." His face crumpled like plastic in a fire, and I wanted to hug him. But we were Ogdens, and sloppy public displays of affection were not our style.

So it was rather strange when I found myself walking around the table to sit beside him and wrapped my arms around him, leaning my cheek against his shoulder. Stranger still when I felt Stu's arm go around my back, and we just sat like that for a few quiet, utterly unprecedented moments, Jake's nose wedged in between our bodies as though he couldn't bear to be left out.

The squeak of the bar's rickety screen door finally broke the moment, and I looked up to see an overweight, sweaty man carrying an armful of food toward us.

"I got chips," he said around the lit cigarette in his lips, flinging a small bag of Doritos to the table without making any comment on our tight clinch. "Fisherman's special"—Stu had a heaping platter—"and fish sticks." He laid a second plate beside my chips, and turned to go back inside without asking whether we needed anything else.

I let go of my brother and scooted a few inches away, staring at the plate in front of me. "I didn't order the fish sticks."

"I didn't know if Jake had eaten."

"Oh. I don't know if he can have fried—"

But Stu had already set the plate on the splintering wooden deck, and Jake surged toward it and was inhaling its contents before I even finished the sentence.

"Whoops," Stu said mildly. "It seems he can."

"Oh, no. Stu!" I chastised futilely.

"He'll be fine. Dogs eat cat poop and drink from toilets." He picked at his fries.

I couldn't stand seeing my happy-go-lucky brother so glum. "Stuvie..." I wanted to reassure him, but I wouldn't lie. "Sasha's scared right now, but she *wants* to want this. She's asked me to help her with that, and I am. We're going to fix this, okay?"

The worry in his eyes lightened ever so slightly. "Really?"

"You two are going to laugh about this someday—you'll tell your grandkids about it when they come to you for love advice."

Obviously my pep talk was working, because Stu started digging into his greasy sandwich with the lumberjack-like delicacy I was used to from him.

"But I need you to stop treating her like she's made of china."

He paused and glanced up. "What? I'm not—I'm just taking care of her. That's the man's job, taking care of his family." As he thumped his chest with his left hand, a chunk of grouper tumbled from the sandwich in his right to the picnic table. Stu didn't miss a beat, scooping it back up and shoveling it into his mouth, as I worked not to gag thinking about the pelican poop encrusted into the wood over the years.

"That is a really lovely sentiment," I said dryly. "From a caveman. But you're freaking her out—she doesn't feel like *her* anymore. Suddenly she thinks everything has changed between you guys."

Stu's dark eyebrows knotted together. "Everything *has* changed."

I dropped my bag of Doritos back to the table before I'd even slitted the cellophane, and pointed a stern finger at him. "No! That's what you have to stop showing her. Change is terrifying her—especially one this big. You can't go from zero to a hundred that fast—let things happen gradually. Organically. Quit pushing her to say yes to your proposal. Don't talk about becoming parents all the time. Don't baby her—she knows what she can handle."

"I'm trying to be supportive. Let her know I'm totally on board. I thought that's what I was supposed to do!"

"Well, in this case it's the wrong response. Treat her like the same old Sasha. Be irresponsible and childish. Keep her out all night on a work night. Manhandle her like a sex puppet."

Stu shook his head. "And you wonder why men don't understand women."

"Right now Sasha needs to feel like she's still the same person and that you two are still the same couple. That nothing significant has changed." I reached for the chips and tore the cellophane, pulling out a single triangle and licking off the nacho cheese. "This change has to come gradually for Sasha or she's going to panic."

Understanding was dawning slowly over Stu's face. "Okay...I see what you're saying now."

Over the crunch of the chip in my mouth I almost missed his next words:

"It's like boiling a frog—you just increase the heat so gradually he doesn't even know he's being cooked."

Chapter Fifteen

After I dropped Jake off that evening, a different passenger rode shotgun on the way home: Confusion filled the car as thoroughly on my way from Ben's as Jake's fluffy white butt had on the drive there.

I'd still been chewing uneasily over Stu's words—*it's like boiling a frog*—as I pulled into Ben's driveway, but my worries lifted as soon as I saw the front porch lights blazing. He was home, and the prospect of spending some time with him instantly cheered me.

After grabbing us a couple of beers from the fridge, Ben filled Jake's bowl and we stood chatting easily as we watched the dog Hoover up his kibble. Afterward he asked whether I'd like to join him and Jake for a quick walk. Which of course I did.

I wasn't imagining things: The connection between us as we strolled along the quiet residential street he lived on was so strong, so effortless and comfortable and good, how could it not be inevitable that we'd end up back together, once the speed bump of Perfect Pamela had been (kindly and gently, of course) disposed of?

When we got back twenty minutes later and I finally announced that I had an appointment to get to, I didn't imagine the disappointment I read on Ben's face—he didn't want me to go.

If I'd been meeting anyone but a client I'd have canceled. But Rae Ann was counting on me, and you didn't let a brokenhearted person down. After one last swishing of Jake's fur on his neck and shoulders, I said good night to Ben and let myself out.

My mind was a jumble as I drove. As cozy as things were getting with me and Ben lately, why hadn't he said anything yet about what was going on between us?

Was he still not sure?

Was he waiting for me to say something?

What I needed was to hash things out with Sasha, the way we always did together to analyze opaque male behavior. But we wouldn't have a chance to talk privately, at least until later. First we had a mission to accomplish.

Since I'd started my new practice, Sasha had been my resident expert in certain areas whenever I needed help with a client I wasn't fully qualified to offer. These topics included fashion advice, hair and makeup consultations, and the exact legal statutes on stalking, vandalism, and breaking and entering. (We all play to our strengths.) She also happened to be fantastic at the social graces. Rae Ann needed a specific type of intervention—and I knew exactly who could offer it. Sasha was an absolute wizard at talking to men.

I'd invited her tonight not just for her social-coaching skills, though, but because I well knew the Rule of Three: No man would approach a pair of women for fear of leaving the wingwoman hanging, and a gaggle of them was too intimidating. Walking up to a trio, though, wasn't as daunting as walking into a pack, and separating one from the herd didn't leave anyone out in the cold. This also seemed like a fortuitous opportunity to get things with Sasha on an easier, more normal footing, and not focus so exclusively on the pregnancy.

Claude's, downtown on Second, was a place Sasha and I had once spent a lot of time. The closest thing Fort Myers had to a singles bar, it was run by an aging expatriate Frenchman—the place was pronounced with a long O sound, "Clode's," and woe to any ugly Americans who pronounced it any other way (though Sasha and I had often sat at the bar, snickeringly referring to it—very, very quietly—as "Chezz Clawed"). The décor was a mix of classic European elegance and modern French pretension, with warm-toned faux-stuccoed walls artfully textured and revealing in places the "brick wall" behind it (which was actually artfully painted drywall). Red tablecloths dotted the dining area, each table sporting a vase (a "vahz," as Claude called it) with a single perfect yellow rose, and accordion-heavy music played softly in the background. The menu, on a chalkboard on the wall, was of course in French. The bar area was vast—it took up more than half the space—and on any given weekend it would be packed wall-to-wall with singles on the prowl, as patrons in the adjacent dining area shouted to be heard over the din of their mating calls.

But on weeknights it was usually a quiet little oasis in the middle of downtown, hopping for happy hour with the denizens of the many law offices in the area, but quickly settling down later in the evening. It was perfect for what I had in mind tonight—giving Rae Ann enough opportunity to talk to men without overwhelming her.

After introductions, and my explanation to Rae Ann for Sasha's presence, we settled in at the bar and ordered—sparkling water for Sasha, a glass of wine for me (with an apologetic glance to Sash, but I didn't want Rae Ann to feel funny about drinking alone), and a bottle of Coors Lite—no mug—for Rae Ann.

"No," Sasha said as soon as my client had ordered.

Rae Ann looked at her, bewildered. "What?"

"Belay that a moment," Sasha said to the bartender, who went to help another customer while she turned back to Rae Ann. "Men snap-judge a woman who drinks beer in one of three ways: She's easy, she's a ballbuster, or she's a lesbian."

I might have taken some offense to that, but Rae Ann beat me to the punch.

"That's crazy!" she protested as the bartender—an exceptionally attractive dark-haired thirty-something with gray-blue bedroom eyes and perfect straight, white teeth—returned with a stem glass and a bottle and began to pour for me.

"Excuse me," Sasha said to him. "What's your name?"

He gave her a slow grin that would have quickened the pulse of a dead woman. "When Claude's here it's Étienne. But otherwise it's Eddie."

"Of course it is," she said, with her own electric smile. Flirting was as instinctive to Sasha as breathing. "Eddie, what are the women who get the most attention from men drinking at your bar?"

He didn't even hesitate: "Cosmos."

Sasha turned back to Rae Ann. "Cosmos say feminine but fun—they're pink, but they're strong. Men *love* a cosmo girl." She turned back to Eddie, who was practically leaning across the bar toward her now; Sasha truly had a gift with men—and I knew she wasn't even trying. "And what about the girls who drink beer, Eddie? What happens to them?"

"They sit here alone most of the evening, or with their girlfriends, usually trash-talking guys—until now and then one of them goes home at the end of the night with one of the left-behind remnants who couldn't find anyone to hook up with before closing time."

I rolled my eyes out of Rae Ann's sightline. I suspected Eddie was exaggerating a fair amount to play into Sasha's obvious script, but it didn't matter—Rae Ann was staring at Sasha with something like idolatry.

"I'll have a cosmo, please," Rae Ann murmured, and Sasha patted her leg.

"Good girl. That's step one. Step two—smile. You have to look approachable before anyone's going to try to approach you, and a smile says, 'I'm pleasant. I'm happy. I'm not scary.'"

"You make it sound like men are the ones who are nervous about this kind of thing," Rae Ann said.

"Oh, honey! They are! Don't you know that women have all the power at this stage?"

"They do?"

"*We* do," Sasha said, winking. "Now let's show you how to wield yours."

Rae Ann was rapt, so I just stayed quiet and let Sasha lead the effort. I knew who was the master here. She reviewed the basics—the smile, eye contact, staying aware of the room and not getting too intent on our conversation, etc.

"So I get that you have to be open enough that they'll come talk to you," Rae Ann said finally. "But then what? I panic. I have nothing to talk about. I'm boring."

I frowned. "Why do you think you're boring, Rae Ann?"

She shrugged. "I don't know. I don't really follow current events. I'm not sparkly. I have a cat."

"Do *not* talk about your cat," Sasha jumped in.

"Yeah, I learned that one the hard way," Rae Ann said dejectedly.

"Honey, again you're underestimating your power here," Sasha said. "It's not up to you to entertain a man. It's on him to impress *you*. This is what they're hardwired for—to impress, to conquer, to *win*. All you have to do is give them the opportunity."

"I don't know what you mean."

I'd bowed out of their exchange again, but not intentionally: I was just fascinated to see Sasha in action. For all the issues she used to have with relationships, she was always a savant out of the starting gate.

She held up a finger to Rae Ann—"Watch"—then turned her gaze to Eddie, who was at the opposite end of the bar chatting with a customer. As soon as she caught his eye, she smiled and he bustled over.

"Do you need something, gorgeous?"

Sasha winked. "You read my mind. Could you tell me about your white wines?" she asked, pointing to my glass. I felt a flare of alarm, but tamped it down—she was clearly doing something.

"Why don't you tell me what you like?"

The look she slanted him might have been suggestive or simply inquisitive—it was impossible to pin down. "You know something about wines, then?"

He flashed a dazzling grin. "Well, I know enough to make some suggestions. I'm studying to be a sommelier."

"No kidding? What drew you to that?"

And they were off, Eddie telling her about everything from his interest in wines sparked from a vacation to Sonoma when he was in his twenties, to his training at a vineyard in Oregon, to his travels through Europe. It was at least another ten minutes in before they even got as far as talking about the house wine list.

"That's a lot of really great info," she told Eddie finally. "You know your stuff. Let me think about it for a few minutes."

"You got it. Let me know when you're ready. You ladies doing okay?" he asked me and Rae Ann. We nodded and he withdrew back to his other patron at the end of the bar.

"And *that* is how you have a conversation," Sasha said, as though there'd been no interruption in her lesson.

Rae Ann looked confused. "But you were just ordering wine."

"No." She indicated the glass of Perrier in front of her. "Notice I have no wine. But I spent a good fifteen minutes getting to know Eddie."

Rae Ann kept shredding the napkin she'd been savaging since we got there. "Well, obviously you're good at talking to people. But I'm not," she protested. "You can't just create the gift of gab in someone if they don't have it."

"*Au contraire.* I barely spoke at all. All I did was ask a few questions here and there."

Rae Ann shook her head. "No, you..." She trailed off, her forehead pleating, and I could tell she was replaying the exchange in her mind. "Oh," she said finally. "You're right."

Sasha gave a very Gallic "but of course" shrug. It was easy to get infected by the spirit of Chez Claude. "Talking to a man is like catching a fish. All you have to do is drop the right bait, and then hold on while he plays the line." It tickled me to see her using a metaphor clearly gleaned from my brother's passion for fishing. "Men just want to feel fascinating—we all do. Find out what interests them, and then...just ask about it. They'll take it from there."

Rae Ann was looking at Sasha as if she were Moses on the mount. "That's amazing."

Sasha put a hand on Rae Ann's to stop her relentless shredding. "And stop doing that. Even if you *are* sexually frustrated, there's no need to advertise it."

...

We wound up leaving Rae Ann at the bar. When Eddie came back Sasha told him she'd changed her mind about ordering wine—but that didn't stop him from leaning across the bar and striking the conversational flint again. To our surprise this time Rae Ann leaped in, asking Eddie about Italy, one of her dream vacations. By the time Sasha and I said it was time for us to head home, Rae Ann blithely waved us on. I suspected Eddie's heart (or his hormones) were following Sasha out the door, but he and Rae Ann were tête-à-tête about Tuscany when we left.

Sasha barely spoke the whole way to her apartment except to grunt agreement at my praise for her conversational coaching, and the sleeping serpent of dread in my belly, curled up and quiescent all night long, began to lift its head. When I pulled into a visitor's spot, I stopped the car and turned to face her. "Okay. What is it?"

"It's nothing," she said, waving me off as she reached for her purse with one hand and the door handle with the other. Quick as a bunny I hit the automatic lock, and Sasha sagged back in the passenger seat and gusted out a sigh. "Seriously, Brook—aren't you bored with my drama by this point? I'm kind of fed up with my*self*."

"I'm never bored with you. *Or* your drama. That's what friends are for."

"Okay, Dionne Warwick. Thanks."

"I'm not kidding. Look," I went on, "what you're facing right now isn't a broken fingernail, or even a bad breakup. This is huge life stuff— the biggest. If you're struggling with it, that's normal. You've got to go a little easier on yourself, Sash."

In the reflection from the streetlight overhead I saw her eyes glistening. "Why are you being so nice about this? This 'struggle' you're being so understanding about? Everything about it has the potential to really hurt your brother. To hurt you. And your family—" Her voice broke on the last word and hung in the dim silence.

"Sasha," I said quietly. "You *are* my family."

Tears spilled over her eyes and streaked illumination down her cheeks. I said nothing else, just rested a hand over hers on the console, and waited at her side while fear and sorrow had their way with her. My every instinct was screaming for me to say something, help her, fix this—but some things, I was coming to learn, I had to let run their course on their own.

Finally she moved her hand from under mine and reached into her purse for a tissue, wiping her face and dabbing at her eyes.

"Being a parent?" she said in a wobbly voice after a few moments. "It's like someone else's life—a grown-up's life." She blew her nose daintily into the tissue. "I don't know how to do that. This—tonight— is what I'm good at. I talk to people for my interviews at work. I flirt. I make party chitchat. But it's *all* I'm good at. How can I be somebody's mommy? I have no idea how to deal with children. I know how to talk to *adults*, not babies."

Her words sparked a sudden memory, and an idea began to hatch in my head—crazy maybe, but maybe exactly what my friend needed. Despite the deflated tone of her voice, I began to grin.

"So I know we said we were going to give Operation Bring It On a rest," I said, "but I might have an idea for something that could help. What are you and Stu doing tomorrow night?"

She frowned. "I don't know. It's Friday, so normally we'd be going out, but we'll probably stay home and go to bed at nine, if your brother has his way. I'm made of eggshells now, remember," she said bleakly. "And you know the worst thing?"

"What?"

"He's right—I'm too exhausted to keep my eyes open most of the time lately. This remora inside me is literally sucking away all my energy." But as she said it she cupped a hand protectively over her belly, and that insistent spark of hope flamed to life again.

"Don't worry about Stu," I told her. "I've got that in hand, and he's going to chill out."

"What do you—"

"Not important. I'll pick you up at bedtime tomorrow evening—I mean nine." Sasha glared, but I just grinned at her, releasing the door lock. When she hesitated, frowning at me, I gave her a gentle shove on the shoulder. "Just trust me. And be ready for a late night."

Chapter Sixteen

Michael was already sitting in one of the chairs along the opposite wall after my last client the next afternoon—on Fridays I wrapped up by four so I could make it to my radio show on time, but today I'd taken my last client at two so we could meet for an hour to discuss how things were going with Michael's plan for my business.

Paige was still at her desk when I stepped out of my office, though I'd told her at lunch she could leave early.

"Oh," I said, stopping abruptly. "I see you two have met."

"Before, actually," Michael said with a wink to Paige, whose expression remained stony. Stonier than usual. "Paige here is a mean plant wrangler."

The peace lily still sat on the floor in front of the window, mute testimony to the door I'd reopened with Michael.

"I can stay for a while longer, if you need me to." She was eyeballing Michael as she said it.

I wanted to smile, but bit it back. Paige had clearly picked up on the history between the two of us and was being protective. Fondness for her flooded me. For all her literalness and serious demeanor, Intern Paige had great instincts and plenty of compassion.

"Thanks, Paige—I really appreciate it," I said sincerely. "But I can handle...whatever's left to do today. I know you probably have homework to tackle."

She frowned. "Well, no, it's not homework. At this stage of my education it's research for my disserta—"

I held up a hand. "Figure of speech. My bad. Thanks, Paige—have a good night."

She gathered her things and left, casting a baleful glance at Michael as she did that made me wonder whether Sasha had been planting a bug in her ear about him. There were few women Michael couldn't manage to win over, and that seemed a likely explanation.

But so did the more likely fact that Intern Paige was utterly oblivious to frivolous charm.

"Come on back," I said to Michael, gesturing toward my office.

He stopped just inside the doorway, taking in the room: My desk, bought secondhand at a business-consignment shop downtown, with its vintage wooden roller chair that I loved (it made me feel like Sigmund Freud). The forest-green chaise along the near wall where my clients sat, a butterscotch-colored armchair cattycorner from it. The IKEA shelves lining the far wall adjacent to my desk, so clients would have something of interest to look at over my shoulder when rising emotions made it difficult to maintain eye contact, and where I'd gleefully unpacked the boxes of books—psychology and otherwise—that had sat in my parents' attic for years. My old Goosebumps books sat beside psych texts from college, Grimm's fairy tales alongside lit classics, several rows of popular fiction above shelves of how-to and self-help titles.

"Wow," Michael said. "You finally got your dream office."

All my life I'd wanted a comfortable, homey, book-lined workspace for my practice, and this room was one of the first things I'd tackled when I started renovating my house.

"You want the chaise, or is that too therapy-ish?" I asked, gesturing toward it. "You can have the armchair if you're more comfortable."

But he remained standing. "Can I see the rest?"

"The rest?"

"Your house. I'd love to see it."

"Oh..." I hesitated. It felt odd and slightly dangerous to bring Michael into my private spaces, but I couldn't think of a reasonable way to turn down such an innocuous request. "Sure. Come on."

I led him back out of the office. "You already saw the waiting room, of course. And the office lavatory?" I indicated the bathroom with an arm.

Michael shook his head. "I haven't seen that yet. That's really nice," he said, peering in at the tile and stonework around the vanity and tub, the shiny glass accent tiles and oil-rubbed-bronze fixtures.

"Thanks," I said, feeling a rush of pride. "That was the first project my dad and I worked on. Out of necessity," I said with a chuckle, remembering. "This wall was eaten up with mold." I pointed behind the tub. "Once we had to tear it all down pretty much to the studs, it seemed a shame not to fix it up as nicely as we could."

"Your dad's always been a magician with stuff like this."

I stopped, turning to face him. At one time Michael and my father had been close, and I was reminded that Michael had suffered other losses when the two of us fell apart. "Yeah. He is."

I took him into the living room next, where he admired the Venetian plaster–textured walls and the stained-concrete floor. He grinned. "Your dad again?"

A sliver of pain sliced into my heart as I remembered Ben with his industrial diamond sander, smoothing the floor into a glasslike finish before we artfully applied the stain; Ben patiently showing me the nuances of the faux-plaster technique, helping me over and over again until the texture actually looked intentional, instead of like a bucket of stucco had exploded on the wall.

"No," I said quietly. "Someone else helped me in here."

Michael turned to look directly at me, his gaze intent. "Someone...you dated?" he asked, and I wasn't surprised that he'd read me so easily. I nodded, and his face crumpled like a sinkhole.

"You dated?" he repeated, as if the words made no sense to him.

"It's been two years, Michael. Of course I dated."

He shook his head. "No, but...someone who did all this...it was serious. Wasn't it."

I looked away, at the cinnamon-colored wall that lit up orange in the setting sun. "It was. For a while."

He made no reply. After a few silent moments he turned away from me, pointing toward the other doorway in the living room. "That's to the rest of the house?"

I was so grateful for the change of subject I trotted right over and led him into my kitchen and den area. "I haven't really done much back here yet," I explained as he took in the ancient pressed-wood cabinetry and Formica countertops, the cracked Saltillo tiles in the adjacent den.

We walked out onto the lanai, furnished with my Big Lots sale outdoor set, and into my overgrown backyard before going back inside. I hesitated at the door to my master bedroom. Jake was in there—for some reason he'd devolved into full-on play mode during my last session, doing the bouncing bunny in front of my last client, diving into a hopeful downward dog, tail wagging, and barking in the man's face. I'd finally had to excuse myself long enough to escort him into solitary confinement in my bedroom so we could finish the session in peace.

"Brace yourself," I warned as I opened the door, and Jake wormed through the opening the moment it was wide enough for his body, nearly knocking Michael over with his gregarious hello.

"You remember Jake," I said dryly.

Michael looked up from where he was stroking the dog's neck. "Jake? I thought your dog's name was Spike?"

My face heated with a blush I was sure he could see. "Um...right. I just sort of said that, actually. He's Jake. And he's not mine. I'm keeping him for a...a friend."

I turned away to avoid Michael's searching look, gesturing into the bedroom. "I haven't done anything in here yet at all, really. Well, except pull up the carpet, as you can see," I said, indicating the gray concrete floor scattered with cheap rag rugs. "It was about thirty years old, and I couldn't fathom putting my bare feet on it," I explained. "And there used to be curtains and a nicer bedspread, but..." I dwindled off, remembering the first night I'd ever had Ben's crazy dog, when a traumatized, confused Jake had eaten pretty much every textile in the room when I'd left him here alone for a few hours. I blinked away the memory, turning a determined smile to Michael.

He looked as if I'd struck him.

"Michael? What's wrong?"

"It's just..." He stopped, cleared his throat, tried again. "This would have been ours. We'd have been the ones doing all this together if I hadn't—"

"No," I cut him off quickly. "It wouldn't have. This house was my reaction to...to what happened. I rushed into buying it to prove—to myself and everyone else—that I was fine. But I never would have ended up here otherwise. You and I never would have bought a derelict like this." I turned away from the bedroom, leading us back out to the living room. I ran my hand along the wall as we walked, Jake weaving through us as if trying to trip us. "It's funny, though," I said, without turning back to Michael. "It's a wreck, and it needs so much work, and I bought it for all the wrong reasons in a terrible state of mind. But...I love it. It's mine."

"It's you," he said quietly from behind me.

It was. But it was also all the people I loved—my dad, Sasha and Stu, who'd worked alongside me on the smaller projects.

Ben.

"Let's go back to my office," I said brusquely.

I took a seat in my chair, Jake planting himself beside me, and Michael sat on the chaise.

"Well, first things first," he said, pulling his laptop from his messenger bag. "They said no."

"Who said no to what?"

"KXAR. I set up a meeting with the general manager and laid out our case for your own show, and he said they couldn't offer you that."

I felt a dull flutter of disappointment, but I wasn't surprised. "Oh, well. We tried."

He snorted. "Tried, hell. I told them you quit."

"You *what*?!"

"Relax. This is how the game is played."

There ensued a good four solid minutes of my haranguing, complaining, and accusing Michael of making huge unilateral decisions without my okay, before he was able to get a single word in.

"They're talking about an offer," he said calmly when I finally wound down.

"What?"

"The station manager is meeting with the owner to discuss what they can offer you, and he said he'll get back to me. That's what I was trying to tell you. You have to trust the power of no."

My heart slowed back to a life-sustaining pace. "Geez, Michael. *Lead* with that next time, would you? And also...*ask* me what to do before you just do it. I thought that's what we agreed on."

"I did ask! You said go ahead."

"I said go ahead on starting to negotiate! Not go ahead and tender my resignation!"

"Fair enough," he conceded. "Then do you also want to see the offer for you to be one of the main speakers for a traveling relationship seminar before I accept it for you?"

"What?"

He chuckled. "It's called Relationship Town Hall—it's run by this dating guru up in New York who takes the show to various towns and hires local relationship experts to be panelists in each city. Attendees come to discuss love and dating, and then afterward there's a mix-and-mingle for them, like a singles event. It's been gaining a lot of traction and media coverage—how have you not heard about this, in your line of work?"

That was a good question. It certainly sounded like something I should have been aware of. "I don't know. How did *you* know about it?"

"I just dug around a little on the Internet. Anyway, I approached the guy who started it—his name's Rod Traynor; maybe you've heard of him? He's on *GMA* a lot and has a column in HuffPost."

"Really—Rod? The dating guru is named *Rod*?"

"You're a child," he said, but he was grinning. "I gave him a rundown on what you do and your CV, and he was really interested—wants to talk about possibly booking you for the panel in the Tampa, Miami, and Jacksonville shows, if you're up for it."

"Holy cow, Michael," I said, stunned. "You really are good at this."

He sighed. "Why do you and Sasha keep sounding so surprised when you say that?"

Where was this motivated, together, *adult* version of Michael when he and I were dating? I couldn't help thinking how different our lives might look right now if he'd found this side of himself sooner. This guy knew what he wanted and how to get it, and wasn't afraid of growing up. *This* guy would never have walked out on his fiancée.

I shook off the thought, turning my laptop so Michael could see the screen.

"Okay, like you asked I made a bullet list of possible topics I could write about as guest blogs. Some of them are based on articles I've done for my column, but I have a lot of new ones too."

He had good feedback—helping me tweak broad topics into sharper focus, and suggesting which ones might be best for initial pitches to the bigger sites—but I could tell he was preoccupied. Finally I looked up from the screen.

"What's the matter? Are these not what you were looking for?" I asked.

He shook his head. "No, they're great."

"Michael." I leaned back in my chair, regarding him. "I know you. What's wrong with this?"

"Nothing, Brook, honestly. It's good stuff." Our eyes had a Mexican stand-off for a few long beats, and then finally he said, "It's... I know you wanted to keep our personal stuff out of"—he made a stirring gesture encompassing my laptop and desk and the area between us—"this. It's harder than I thought. I'm a little thrown by the guy who helped you fix the house. That you seriously dated another guy."

"Two, actually." I said it without thinking, but a hot flush of shame rose in the words' wake as his face fell. Despite my professed forgiveness of Michael, I wondered whether part of me was still deliberately trying to hurt him.

"You've had *two* serious relationships since us?"

"Hey!" I said sharply. "*You're* the one who called things off. *You're* the one who left and never looked back, as far as I knew. What the hell did you expect me to do, Michael, sit around nursing my broken heart?"

"Of course not. I know you had to move on. But—"

"But what? You thought I'd just have hookups and crappy first dates while I waited for you to get your shit together and come back to me?"

"No! Jesus, Brook, I know you better than that. I knew when I left that you'd be back on the horse probably the next week. That as far as anyone else would see, nothing had touched you. That's who you are—you don't let anyone in far enough to hurt you."

That stung. "*You* hurt me, Michael," I said with venom. "You pretty much broke me in half."

Silence crashed over us like a wave.

"So yes, I tried to move on," I said, more quietly now. "And yes, I had relationships. But they blew up. Because of you." I looked directly at him and said levelly, "Because when you left it just about destroyed me—but I never let myself deal with that."

"Why didn't you tell me?" It was a plea.

I gave a dry laugh. "Well, for starters, you went AWOL." He acknowledged that truth with an inclination of his head, silent apology written across his face. "But even if you hadn't I wouldn't have told you. For the reason you said—I never wanted to let anyone get close enough to be able to hurt me. Which was foolish, I've come to learn. Because hiding your feelings doesn't protect anything—and keeping my heart under such tight guard was exactly what blew up the thing I wanted most."

I wasn't sure who I was talking about anymore. I felt his eyes on me as I stared into the bookshelves I'd deliberately positioned to help my clients deal with overwhelming feelings.

"You've changed so much, Brook."

"Yeah. So have you."

"Jesus. I was such an ass."

At his words I couldn't help the grin that crept across my lips, and I shifted my gaze to him. "Speaking of which...Want to see something?"

His eyebrows bunched. "Yeah...?" he said cautiously.

I put my computer on the desk, then shrugged out of my gray suit jacket. Michael watched with an expression I couldn't read as I turned farther to my right to expose to him my bare right shoulder in the halter-neck blouse I wore.

"What is that?" he asked behind me. "A bruise?"

"Look closer," I said, knowing that the embarrassing tattoo I'd gotten one drunken night in the lowest part of my breakdown in the aftermath of Michael's decampment wasn't quite eradicated yet, despite the months of tattoo removal I'd already undergone.

I felt Michael's breath warm on my shoulder as he stood and leaned closer to see. "What does...Oh, my God."

I didn't even remember getting the giant donkey tattoo, let alone directing the tattoo artist to endow it with massively engorged genitals. But the caption I'd had inked underneath it certainly sounded like me at the time: "No more jackasses."

When I shrugged the jacket back on and turned to him, I had to give him points for how hard he was trying not to laugh.

"Well, Brook, everyone has the right to express themselves. I applaud your originality and willingness to take risks."

I shoved him. "Shut up. I was drunk off my ass."

"No pun intended..." Michael shot me a sly grin I couldn't help returning.

And then, contrary to every tenet I once held about keeping things to myself, I plunged into the full story of my rebound relationship with

Kendall Pulver, who'd dumped me via text message when things seemed to be moving faster than he was ready for. After Michael, it was the proverbial straw that broke the stoic's back, and my spectacular breakdown had ensued, complete with drunk-dialing, stalking, snooping, the infamous tattoo, and finally making an enormous public embarrassment of myself by screaming and hurling a drink at Kendall at a bar downtown in our final showdown, when he revealed that he'd been married for the first several months of our relationship.

"It was the lowest point I'd ever been at," I said to Michael, who'd sat on the chaise mesmerized during the whole sordid tale. "And yet, in a weird way it was the best thing that ever happened to me. It sort of...I don't know. Shook something loose here." I popped a fist to my chest in a mini Celine Dion. "As Sasha said, it was like someone who'd been deaf all her life had suddenly had her hearing restored."

"Trust Sasha to provide a colorful metaphor."

He used to know her so well. I'd lost a lot when Michael and I broke up, but he'd lost an entire social network.

"And what about the other relationship?" he asked. "You said there were two."

I stood, busying myself shutting down my laptop. "That one didn't work out either."

I could feel him watching me. "That was renovation guy?"

"Yes."

"What happened with him?"

I swiveled around, planting a playful smile on my face. "Uh-uh. I told you one of my stories. Now you have to tell me one of yours."

"You mean from after we...after I left?" He shrugged. "I don't have any to tell you."

I raised my eyebrows. "Come on, now. From your reaction earlier I'm guessing you didn't get serious with anyone—and God knows I don't want dirty details—but let's hear your lowest point. Which meaningless hookup with a skank finally told you you'd hit rock bottom?"

"None of them. I mean, they didn't."

I leaned back in my chair, arms folded, and shot him a mock glare. "Fine. You don't want to confess? Let me guess, then. An underage band groupie. A half-passed-out girl hopped up on E? Oh, my God—a dude? No judgment if that's what—"

"There's no story because there were no hookups, Brook. I haven't been with anyone else since you."

Air drained out of me as if someone had pulled out a stopper. "Two years?" I asked, incredulous. "You haven't had sex in two *years*?"

He held up his right hand, wiggling his fingers. "Are we counting—"

"No," I stopped him quickly. "Jeez, Michael. Are you about to explode?"

He shrugged, and now it was his turn to focus intently on my book titles. "At first I had no urge. Like, at all. I could barely remind myself to eat, let along summon up any kind of..." He made a vague gesture toward his torso.

I held up a hand. "I get it."

"And after that...I don't know." He pushed to his feet, walking over to the shelves closest to the far corner, pulling out a book. I was distantly amused to note that it was *Women's Bodies, Women's Wisdom.* "I just...didn't do it. It's sort of like when you get the yips in baseball, and pretty soon you're on a real losing streak. After a while you don't even have the game in you anymore—you've whiffed before you even step up to the plate."

He opened the book, thumbing through pages I was certain he wasn't seeing. I watched him, sympathy I hadn't thought I could feel for him tugging at me.

"I smoked a lot," he went on as if speaking to the pages of the book. "Too much. Too many different things. Drank myself into a blackout most nights. Who'd want to be with that anyway?"

"You were punishing yourself," I said.

"No."

"You still are."

Finally he looked up and met my eyes, and I caught my breath at the naked anguish in his. "Shouldn't I be?" he said softly.

Two years ago I would have said yes without hesitation. With my clients I was quick to root out areas where they were beating themselves up, causing themselves more pain and making healing that much more difficult. But Michael hadn't been a client. He'd been the love of my life, or so I'd thought, and he'd done me the greatest of wrongs. If he'd told me then that he deserved to be punished, I would have wholeheartedly agreed.

But so much had happened since then—between us, and to me. And what I saw in front of me now wasn't the man who'd broken my heart and ruined my life, but someone I'd once cared about deeply—and still did. Someone I couldn't bear to see launching missiles at himself.

"No," I said firmly. "You shouldn't. Don't you think I know that you weren't trying to intentionally hurt me?"

"But I did. And I screwed up your whole life."

"You're giving yourself an awful lot of credit there," I said dryly, but Michael didn't crack a smile. I pushed up off my chair, standing to face him. "Who can say if things got screwed up? I wouldn't be where I am if that hadn't happened." I would never have met Ben. "I wouldn't have my Breakup Doctor practice. And I love it, Michael—it's literally my dream job. And you said I've changed since then—I have, in ways I like. I don't think I would have without going through...what we went through."

"But the way I did it..."

"Sucked. And was cowardly."

Shame filled his face. "I know that."

"But it was the best you could do at that time. Wasn't it." It was hard to believe I was defending his actions—to the very person responsible for them, who'd crushed me—but I meant every word. "I forgive you."

"No." He looked as if I'd hit him.

"Yes," I insisted. "I forgive you. I did a while ago—when you came back and we talked. And it felt like the greatest gift I'd ever given myself, to let go of all that anger and hurt and pain. I should have told you that then."

"I don't deserve your forgiveness."

"And yet I'm offering it."

"Stop it."

"I forgive you, Michael," I said inexorably, stepping closer. "Now forgive yourself."

He stared at me with a wash of emotions crossing his face—disbelief, anger, denial. And then his face eased almost imperceptibly. "Forgive myself," he said, as if trying the thought on for size.

"Yes. I can't believe I'm the one exhorting you to do that, but I mean it. Forgive yourself and, in the wise words of Elsa, let it go. That's the only way you're going to move past this." I put a hand on his wrist where he still held the book, felt his pulse beating under my fingers. "That we are."

The ghost of a smile played across his lips, and he finally closed the unread book and slid it back into its spot with the hand I wasn't touching. "Okay. You're the expert. I'll give it a try."

"Good." We shared a smile that reminded me of old times, and before I realized what I was doing I closed the small gap between us and reached to hug him.

His arms came around me immediately, as if they'd only been waiting for me to initiate, and he held me close. His familiar scent filled my nose; his warmth seeped into my skin from chest to thighs through our clothing.

I pushed closer, relishing the strength of the arms holding me, the feeling of being wanted, cherished. Stroking his back, I found muscles that hadn't been there before, but knew exactly where my fingers would encounter the raised mole under his left shoulder blade. Something tightly coiled inside me began to unwind as our bodies pressed together.

And then something else pressed insistently into me too.

I jumped away as if he'd burned me, my heart suddenly racing, my face on fire.

Michael reached out a hand to touch my arm, but I took a quick step out of range. "Brook...I—"

"No, no, it's...I shouldn't have...I mean, especially given your, um, you know...dry spell..." I gave an awkward laugh. "I know the chamber must be loaded and the safety off." I moved to my desk, desperate to avoid his searching gaze, my own rattled emotions. "So, I'll fine-tune these proposals and get them to you ASAP?"

"Okay. That'll be good." I heard the words, but didn't see them through the curtain of my hair as I kept my gaze determinedly focused on shutting down my laptop. Slowly.

It felt like a long, long time before I heard footsteps and then a soft click, and only then did I dare to look up, staring at the door that had shut behind Michael.

Chapter Seventeen

Michael had decreed that I could do my radio show that afternoon, with the caveat that if the offer from the station was lacking, I would be willing to play hardball and sit out further appearances while he negotiated.

I was ridiculously grateful not to have to miss it—particularly today. I need to take my mind off of what had just happened.

I'd known that whatever had once been between me and Michael had never fully died on my part. And he'd made it perfectly clear since he'd come back that his feelings for me were very much alive as well.

But the clear physical evidence of it had made everything feel much more real. And immediate.

I couldn't put off letting him know my decision forever.

By the time my ninety-minute radio segment was finished, my thoughts had begun to settle and the ground underneath me felt solid again. I couldn't imagine if I had to give these shows up as a bargaining chip in Michael's business plan. I loved when someone who called in sounding broken or defeated hung up after our conversation with a burst of strength in their tone. With the radio shows I was able to help more people—at least on some level—than I could reach in that amount of time any other way, and I thrived on that.

I worried that Michael and I would find that I needed the show a lot more than the station needed me.

As soon as I went off-air at six thirty I trucked back down Winkler to my house and picked up Jake. No matter how brief a time I was gone, he was always as happy to see me as if I'd been away at war.

This was why people loved dogs, I thought as I clipped his leash on and wrangled him into my Accord: because we got enough uncertainty and indifference from the people in our lives—at least our dogs made no secret of their giddy delight in our company every time we showed up.

Unlike their humans, I thought disappointedly as I pulled into Ben's driveway, the front of the house dark. He must be working especially late tonight, but I was surprised he hadn't texted to tell me so.

Although maybe it was for the best, I reflected as I fetched the key from under the paving stone. I'd been able to back-burner my muddled thoughts while I handled other people's problems on the show, but as soon as we were off the air, worries swarmed my head like no-see-'ums.

I'd been trying to keep things on an even keel with Michael, hoping to move slowly, not only to find out what might still be there between us, but to give myself time to figure out what was going on with me and Ben.

But I was no closer to an answer.

I fumbled with the lock in the deep shadows on the porch, reaching inside to grope for the light switch so we didn't stumble in the pitch-black. But as Jake pushed past me, pushing the door wider, I noticed a faint spill of illumination from the back of the house.

Ben never left lights on.

Suddenly I heard voices.

A chill passed through me, literally raising the hair on the back of my neck. Jake, whose vaunted Pyrenees hearing and finely honed guard instincts were responsible for his endless alert barking in the middle of the night, somehow failed to respond to this actual threat, glancing up at me contentedly and wagging his tail.

I knew what you were supposed to do with a suspected intruder: Leave the house immediately and call the police. But that excellent advice fails to take into account the surge of adrenaline and outrage that courses through you when someone has breached the security of your home—or the home of someone you care about—and before I could stop myself I had in my hand the canister of pepper spray I always carried and was charging back to where the voices were coming from.

"Get the hell out of here!" I barked in as ferocious a growl as I could manufacture, my lips pulled back in a snarl as I rounded the corner still holding Jake's leash in one hand, wielding the pepper spray in the other like Lady Liberty with her torch.

Only to find Ben and Pamela standing in the kitchen, a bottle of red wine open on the counter between them, one glass held in Perfect Pamela's beautifully manicured fingertips. Her perfect mouth was open in a perfectly round O as she took in my aggressive entrance, and Ben was looking at me as if I'd walked in with my hair on fire.

I felt my face heat. "Oh—sorry. I thought you were a burglar."

"Hi, Brook," Pamela said, recovering her composure in an instant. Of course.

"Hello, Pamela," I said brightly, trying (and failing) to match her poise. "How lovely to see you. You're looking great. As always!" And she was—in a black-and-white wrap dress that hugged her wasp waist before flaring out in a feminine spill, and perfect sensible black low-heeled pumps. Instead of the jeans and well-fitted cotton shirt I'd grown used to in the last week, Ben wore khaki pants and a white button-down.

Understanding dawned. He had a date.

With Perfect Pamela.

And I'd walked in on the middle of it.

Nausea boiled up in my stomach.

I laughed somewhat maniacally as I tried to casually drop the pepper spray back into my purse, as if it were a lipstick I'd just used. I was thrown by the homey, intimate scene, Pamela occupying the position against the counter I'd already come to think of again as mine, Ben standing a few feet away, hands jammed into his pockets.

He was frowning. "Why did you come tearing into the kitchen if you thought we were intruders, Brook? That's dangerous. You should have left and called the police."

I rolled my eyes. "Yes, I know. Good thing I didn't, though, right? Wouldn't want you two hauled off to the pokey together or anything— ha, ha, ha! Oh," I rambled on. "Congrats on the Doctors Without Borders interview, Pamela. I hope you win! I mean, I hope you get it. Get chosen, I mean. Not that I want you to move halfway across the world or anything! Ha, ha, ha!"

Ben was eyeing me with concern. "Would you like a glass of wine, Brook?"

No, but maybe a Valium? I thought wildly.

But Pamela, of course, was gracious enough not to react to my verbal incontinence, just arced a glance across to Ben with a secret smile that sent a sudden shard of ice sliding into my belly. "Funny you mention that," she said. "We were just talking about it. There's a partner program that works with the Doctors Without Borders organization to help build the clinics in various villages. That sounds right in Ben's wheelhouse, doesn't it?"

The ice spread to my fingers and toes, and the bottom dropped out of my stomach. Ben was thinking of going with her?

To freaking *Africa*?

If I'd needed clarification about the mixed messages I thought I'd been getting from him, they'd just become utterly, painfully clear.

Suddenly I was more than a little concerned about the prickling heat building behind my eyes. I might be able to pass off my mania as an overindulgence in caffeine, but it was going to be a lot harder to explain to Perfect Pamela why her boyfriend's pal and dog-sitter was blubbering in his kitchen.

"Brook?" Ben asked, his eyebrows bunched together, and I realized I hadn't made any response in too long a time.

"Oh...mm-hmm," I managed, having long forgotten Pamela's question and hoping it would do as an answer. All I wanted to do was get out—quickly, before I embarrassed myself. And Ben. "Well, I don't want to horn in on...I mean interrupt...Friday night—date night, amiright?" I sounded like a bad Vegas comedian. "I've got plans of my own! Definite plans. I need to get going. Catch you later!" I said inanely.

I turned on my heel to block out the sight of Pamela and Ben and Jake in a happy huddle in the kitchen, but the cozy scene was still burned onto my retinas. The only thing intruding on the sweet little picture of domestic bliss was *me*.

I was moving so fast that I had the door to my car open before I heard the hydraulic arm of the screen door slam it shut behind me.

...

My phone rang just as I pulled into my garage—Ben.

I debated whether I should answer. I pictured Perfect Pamela standing at his elbow, an expression of concern across her lovely face as she kindly exhorted Ben, *You should call her and check on her. She seemed upset.*

But not answering would only confirm it. Swallowing, I closed my eyes and hit answer.

Sure enough: "Hey...just wanted to make sure you were okay."

Mortification heated my face.

"I'm sorry about that," I said. "I know that was weird."

"It wasn't weird," he protested halfheartedly.

"It was weird."

"It was a little weird."

"Sorry. I...I had a long day," I said. "A long week."

There was a pause, and then: "Listen, about what Pamela said..."

"Yeah, sorry, I was just...It was unexpected. You didn't mention you were considering that."

"That's because I wasn't. She just mentioned it to me before you came in."

There was a long silence in which my grief warred with relief. So this hadn't been planned all along. And Pamela had asked *him*...not the other way around. I wondered whether he was clarifying that on purpose. And whether Pamela was right next to him, hearing everything both of us said.

I didn't know whether Ben had ever told her we'd dated. Knowing him, I assumed so—he wasn't a big fan of keeping secrets (as I knew from painful firsthand experience). And in that case, she was too smart not to realize that my freakish reaction could only mean that I still had feelings for him.

If so, I'd put him in a very awkward position. And he wasn't making it any better by calling me with her there. Whatever this meant, now wasn't the time to talk about it.

"I really need to go, Ben."

"Listen, Brook…" There was another lengthy silence, the sound of an exhaled breath, and I finally understood the phrase "heart in mouth" as I waited to hear his next words. "If you'd rather not watch Jake on Monday—"

"No! I'll watch him."

"Are you sure? I can—"

"I'm sure." I had only a few more days before Adelaide came home. A few days left to find out whether there was any hope at all for me and Ben.

"Well, then…thanks. I'm glad."

"Me too," I said. Relentlessly, I wondered whether his words were only borne of gratitude.

"Okay, well," I said finally, "you guys have fun tonight."

"You too. What are you—"

I broke the connection.

Chapter Eighteen

Nine thirty that night found me at a place I never thought I'd come back to.

Sticks and Stones was a local S and M club filled with both curious *50 Shades* looky-loos and hard-core BDSM devotees. I liked occasional silk-scarf blindfold-and-bondage recreation as much as the next person, but I fell into neither category: My ill-advised trip to the club last summer was a result of following a shy, circumspect client here to stop her from doing anything she might regret in the desperation of her relationship woes.

Which I had, but that was also the night I'd run into Chip Santana, a former client and inappropriate crush I'd nearly crossed ethical lines with once before, then severed contact with to maintain professional boundaries. Seeing him here had reopened that explosive can of worms—which had ultimately resulted in my breakup with Ben.

Good times.

I pushed all that out of my head, though, as I pulled my Honda into the ill-lit concrete lot outside the club.

"What the hell are we doing *here*?" Sasha asked from the passenger seat.

She and my brother had her own history with the place—after my memorable-in-the-bad-way evening here, they had decided to check things out for themselves, because apparently there was no sexual line they would not gleefully leap across (and then insist on telling me about in unwelcome detail). But Sticks and Stones proved too much even for them—they got groped like the newest inmates at Sing-Sing, and pushed their way back out the doors minutes after they'd gone in.

"Trust me, you guys—there's a reason we're here," I said. It felt good to be doing something in my comfort zone, where I felt in control and competent, not the idiotic boob I'd acted like earlier in front of Ben and Pamela. I let myself out of the car and turned to open the back door, where Stu was still sitting, making no move to get out.

"Come on, baby bro. Trust big sissy," I cajoled.

He looked to the front seat, where my best friend was also still planted. "Sash?"

"What are we doing here, Brook?" she asked again.

I leaned down to look at her directly. "I can't tell you. I just have to show you. Come on."

Sasha's arms were crossed over her chest, her eyebrows pinched together. "Stu?" she asked. "What do you think?"

I watched my brother take a deep breath and manufacture a game smile. "It's up to you, babe. If you want to go in, I'm with you."

Sasha's face relaxed like she'd had a mega injection of Botox, and then pulled into the reckless grin I absolutely adored. "What the hell. Let's do this."

I wanted to hug my brother: Stu had taken my admonition to heart and was trying to stop babying Sasha—pun unavoidable—and she looked like her old self again.

The inside of the club was just as I remembered: wall-to-wall bodies that seemed to close in as we made our way through the crowd, dim lighting, thunking bass, and hands roaming all over us, their owners invisible no matter how much we scanned our surrounds. The cool, moist air carried a musky scent and the underlying sharp tang of bleach. I turned to Sasha and Stu and made vague military hand signals—*You two, with me, that way*—and we pushed through to the back of the club and the warren of semiprivate rooms where the boldest took things a step farther, and the voyeurs watched.

It got quieter in this part of the club, the walls sectioned off with office-cubicle partitions carpeted in thick sound-absorbing black carpet, and the crowd thinned the farther we ventured as the various fetish rooms winnowed out their aficionados. Finally we came to a back room, moving almost freely through the makeshift halls now, and we stood in the doorway taking in the scene.

At first it seemed like a toga party where only some of the guests had bothered to come in costume. But it took only a moment to figure out what we were looking at: About half the bodies milling around in the fifteen-by-twenty room were in street clothes; the other half wore diapers.

"What. The. Fuck," I heard Sasha say beside me.

I let out a self-satisfied grin. "You said you're afraid of babies and you only know how to talk to adults. *Et voilà*: adult babies!"

Stu looked shell-shocked. "That's a thing. It really is a thing," he was repeating, as if he couldn't believe it.

"It's a *lifestyle*," I corrected. "And what we have here are a group of babies that Sasha can *converse* with. I thought it might be a good way for you to learn to interact with infants in a way that feels more comfortable," I said to Sash.

She turned a flat stare on me that I couldn't read. "You are a total idiot," she said calmly. "And also possibly a genius. This is insane, Brook—but it might be the perfect thing. Let's do it." And into the room she went.

It took Stu a few more moments, and possibly a loving shove from me, but eventually he followed her in and I trailed behind them, ready to help grease the conversational wheels if need be.

But I should have known that Sasha would take care of things herself—this was her gift, meeting strangers from every walk of life, offering them interest, respect, and no judgment, and getting them to open up to her. By the time Stu and I caught up to her she was already deep in conversation with three people—a tall, bald man in street clothes, a man wearing only a diaper and clutching a blankie over his shoulder like Linus, and a woman in what appeared to be a full-size onesie, a pacifier in her mouth.

"Hey, guys," Sasha said casually as we approached. "This is Richard." The bald man nodded in my direction and reached a hand to Stu.

"Hey, man."

My brother managed the handshake and even a tepid smile. "Hi."

"And this is his...what do I say?" she asked Richard.

"My baby," he supplied helpfully, wrapping an arm around the woman. "Little Lulu."

Sasha nodded. "This is Lulu," she went on, "and this is Johnny B. Guys, Brook and Stu."

Lulu just waved, fingers opening and closing as she sucked on her binky, but to my surprise Johnny B offered a hand to both of us.

"Welcome!" he said. "Sasha says you're new at this."

"Entirely," my brother said.

"Don't you have to talk baby-talk?" I asked, confused.

He grinned. "Nah, there's no rules. You do what feels right, you know? Sasha here says she's not real comfortable with kids and is trying to learn to be, so I turned it off for now."

For a fleeting moment I wondered whether she'd actually told this group she was pregnant. If she had, it was the first time she'd said it to anyone besides me and Stu.

"So, what is it you want to learn about?" Johnny B asked, and then he reached into the front of his diaper.

My eyes widened in alarm—things were about to get weird—but he drew his hand right back out, holding a pack of Marlboros. "Smoke?" he offered us.

"Thanks, not for me," Sash averred.

Stu and I also declined. Johnny B pulled a Bic lighter from the pack, but Richard put a hand on his to stay him.

"Hey, man, not in front of the baby—you mind?" he said, nodding toward Lulu.

"Oh, sorry—my bad," Johnny B apologized, and the cigarettes vanished back into his diaper. "So what can we tell you, hon?" he asked Sasha.

His avuncular manner and demeanor coupled with the diaper and blanket were a bit disconcerting, but Sasha plunged ahead as if they were chatting at a family reunion.

"Well...I guess, why do they have to fuss at you all the time? What do babies *want?*"

Lulu giggled and batted the air, offering us a giant, vacant grin. Sasha lifted her eyebrows and turned back to Johnny.

His fingers snaked down into his diaper again, I hoped for the cigarettes, and then he seemed to remember the presence of Little Lulu, bringing his hand back out and instead raising it palm-up with a shrug. "Same thing anyone wants, really. Babies are just preverbal humans. We want the basics, of course—not to be hungry or thirsty or cold or wet. But we also want to feel safe and loved."

Sasha frowned. "But what does that *mean*? I mean, I get feeding an infant, giving it a bottle, changing its diaper, et cetera. But...you can't talk to it, or teach it anything, and it can't tell you what it wants. What are you supposed to do beyond seeing to its basic needs?"

"Every baby is different," Richard piped up. "My Lulu is a quiet little thing—no trouble at all. She just wants affection and to play and to be taken care of." As he spoke he pulled Lulu in closer, and she snuggled up against him, cooing softly behind her paci. He leaned over and kissed the top of her head. "And that's my sign to get my baby girl home to bed," he said to us with a beatific smile, and then gently led her toward the doorway with a protective arm wrapped around her shoulders.

It was actually kind of sweet.

Sasha seemed to consider his words for a moment as she watched the cozy pair walk away, and then she cast a quick, apologetic look to Stu. "But how do you know you'll be any good at it?" she said to Johnny, so quietly I almost didn't hear her. "How do you know you have it in you to care enough about some helpless, demanding creature that you'll actually do all that?"

My brother's face blanched, but he stepped closer and rested a hand in the small of her back. I loved him for supporting her even when it clearly hurt him to hear her doubts.

Johnny smiled and gave her a kindly wink. "If you don't mind my saying, hon, I don't think you need to worry." He brushed a quick comforting pat to her arm—thankfully with the hand that hadn't been investigating his diaper. "If you didn't have that in you, I don't imagine you'd be standing here with us, working so hard to figure things out."

Sasha's face softened like butter left in the sun, and she blinked at him a few times. "Thanks," she said quietly, and I saw Stu squeeze her waist.

Suddenly a cloud shifted over Johnny B's expression and his eyebrows furrowed in concentration or consternation—I couldn't tell which. His mouth slackened slightly and his eyes lost focus, but just as I grew alarmed that he was having an epileptic seizure, his face cleared and he smiled like the sun had come out. "Oopsie!" he said in a high, silly voice. "I made a poopy in my di-di! I have to go get Mommy." He skipped away from us into the crowd.

The three of us stood in stunned silence for a moment.

"Did...did that dude just *shit his pants* while he was standing here talking to us?" Stu said finally, his face poleaxed.

Sasha was watching where Johnny B had headed over to a very tall woman with a blond helmet hairstyle straight out of the sixties and was tugging on her arm for her attention. "Well, no, because technically he's not wearing pants," she said calmly.

The woman nodded and indicated a corner of the room, where she led Johnny B by the hand. When they got there, he dropped out of our sightline while she rummaged in her enormous bag and came up with a box of Handi Wipes and what looked like a folded sheet.

Stu's face convulsed. "That's not...She's not actually going to change his diaper right here, is she?"

Through the crowd I suddenly saw a pair of bare, hairy men's legs shoot into the air, and the woman lowered herself to her knees in front of them.

"That's it—I'm out," Sasha said, and streaked toward the door.

Stu and I were right behind her.

Chapter Nineteen

When we pulled into Sasha's parking lot after fleeing Sticks and Stones, she was barely able to muster a good-night for me. Stu hung back as she trudged into her apartment.

"I didn't think we could make babies *more* frightening to Sasha," he said conversationally, leaning down into my window. "Solid work, there, Doc."

"This may not have been the best idea. I see that now," I admitted. "But I mean, on the plus side, you know, there was a moment when..." I caught Stu's raised eyebrow and didn't finish the thought. "But overall, yeah, I guess maybe watching a grown man get his butt wiped in public isn't the best—"

"Stop," he said abruptly, shuddering. "I can't have that picture back in my head again."

I grimaced, then sighed. "You're right. I'm sorry."

Stu glanced down to the asphalt, where I could hear his feet scuffing on pebbles. "Please don't give up on her, Brook," he said quietly, not meeting my eyes.

The irony struck me—Stu and Sasha had completely switched positions. Before they got together, it was Stu who'd always danced lightly around anything that smacked of commitment, and Sasha who'd spent her whole life chasing it. Now everything was backward—and they were both counting on me to make it right.

I put a hand over his on the windowsill. "I won't, Stuvie."

But failure weighed like lead in my belly.

...

My stomach clenched as soon as I saw Michael's name on my caller ID Saturday morning. I wasn't ready to talk about what had happened between us yesterday.

But he made no mention of the new vibe that had come up between us (literally), just shared unsettling news—the station was dragging their feet on an offer, and he thought it was time to play hardball.

"I think you should sit out the show on Monday," he said.

I'd told him I was willing, but now that the decision was here I choked. "Two reasons why that's a bad idea," I protested. "A. I'll lose momentum with my audience. And B. I'll burn a bridge with the station."

"A. No, you won't. And B. No, you won't," Michael replied. "You're highly visible through your column and no one's going to forget about you in a week. And you're not going to piss off the station—this is how negotiation *works*, Brook. You have to show that you have a bargaining chip in your corner or we're at their mercy. Quit underestimating yourself—you're the commodity here. They know that. Trust me."

And weirdly, although it was something I never thought I would be able to say about Michael again, I was beginning to.

Meanwhile, he said, he wanted me to write a couple of the articles from the ideas I'd shown him for him to pitch to major media outlets with a slant toward dating and relationships. I suspected he was just trying to keep me occupied so I wouldn't freak out about the radio station, but I was grateful for the distraction anyway—grateful that we seemed to be back on a casual, easy footing—and spent the morning brainstorming as I got ready for my Saturday group therapy.

With twelve other people's issues to concentrate on, I had no time to sit and masticate on my own, and at the end of the three-hour session I was feeling juiced—invigorated by the progress some of the participants were making in moving past their heartache.

But that feeling lasted only until I got in my car and last night came crashing back. After the disastrous end to the evening, I knew my next approach with Sash needed to be much gentler.

And so that afternoon found us in the outdoor play area of Fort Myers Pet Rescue on Six Mile Cypress, watching a crazed horde of dogs of every breed and age tearing around the confined area, giddy with their freedom.

"We depend on our volunteers to help care for and play with the animals," my friend Angela told us, pointing at two women in their mid-thirties running the perimeter of the grassy area with a mini pack of dogs chasing after them. I'd met Angela at UF when she was studying to be a vet; she was now working as the shelter director, and had offered to give us a guided visit. "We're overfilled and understaffed, and the more we can interact with and exercise the dogs, the less chance they'll get kennel crazy."

"Kennel crazy?" Sasha asked, frowning.

Angela nodded. "Barking, drooling, licking themselves raw—sometimes they just circle over and over. That can make an otherwise healthy dog unadoptable, and then...Well." Her face darkened, and I knew she was talking about euthanasia—and judging by the dismayed look on Sasha's face, so did she.

Time for a subject change. "Can we go see the puppies?" I said with hearty cheer.

Inside was a bit dreary—three-by-five gray concrete-block kennels were lined up at least twenty deep in row after row in the cavernous interior, and a cacophony of shrill barking echoed off the concrete walls and corrugated-metal ceiling. Sasha blanched and covered her ears, and I started to worry that this idea, too, would backfire.

Angela led us farther into the building and through a set of double doors that led to a linoleum-floored area separated into larger cages by chain link. The noise decreased substantially as the glass doors swung shut behind us. Inside each fenced-off area, little squirming balls of fur wrestled and rolled and jumped all over one another. Sasha finally let out a smile.

"This is where we keep the puppies, so they're not too scared or overwhelmed by all the noise and activity out there with the older dogs," Angela explained. "As you can see, we get a lot of babies, but luckily they're the easiest to adopt out. As they get older, it gets harder."

Sasha snorted. "Even dogs suffer from age discrimination."

"Can we play with them?" I asked.

"Sure," Angela said, and reached to unlatch the cage nearest to us. "Go on in."

I'd thought ahead, and warned Sasha to dress in casual clothes she didn't mind getting a little dirty. Good thing—as the door swung open, a sea of furry bodies swept our way like Tribbles, schooling around our feet and yipping for attention.

I thought she'd be put off by the smell and the mess of dozens of not-yet-potty trained puppies confined in this room, but to my surprise Sasha's face lit up and she bent over immediately, coming up with a puppy in each hand.

"I want them *all!*" she said, holding up first one, then the other to her face so she could nuzzle into them.

I grinned and reached down for two puppy handfuls of my own. "Look at this little guy," I said, holding a white one over to her so she could see the dark splotch circling his left eye. "He's got a black eye."

"Look at her," she said, proffering one of her own, a dog whose face was nearly lost amid the puff of reddish-brown hair covering her body. "She's more fur than dog!"

We babbled on this way for a while, cooing and exclaiming over each dog's attractiveness and endearing quirkiness and general goodness, and when we finally plopped ourselves down on the bare floor to let the sea of tiny warm bodies swarm all over us, Angela grinned and joined us. We repeated the same sort of nonsense in each of the four cages, so that no puppy felt forgotten, and when we finally stood and stretched our cramped muscles to leave, more than an hour had gone by.

I walked a step or two behind the two women as Sasha chattered happily with Angela about pitching a story to the paper to help draw attention—and hopefully funding and volunteers—to the shelter.

Dogs barked and jumped and clamored for attention on either side of us as we walked down the aisle lined with kennels, but as I passed one concrete pen, a brown-and-black medium-haired dog caught my eye because he simply stood wagging his long tail, watching us pass with intelligent brown eyes.

"Well, hi," I said, stopping. "You're very well mannered." I reached over the low gate to pet him, forgetting until too late that we weren't supposed to do that.

But I wasn't going to pull back now, as the dog moved more fully under my palm as if granting me easier access. I couldn't tell what breed he was—he had the elongated nose and triangular ears of some kind of shepherd-y mix, but the tips flopped over like a spaniel's, and one was set crooked on his head. I smiled, rubbing his ears and neck and cheeks as he never broke eye contact with me, and his feet never left the floor.

"Hey, Angela," I called to where she and Sasha were almost at the end of the row, and they turned. "Who's this guy? He's so good."

She walked back toward me, Sasha following. "Oh," Angela said, "that's Slick. The intake staff named him that because he'd been totally shaved when they found him. Probably fleas. No one's even taken him out to consider him since he got here a few months ago."

I frowned. "Why not? Look how calm and well behaved he is. No sign of kennel craziness, even after all this time. He'd be a perfect pet."

Angela arched an eyebrow and slanted a plotting smile at me. "Want to adopt him?"

I straightened and took a step back. "Oh, no, not me. Way too much commitment, and one that's guaranteed to break your heart," I added, remembering our family's shepherd, Mugsy. Except for Sasha, Mugsy had been my closest friend, confidant, and playmate all my life. At age eleven, when he stopped eating and began wasting away, Mom took him to the vet and found out he had cancer—and Mugsy never came back home. I'd cried for weeks, until my mother finally barked at me to stop wallowing and "cowgirl up."

"Too bad," Angela said. "This dog's older—probably around four, and most people want young dogs. And he has heartworm. He'd have to be treated, and that adds expense to his adoption fee—we don't treat infected dogs unless they're adopted, because we just don't have the resources."

"And that's why I want to draw more attention to the shelter," Sasha said, turning her back on me and continuing her conversation with Angela. "I'd like to bring a photographer in when I come, to add impact to the story, and..."

Their voices dwindled as they walked back down to the end of the aisle toward Angela's office, but I lingered with Slick for a few moments.

"That's a terrible name for you, buddy," I told him. "It doesn't suit you at all."

He tilted his head as if considering that.

"You know, you might want to work on your showmanship a little. These guys are upstaging you. You gotta make people notice you when they come in looking for a dog, so you can get the treatment you need."

He dropped his haunches and sat calmly, as if directly refuting my argument.

I reached in with my other hand so I could give him one last thorough head rubbing. "I know a dog who could teach you a thing or two about getting attention," I told him. "Although from what I gather just from the little I know of you, Jake's techniques might be beneath your dignity." I stood to leave, and the dog rose to all four of his feet too, like a gentleman whose date had excused herself to the ladies' room. He looked directly into my eyes with a gentle, inquisitive gaze, as if wondering why I was leaving when we were having such a lovely time.

"Take care, pal," I said through a suddenly thick throat. "Good luck to you."

•••

Sasha chattered about the article she planned to write as we walked out to the car, the whole drive home, and as we sat in front of her apartment building when I dropped her off. When she finally wound down and looked over at me, her animated expression morphed into suspicion.

"What?" she said with a skeptical look.

"What?"

"You're grinning like a damn fool."

I spread my hands palm up, unable to remove the offending expression from my face. "You're glowing."

"Brook." Sasha blew out a long breath, looking at my car's headliner. "You ever feel like you know exactly what you're supposed to be doing? And you absolutely love it?"

"Every damn day since I started my Breakup Doctor practice."

She nodded emphatically. "I know. And I feel like that every time I write a story." She laid a hand over her abdomen, casting me an apologetic look. "But not about this. I think that's telling me something. Don't you?"

Panic shot up in me, bright and hot as a flare. "What? No! Sash, we talked about this—it's just fear, perfectly normal."

"No, Brook, I think it's more than that. I—"

"Sash, listen to me—this is totally new, totally unknown, and I get why it's freaking you out. Of course you aren't excited about it yet—of course you don't know whether you love it. You haven't experienced it! You didn't know before you turned in your first story that you were going to feel all those things, right?"

"I'd been writing in a journal since I knew how to write, Brook. I always loved it. I always knew it was my passion."

"Sash, honey, this is..." I floundered for words to convince her, to quell this hiccup of nerves. "The way you were with those puppies...you came alive! You loved them! And you didn't necessarily know you would."

"Everyone loves puppies."

"That's not true," I protested.

"Pol Pot loved puppies. *Hitler* had a dog."

"Honey, you have to trust me here. You asked me to help you, and I am. Sometimes other people can see things a little more clearly when we're too deep in our own concerns to be objective. You've got to just sit with this, okay?" I sounded wheedling, and I schooled my tone into something more confident. "Just wait it out. I know you. You know I do. I wouldn't say all this if I thought that deep down, you really think marriage and kids are the wrong path for you."

She chewed the inside of her lip. "Well...maybe..."

I laid a hand over hers. "Hey...who's the barber here?"

It was a lame joke—a reference to an old *Saturday Night Live* sketch that always cracked Stu and Sasha and me up, where Steve Martin played Theodoric of York, medieval barber/physician, whose answer to everything from plague to severed limbs was to give his customers a good bleeding.

"I know you're a professional," she conceded. "But—"

"No buts. You've got to trust me, honey." I squeezed her cold fingers in mine. "Hang in there, Sash. Everything's going to work out just the way it's supposed to."

Chapter Twenty

After my little freak show in front of Pamela Friday evening, I wasn't at all certain that Ben and Jake would be at Dog Beach for our Sunday-morning get-together, but when I rounded the corner from the mangroves to where the dog-infested spit of sand stretched out to the gulf, I breathed out a sigh as I caught sight of Jake, standing at the water's edge as a tiny Jack Russell terrier ran lightning-fast laps around him. Jake was barking intermittently as he kept whirling to try to follow the little blur of a dog, and his confounded expression made me laugh aloud.

"That's been going on for about ten minutes now," said an instantly familiar voice to my left, and I turned to see Ben standing in the surf, the gentle incoming waves swirling around his bare ankles.

I couldn't control the pang that shot into my chest at the sight of him, jeans damp at the cuffs and crusted with sand where he'd rolled them up his calves, a moss green t-shirt with his company logo stretched across a torso I knew from our one memorable marathon evening naked together was hard and muscular. Sand peppered his tanned forearms, and I figured he'd been wrestling with Jake before I arrived. His hair was tousled from the breeze that blew in off the water with the musky, clean scent of the sea that I loved.

"Hey," I said, and felt the weight of the last week roll off of me.

"Someone's been eager for you to get here," Ben said with a smile, and my heart jumped—until he dipped his head toward Jake.

I looked up just in time to brace for a hundred pounds of furry wet dog barreling into my legs, and even so I had to stagger back to keep my balance. "Mmmph! Hey, buddy," I said, leaning over to pet his damp head. Rubbery ropes of slobber hung from the corners of Jake's panting mouth, his tongue lolling out in a delirious grin. "You look like you've been having fun!"

He shook his big body, sandblasting me as remnants of his roll in the surf centrifuged off his fur, and then tore away back to his playmate.

Leaving me standing awkwardly with Ben, silence thick between us as we watched the army of dogs frolicking on the beach, their owners milling among them, or sunbathing, or—I grimaced—swimming in the fecal-festooned water of dozens of off-leash dogs. Barking filled the sea-scented air, along with distant conversations and the occasional shouted command of the owner of a wayward pup.

"I wasn't sure you'd be here," Ben said finally.

"Of course I came," I said lightly, wondering whether he'd read my mind. "I wouldn't miss my weekly date with Jake."

Ben was staring out over the water, not looking at me. "I meant after the other night."

My face burned, and not from the sun blazing overhead. "Oh. Yeah. Sorry. Like I said...it was a rough week."

All the images I'd been trying to avoid pushed their way into my brain—Pamela's hopeful, guileless smile as she told me about Africa...the romantic dinner she and Ben must have shared somewhere after I left...the bed they'd probably shared after that.

For all I knew he'd left her sheets just an hour earlier, disentangling himself from her to come meet me.

For the first time it occurred to me to wonder what she made of our Sunday-morning ritual.

Had they talked about things after I left? Did they discuss her invitation for him to join her halfway across the world, doing good for those who needed it?

Was he going?

"Not at all," Ben answered, and it took me a moment to remember what I'd said. "I was...worried about you."

He was looking over to where Jake was now lying on his back, wrestling with the much smaller white dog, who was literally walking all over him, and I couldn't read Ben's eyes.

I took a deep breath, filling my mouth and my lungs with the thick, salty, humid air, and let it out again.

"I'm really sorry about that," I said finally. "I know I acted like...like a crazy person," I said lamely, with a dry laugh. I pushed ahead before he felt he had to politely deny it. "I just...I didn't mean to embarrass you or make things awkward for you...or for Pamela. I really value your friendship, Ben."

His face was drawn into stiff lines, and I couldn't help feeling that I'd disappointed him.

Finally he turned to face me. "I'm having a hard time being friends with you, Brook."

Hot shame flooded through me at his words, along with a breathless flare of panic. "I know. I'm sorry," I repeated, as if the words were on an endless loop, but it still didn't feel like enough.

I was the one who'd finally broken the six long months of radio silence between us. After our terrible breakup I knew I needed time on my own. I'd been so lost, consumed by fear and anger and pain after all I'd been through with Michael and then Kendall, and I needed to find out who I was outside of a relationship...what I really wanted out of my life—and love. Half a year had gone by while I figured that out, and I'd heard nothing from Ben at all.

I hadn't been entirely surprised. I'd hurt him—badly and, I'd come to realize as the months went on, possibly irrevocably. But I'd begun to accept that not hearing from him was for the best—despite my desire to be on my own, I'd still had strong feelings for Ben. If he had called I was certain I wouldn't have risked losing him twice—I'd have gone back before I was ready.

So I waited. And finally, when I knew I'd let go of all my old demons, that I was emotionally and psychologically ready to have a healthy, committed relationship, I'd called him.

Only to find out that I'd waited too long.

When we struggled through that first awkward conversation, I'd nervously asked how he'd been, what he'd been doing. And he'd told me shyly, almost embarrassedly, that he'd begun seeing someone recently.

I should have told him then, when things were newer between him and Perfect Pamela, that I still had feelings for him. I should have begged him to give us another chance, not to go another step down that path with anyone else but me.

But I'd been so surprised—so illogically hurt by the news that a genuine, emotionally available guy like Ben would have moved on to someone who was ready to offer what he was looking for—that the words stuck in my throat. Instead I'd told him—probably too enthusiastically—how happy I was for him. How much I'd love to meet her. I'd asked all about her, digging my nails into my palms so hard as he finally caved in to my relentlessly cheery inquisition that I'd had little crescent-shaped scabs there for a week after we hung up.

I'd never told him that I still loved him.

If I told him now...if I kept pushing for something more than what Ben was offering, when he was in a relationship with another woman—one who was everything anyone would wish for someone they cared about—then I hadn't learned anything at all about honesty and commitment...and love.

I'd spent most of the last year trying to learn who I was and what I wanted, yes. But I'd also been working on what kind of person I wanted to be. And that wasn't someone who jeopardized another person's happiness in the blind pursuit of her own. Whether that meant Ben or Pamela. Or both.

"You've got every reason to be angry with me," I said finally.

A shadow flitted across his face. "Brook—"

"I didn't mean to make things awkward or difficult for you," I cut him off, afraid to hear what might be next. "And I never..." I stopped, swallowed, started again. "I never wanted to make Pamela feel uncomfortable either."

He frowned, staring down at the sand. "No. Neither do I."

I nodded, blinking at the bright rays of the sun making my eyes water. "I'm—" *sorry*, I stopped myself from saying for the fourth time. "I wish things hadn't gotten so complicated," I said instead, quietly.

"I do too."

I glanced over at his low tone. "I care about you...so much, Ben."

It was all I could risk, and I barely breathed the words, but a pressure I hadn't known was in my chest seemed to ease. It felt good to be honest with him about my feelings—even if I couldn't be *totally* honest.

"I don't ever want to complicate your life," I went on quickly, before he felt obliged to answer. "Like...this." My hands drifted upward in a vague gesture I meant to indicate our present awkward reality. "I really want to be your friend." *And I will be*, I swore. "But if that's not a great idea for you right now..." My throat suddenly seemed to close up, but I pushed past the constriction. "Well...just tell me, okay? Maybe..." I swallowed again. "Maybe it's too soon."

He said nothing, just nodded.

Inexplicably my eyes filled with tears, and I moved my gaze back over the water to mask them, wishing for my sunglasses.

...

I don't know what I was hoping for at family dinner that night—probably, knowing me, that Sasha and Stu would giddily announce their pregnancy, along with their engagement, and everything would be magically fixed. But our evening was just as they always were—except that as we kids pitched in getting ready, my dad actually stayed in the kitchen working as Mom's sous chef, rather than puttering in the garage on some woodworking project.

Lately I'd noticed more secret looks passing between them, the way I used to when they were kids. When I was little I was convinced they could read each other's minds, because a brief glance between them was enough to yield a mysterious smile I didn't understand, or to bring them together for a kiss out of nowhere. In those moments a childish panic would grip me momentarily, as if for that second they'd forgotten Stu and I existed, but it had been a long time since I'd felt as if we were merely orbiting their world of two.

Instead of fear, though, now these moments of connection suffused me with warmth.

That quickly dissipated, though, when Mom went around the table for our usual Sunday-night grilling of each of us, and Sasha and Stu reported only unusually dull work events.

It scared me—the longer they didn't tell anyone about anything, the more I worried it was a very bad sign.

Chapter Twenty-one

I woke up antsy on Monday morning. This was the day I had to sit out my radio show, and despite Michael's assurances, I wasn't at all sure that I wasn't going to irrevocably lose ground by skipping it.

I was nervous about seeing Ben too. After our talk on Dog Beach, I wasn't sure whether, after thinking it over, he'd agree it was too soon for us to be friends. Adelaide was coming home tonight—there was no real reason for him to bring Jake to me this last time.

But he'd texted when I got home from my parents' last night—just a brief, *How late do you need me to drop Jake after your show?* And the brief words filled me with relief out of proportion to the message.

And that told me more about my feelings for him than any jolt of attraction ever had.

Not doing the show, I'd texted back with unsteady hands. *Anytime's fine.*

All morning I was jumpy, thrown by not having to lurch out of bed at four thirty and hustle to the station, and slightly sick to my stomach at hearing Jim Veneer glibly pattering about dating. "You had a great date, but he never called! What's it mean? Guys, give us a call and weigh in...." Clearly the station was perfectly content to fill the relationship niche without me, and it was all I could do not to call Michael and blast him about his stupid plan backfiring.

By the time the doorbell rang, I felt like no-see-'ums were biting my ankles.

I didn't greet Ben at the door with coffee in a travel mug this time. I knew that cozy, intimate gestures like that were part of what was complicating matters and making it hard for him to be friends with me.

But as Jake streaked inside as soon as I opened the door, I heard myself inviting him in for a cup. It was a foolish impulse—but I was surprised when he agreed.

Embarrassingly, as we came into the kitchen the show was blaring from my computer's speakers, where I'd been glued to it all morning. I hustled to click it off.

"Leave it on," Ben said, settling easily onto a stool at my kitchen island. "I'm curious to hear how inane Veneer gets without you."

I looked over from reaching another mug down from the cabinet over the coffeemaker. "You still listen?"

He shrugged. "You know my mom's your biggest fan—I have to stay current on your calls so she can hash them all out with me."

I determinedly focused on pouring his coffee, bringing the sugar over to him rather than making it the way I knew he liked it. I had to stop looking for encouragement and signs in every comment he made. Ben was a good man. He said nice things. That was all.

Jake came out of where he'd gone into my bedroom on a scouting mission to make sure all was to his approval since he'd last been here, and sat in front of my sliding glass door to the lanai, looking back meaningfully at me. I walked over and slid it open for him, and he barreled out onto the porch, bulling open the screen door and charging into my yard.

Ben watched with a tiny smile I couldn't read. "He certainly makes himself at home here."

I gazed fondly after the dog. "It only really feels like a home when he's in it," I said without thinking, then felt my face heat.

Ben let the comment go.

"Do you mind if I ask why you're sitting today's show out?" he asked as he stirred a single spoonful of sugar into his cup.

I looked up, startled. Of course he didn't know. When things had seemed to be going so well with Ben I didn't want to jeopardize that by telling him about my ex-fiancé's return—Michael and I were nothing but friends, colleagues of a sort, and there had seemed no point in giving Ben any reason to believe that I wasn't totally available.

Now…was there any reason not to tell him? Probably not. And yet I found that stubborn piece of me that wouldn't completely give up hope made me edit the truth.

"I'm hoping for my own show—trying to convince the station to put their money where my mouth is," I said. "They're balking a little, so I figured I'd sit one out to call their bluff."

The muscles of his forearm and biceps flexed and relaxed as he stirred his coffee. "That's a good strategy."

Ironic that he was actually complimenting my ex-fiancé, who'd indirectly caused him so much grief.

"I don't know. From what I've heard this morning," I said, tipping my head toward the speakers, "they're getting by just fine without me."

Jim Veneer was pattering away, soliciting callers and promising "juicy deets" about dating fails after the next commercial break.

Right then a woman's voice came over the air: "Where's the Breakup Doctor?"

Ben and I both turned toward the speakers.

"Don't you worry, caller," came Jim's hearty reply. "We've still got all your dating questions covered. So…I'm betting you've been stiffed by a guy you had a great date with, right? Tell us all about it."

"I wanted to talk to the Breakup Doctor. Why isn't she on?"

"We're still talking love and relationships, caller…Let's hear your story!"

A long moment of dead air followed, and I pictured Jim—who hated radio silence—squirming.

"I'll wait till the Breakup Doctor's back," the woman said finally, and we heard her sever the connection.

Ben turned back to look at me, and this time I could easily read the expression in his eyes—amusement. "They may not be getting by just fine without you after all," he said, a smile tilting one corner of his mouth.

I just shook my head, almost fearful of cursing it if I agreed, but I couldn't keep an answering smile from my face as we sat sipping our coffee, listening together to the show.

...

Contrary to my fears that things between me and Michael would be awkward after our little erectile misfunction in my office last week, if anything the episode seemed to have broken a barrier between us.

We met downtown at the First Street Grill after work on Monday and sat on the front patio so I could bring Jake. Adelaide's plane would be landing right about now, and Ben was picking her up at the airport on his way home from work. Tomorrow Jake would go back to staying with his grandma during the days.

I squinted at Michael against the glare of the sun just sinking behind the arched white Florida Repertory Theatre building across the street. "So what was the station's offer?"

We sat at a glass-topped wrought-iron table, cold bottles of Swamp Ape IPA in front of us both.

One corner of his lips turned up. "Step off, Veruca."

It was an old joke between us—Michael had always called me Veruca Salt, because, as he said, "You want everything *now*!"

"Some things don't change. What did they say?"

"No word yet. We have to be patient."

"What do you mean, no word? Jim *tanked* this morning! Listeners were literally begging for me. What more do they want?"

"These things take some time, Brook. Right now they may still be thinking that Jim will get his wheels under him and gain steam." He took a long sip of his beer and leaned back. "But don't worry—what you do isn't easily replicable, and they're going to figure that out."

I folded my arms across my chest, scowling. "You said play hardball. You said sit out *one* show. How long are we supposed to wait for the station to decide they need me after all?"

He took another sip of beer so maddeningly calmly and leisurely I wanted to lean forward and shove the bottle into his teeth.

"As long as it takes."

"Dammit, Michael!"

At my raised voice Jake stirred from his comfortable curl under my feet, and I leaned over to soothe him, cutting an apologetic glance to the three other patrons nearby.

"Brook..." Michael put the bottle down and leaned forward to meet my eyes. "Please trust me. And if you can't do that"—he picked at the damp label of his beer—"at least have faith in *yourself.* You can do this. You're worth more."

I leaned back and blew out a long breath. "Fine. I'll be 'patient,'" I said, with air quotes. "What's next on your terrifying bucket list?"

"I want you to ask the newspaper for a raise."

"What?"

That little stand-off resulted in another fifteen minutes of spirited back-and-forth. But he was like speeded-up time-lapse photography of water wearing away stone, smoothing down every hard edge of my resistance with unexpectedly solid, reasoned arguments that left me no rational option but to agree.

"You are *killing* me, Michael," I grumbled, but I didn't mean it.

Lisa Albrecht's head was going to explode, but I was going in there to stipulate more money for continuing my column.

I couldn't help a smile; I had to admit that I loved Michael's view of me and what I did—his confidence in my abilities and their value. And it was so good to be able to talk to him like this, after so much bitterness between us. I reached across the table for his hand where it still worked at shredding the beer label.

"Thanks, Michael," I said fondly. "I'm really glad you came back."

He looked up, meeting my eyes, and for a moment the guileless directness in them felt as though we were sitting there naked in front of each other. My heartbeat quickened as neither one of us averted our gaze, and he slowly moved his hand so it engulfed mine, twining our fingers together. Relishing the warmth, the connection, I let him.

"Brook?"

You know how you can be really familiar with someone—your regular checkout person at the grocery store, say—and then when you run into them out of context, in a restaurant or at the beach or a concert, you have the disorienting feeling of knowing you know this person and yet not quite being able to place them right away?

That was what I felt when I heard an instantly recognizable voice calling my name in a place where I had no reason to expect to hear it.

Ben's mother, Adelaide, and I had gotten close when I'd dated Ben. Laid up with a bum knee while her son was working out of town and I was watching Jake, the vibrant, active woman had been lonely enough that I'd taken to bringing the dog by and visiting with her a few times a week. Her warmth and acceptance filled the hole where I'd always wanted my mom to offer those things, and when I'd broken Ben's heart, losing her friendship was one of the hardest casualties of war to bear. I hadn't seen her since, though I always hoped that one day we'd run into each other.

But not here. Not now...while I was sitting at a table with a man who was not her son, in what looked like a cozy little moment of intimacy.

And not when Ben stood beside her on the sidewalk not fifteen feet away, still as a statue as he looked at Michael and me with shadowed eyes I couldn't read.

But I didn't have long to try to interpret his reaction—the moment Jake heard Adelaide's voice, the dog leaped to his feet so fast that his big, broad back shot up against the edge of the table. He lunged toward Adelaide as the table jostled, upsetting our drinks and sending both bottles crashing to the pavement. Chilly liquid splashed my ankles along with a sting like fire ant bites—glass shards, I registered dimly as I vainly tried to control the ecstatic dog yanking against his leash so hard my shoulder practically dislocated.

"Are you all right?" Michael yelped, shooting to his feet as Jake finally pulled me out of my seat and sent me catapulting toward Adelaide, on the other side of the flimsy roped-off patio area.

Strong arms somehow caught me just before I went facedown into the sidewalk, and I looked up to meet Ben's bewildered eyes as his hands gripped my shoulders to steady me. I'd seen this look in them once before—the morning after we broke up, when he'd surprised me and Chip Santana in partial flagrante on my back porch.

"You're supposed to be at the airport," I said nonsensically.

"Mom caught an earlier flight." The words were clipped.

Jake had dropped his butt to the concrete with a single upraised hand from Adelaide—no one else could control the beast the way she did—and she gently stroked his head as behind me I heard a phalanx of servers flock to the scene to clean up the mess.

In that frozen second I locked gazes with Ben, wanting to explain, yet wondering why I felt I needed to.

"You're hurt," he said.

I nodded, heat filling my eyes. "Yes. But so are you."

He frowned and looked down at the hem of his spotless khaki pants. "No—it didn't get this far." He let go of my upper arms and pointed to my ankles.

Little pinpoints of blood dotted my skin from the shattered bottles, a few thin rivulets streaking down in places.

"Oh," I said. "It's...nothing."

"You need to make sure to get the glass out, Brook," I heard Adelaide say, and I turned to her.

"Adelaide. It's so good to see you. Welcome home." My smile wobbled. I hadn't realized how much I'd missed her till I saw her. She looked just the same—maybe tanner from her cruise, a little bit thinner, but so dear and familiar I wanted to lean over and hug her.

Michael interrupted before I could. "Hey, there—friends of yours, Brook?" He came up behind me, standing too close, but I couldn't step away without practically throwing myself into Ben's arms where he still stood in front of me just across the rope barrier.

There had been a half a dozen times that I'd considered telling Ben about Michael being back in town, but I hadn't. I'd been afraid that mention of my former fiancé would bring up every doubt, every bit of mistrust I'd earned after the Chip Santana debacle.

Now that I was about to be forced to introduce the man I'd once loved to the man I still did, I would have given anything if I'd said something before.

"Adelaide...Ben," I said, nearly choking on my own tongue. "This is Michael." I muttered the name, but I saw from the way Ben furrowed his eyebrows and then blinked and recoiled slightly that he'd made the connection.

"Sorry to interrupt," Ben said, not quite looking directly at me. "Mom wanted to grab a bite on the way home. I can take Jakie now, if you like, so you don't have to cut your evening short."

"No, I don't mind bringing—"

"It's all right. If I take him I can save you the trip."

"This is your dog?" Michael asked behind me, and in the tight sound of his voice I heard his understanding of who Ben was. Who he was to me.

He stepped up next to me, but his eyes were glued on Ben, who met his stare with a direct one of his own.

For a moment it was a strange little stand-off, Adelaide and me on either side as the two men seemed to be sussing each other out, each one clearly knowing exactly who the other was. I wanted to fix it—to assure Ben that nothing was going on with me and my ex, regardless of how it looked; to assuage the hurt I'd heard in Michael's voice. But anything I said to either one of them was only going to make things worse.

Adelaide gave me a long glance with none of the accusation or even disappointment I deserved. Just a gentle acceptance. "I'm awfully tired, dear," she said to Ben, laying a hand on his arm, though her eyes stayed steady on mine. "I think I'd just like to go home."

Ben seemed to remember she was there only when she touched him. He started, breaking eye contact with Michael and moving his gaze to me.

"I don't mind bringing Jake over later. Really," I said to him softly, but I heard the desperate edge to my tone. I needed a reason to come talk to him alone. To explain.

But he simply reached for the leash, his warm fingers brushing my wrist and then, to my surprise, giving a slight squeeze before he gently took the lead from my hand. "I'm only trying to make things easier on you, Brook," he said quietly.

"We should go, dear," Adelaide said to Ben, offering me a smile that didn't match the sad look in her eyes.

I watched them turn and move along the sidewalk back the way they'd come, Jake not even glancing back in my direction, Adelaide's thin, strong hand touching her son's shoulder briefly before they turned a corner and were out of sight.

Chapter Twenty-two

"That was him. The guy you wouldn't talk about."

We were sitting at our table, and Michael asked the question to my bent back as I leaned over to clean my cuts with a wet cocktail napkin and check for glass. He'd offered to do it, but the intimacy of that had made me recoil—and I needed something to focus on to avoid his searching gaze.

His question wasn't accusatory—it sounded more like a statement, and I simply nodded, unwilling to raise my gaze and meet his eyes.

"You still care about him."

"It doesn't matter," I said dully.

"You had his dog...obviously you're still friends." There was a long pause, and then: "Why are you here with me instead of him?"

I glanced up at him, confused. "You're...you're helping me. We're friends."

His lips tightened and he crossed his arms. "It's more than that, Brook, and you know it."

I shook my head. "No. We said—"

"I don't care what we said! Are you really telling me you were totally unaware of what's going on? All our banter, falling into all our old habits so easily? You ask me about my sex life since I blew things up with us...And then the way you hugged me in your office...And tonight? Honestly, Brook? Who are trying to fool—me, or yourself?"

I stared at him, my mouth open, but nothing coming out of it.

"Um...would you like us to bring you more drinks, or should we release your table?"

Our server was standing beside us, our mess having been neatly tidied, and I realized the other patrons on the patio were now watching me and Michael like we were a dinner theater show.

Which we were being, with all the drama that had played out in the last five minutes. I swallowed, mortified. Public scenes weren't my thing, and reminded me unpleasantly of my rock-bottom with Kendall.

"No...thank you," I told the server. "We're going." I stood and reached toward my purse, still hanging on the back of my chair, but Michael had beaten me to the punch, throwing a twenty on the table and taking my elbow to lead me out.

I wasn't processing what had happened—it had all gone too fast. Adelaide was back and Jake was gone and now I had no reason to see Ben except at our regular Sunday meeting at Dog Beach—and I had no way of knowing whether he'd show up for that again. What was the look in his eyes when he'd caught me from falling? Beneath his confusion I almost thought I'd seen hurt—but why? Just because the scene reminded him of the last time he'd happened upon me with someone else, before everything between us came to a crashing end?

I mindlessly let Michael walk us all the way to Hendry Street before I finally stopped to look at him.

Meanwhile here was another man I'd once cared about—wanting a new beginning. A desire I'd been pretending not to see so I didn't have to make any choices...and risk making the wrong one.

"I'm sorry," I said, looking up at him.

He looked confused, then cautious. "Why are you sorry?"

"You're right. I knew there was more going on. With us. I just..." I blew out a long breath of air, looking up to the Cigar Bar, where Sasha and I used to swagger in once in a while and choose stogies from the chilled vault and sit at the bar smoking them like mafiosos. Back when you could still smoke inside. Back when we were younger. When the biggest choice we had to worry about was whether it was worth making ourselves nauseous from the cigar smoke.

I looked back to Michael, who was watching me with no trace of his usual levity. Waiting.

"I was trying not to...to rush into anything," I finally finished, searching for a truth that wouldn't hurt either one of us.

One corner of Michael's mouth lifted in the grin I knew so well. "Brook, I was asking for a date, not a lifetime commitment. Not yet," he added quickly. "But I mean, not necessarily either, unless that's what we—"

Despite everything, I laughed. "It's okay. I know what you mean." I threw my hands out to the sides in a giant shrug. "Jesus, I'm so tired of this minefield between us."

"Yeah. Me too."

What had I been thinking? Michael had come all the way back across the country to make things right between us, to show me he'd changed...to ask for a second chance. And I'd been keeping him at arm's length, in reserve, while I chased after someone who'd long since moved on. Making an idiot of myself.

Someone passed by too close, bumping my arm. "Sorry," the girl called with a backward wave, shiny hair swaying behind her like a liquid curtain.

I turned to Michael. "Ask me out."

"What?"

"Ask me on a date. Right now."

His eyebrows lifted. "A little bossy, aren't you, Veruca?"

"Come on," I said, filled with a strange urgency. "Do it."

He looked to the sky as if for divine intervention. "You know, I'm only feeding the demon if I cave to your demands. This kind of thing has to be organic."

I just faced him, hands behind my back.

He crossed his arms and leveled an implacable look at me, but I could see he wasn't trying that hard to outwait me. "Fine," he said. "Brook. Will you please go out with me?"

I rolled my eyes. "That sucks. You have to be specific."

"I don't remember you being this high-maintenance."

"Come on."

He let out a long-suffering sigh. "Brook...will you please accompany me to dinner this Friday night, March fourth, at seven in the evening, for dinner and cocktails?" He raised one eyebrow. "Do I need to specify the menu?"

I swayed into him, bumping his shoulder with mine. "No. That was really good. Yes, Michael," I said fiercely. "I'd like to have dinner with you."

"Good God. That was harder than the Israeli-Palestinian peace talks." But he was smiling at me, his eyes warm.

We walked side by side back to our cars, and I managed to keep the smile on my face until I waved goodbye and pulled away.

Chapter Twenty-three

With one major exception last year during the most mortifying of my breakup breakdown, there hasn't been a single decision, piece of news, or life development that I haven't shared with Sasha.

Except this one.

It wasn't that I didn't *want* to. Partly I just felt stupid—I'd done exactly what she told me not to in pursuing a friendship with Michael, and it had wound up backfiring, exactly as she said it would. And if I told her that afterward I'd finally agreed to an actual date with Michael...well...I knew what she'd say. And I didn't want to hear all the reasons my decision was foolish.

I already suspected it was.

But I had the rest of the week to worry about that. For now, I could focus instead on work—always my comfort when my personal life was overwhelming. Michael had tasked me with asking Lisa Albrecht for a raise, and that was a battle I needed my loins well and truly girded for.

"I have four things on fire and exactly three and a half minutes for you, Brook, so enter talking," Lisa said without looking up from her monitor as I walked into her office at lunch on Wednesday afternoon for our appointment.

"And hello to you too, Lisa."

She let out a long-suffering sigh, but finally glanced at me. "Really? Every single time?"

"It's a social nicety. And it makes people feel as if they matter to you."

She made a dismissive gesture in the air. "Why would I lie to them?"

I crossed my arms and leaned against her cubicle opening, perfectly willing to wait the abrasive woman out.

Another gusty sigh, and then: "Fine. Hello, Brook. How are you today?" She said each word woodenly, as if it were a memorized script, but I considered it progress that Lisa actually made an effort.

"I'm good, thanks for asking. Sounds like you're having a tough day."

She leaned back in her upholstered seat, motioning for me to sit on the chrome-and-fabric chair opposite her desk that took up most of the rest of her cubicle. "A sick photographer. A reporter who's lost somewhere in Cape Coral and missing the ridiculously non-newsworthy dog parade that we nonetheless are supposed to be covering. A story that's such a mess, I'm wondering whether my reporter actually understands English. The usual. Tell me you have something good for me."

This was not going to fall under that category. But if I waited for Lisa Albrecht to have a good day before asking for my raise, I'd never make an additional dime.

I led with: "I wanted to thank you for running my article."

"What article?"

"The one you came to my office about? Two weeks ago?" Her expression was still blank as a whiteboard, and my eyebrows rose to my hairline. Lisa was truly hectic if she'd overlooked a chance to lord her largesse of spirit over me in reconsidering something. "About forgiveness?" I tacked on.

"Oh, shit. Did you actually keep that in?"

I opened my mouth but nothing came out of it, and then Lisa's poker face hairline-fractured into the trace of a smile, the equivalent, for her, of a loud guffaw. "I'm just crapping you. Yeah, whatever." She waved a hand. "I thought about what you said. I can forgive that jackass." She fixed me with a hard glare, raising one warning finger. "I do *not* forget. But I can forgive. And as far as columns go, it wasn't total shit."

"Aw, Lisa, you say the sweetest things." She just rolled her eyes, unamused by me. "Actually, my column is the reason I'm here."

"Let me guess. You want a raise."

My eyebrows shot up. "Yes, that's exactly what I wanted to talk about. How did you—"

"Please. As soon as your little Bobbsey twin asked for one, I knew you weren't going to be far behind. Why don't you two just make out already? You're not fooling anyone."

I knew Lisa wasn't serious about me and Sasha; sarcasm was just part of her natural reaction to stress.

"I didn't know Sasha asked for a raise, actually," I confessed. "But she deserves one, don't you think?" I knew she was one of Lisa's best reporters—a terrific writer who dug deep for the story and never missed a deadline.

Lisa kicked away from her desk, sending her chair wheeling back against the wall with a thunk. "Deserving or not, I can't compete with the *Tribune*."

I frowned. "What do you mean?"

"Trust me, she's one of the few semi-competent reporters I have— if I could meet her asking price, I'd do it, even though in this economy I could get three reporters to fill her shoes for the same salary. But the *Tropic Times* doesn't have the kind of budget a big-city paper does. I suppose you're going to threaten to jump ship for Tampa too?"

I just stared at her blankly until finally I came up with, "What?"

"Don't tell me your girlfriend hasn't mentioned this to you?" Lisa smiled and crossed her arms over her chest, looking infuriatingly smug. "Well, that changes things. I'm calling her bluff. If she hasn't told *you* about it, then she's not really going."

Except the sick feeling in my stomach filled in the rest of the story that Lisa didn't know—if Sasha hadn't told me about this, then it more likely meant that she was considering career advancement and relocation—over marriage and motherhood.

Did Stu know?

I reached blindly to my feet until my hand found my purse, and rose. "I have to go," I whispered numbly.

"What, did you accidentally tip your buddy's hand?" Lisa crowed. "If she can't have her raise, you're not going to push for yours? Come on, Brook—don't be a total patsy. I'll throw you an extra fifty a week. Brook? Brook! This is a onetime offer!"

But I was already halfway down the hall toward Sasha's end of the building, and Lisa's words fell away behind my retreating back.

...

Fifty feet later I stopped, leaning against the wall and breathing hard.

I wanted to confront my best friend. To charge into her cubicle and demand to know why she'd been keeping to herself such a monumental decision—one that had potentially life-altering repercussions for her—for my brother, my family...and me.

Except...it didn't, a voice spoke up inside my head. For all that I was deeply involved, deeply invested in Sasha and Stu and whatever future they might have, it was Sasha who would bear the greatest weight. Stu had built his landscaping business up over years of networking—he wasn't about to move to Tampa and start from scratch. It was Sasha who would have to turn down a job that could take her career to levels that would never be possible here in Fort Myers. And though I had no doubt my brother would be an involved, hands-on daddy, Sasha would carry this child for nine months, would be the one breast feeding for who knew how long, would probably, realistically, wind up being the prime caregiver for a child she feared she wasn't ready for.

I'd told her that everything she was getting was everything I wanted. But was it? At least at the moment?

I tried to put myself in her shoes. How would I feel if right now, overnight, I were facing all the responsibilities and demands she was? If, in the middle of my career's seemingly steady upward trajectory, I had to put everything on hold and completely switch gears?

I couldn't imagine it. I wasn't ready to. I couldn't even fathom getting a dog.

Of *course* I could understand Sasha's reactions.

Yet it didn't change my feeling of hurt.

But right now, freshly stung from it, wasn't the time to confront her. And the offices of the *Tropic Times* certainly weren't the place. I straightened, took a deep breath, and made myself turn around and head toward the exit.

The thought didn't strike me until I was in the parking lot and climbing into my Honda: Was I angry and upset because my best friend had apparently decided that marriage to my brother and motherhood weren't for her?

Or because she'd made this decision without me?

...

Despite the fact that the sun was low in the sky and shadows filled the car, I kept my sunglasses on when I got to Ben's. I didn't want him to see my eyes, still red and sunken and bleak when I'd checked them in the rearview mirror.

I wasn't entirely sure why I was here...or even when I'd decided to come. After seeing Lisa, I'd gone home to finish out the rest of the client appointments I had scheduled, but as the day wore into early evening, with no Paige, no Jake, no one in the house except me and my agitated thoughts, I couldn't bear to be there alone anymore. I got in my car and drove—and as if from muscle memory from the last week dropping off Jake, I'd ended up in Ben's driveway.

But I couldn't make myself get out of the car. I didn't have his dog anymore. I hadn't even remembered to grab Jake's things, so I'd have at least the excuse of dropping them off. Not that there was much to return—the dregs of a bag of dog food and a couple of chew toys I knew Ben cycled through on a regular basis. There was no reason for me to be here.

Except I wanted to be. I wanted to talk to Ben about what he'd seen downtown, with me and Michael—clarify things. And I needed to talk to someone about what I was feeling about Sasha—and the only person besides my best friend who I wanted to confide in...was Ben.

I looked up at the house, the lit front porch light telling me he was home. I could knock on the door and tell him...what? That I hadn't been dating Michael when he ran into us, but apparently I was now? That my best friend and my brother were pregnant, and I had no idea what was going to happen? I couldn't say any of those things. And I couldn't imagine why he'd want to hear any of it anyway.

I didn't belong here.

I jammed the car into reverse and turned to back out of the driveway, when a knock on my driver's-side window startled me so badly I mashed the gas and shot backward almost into his mailbox.

"Jesus!" I stomped on the brake and came to a screeching halt, my head jerking back, my hands shaking on the wheel.

Ben stood a few feet in front of me, Jake on a leash at his side, Jake's panting and the dark spots dotting Ben's shirt telling me they'd obviously just come back from a walk. My heart still thudding, I lowered the window. "You scared me."

Jake's tail started swishing so fast it blurred, and he pulled toward my car, but Ben kept him firmly at his side. "Brook?" he said. "What are you doing here?"

I shook my head and gave a weak smile, waving away the question. "Oh, I just...I meant to bring back Jake's stuff, but I forgot it...Silly. It's not much anyway. I can just bring it over another...Or not. It doesn't really matter. I..." I ran out of words, blinking. I wanted to put up the window and speed away, but Ben had moved closer, dipping his head to peer directly at me.

"What's wrong, Brook?"

Hot tears speared into my eyes and spilled over.

"Hey...Hey," he said, face creasing with concern, and then my door was opening and he was kneeling beside me, Jake's wet nose pressing against my shoulder as Ben released my seat belt and took me into his arms.

It was so exactly where I'd wanted to be again for so long. It felt so comfortable and familiar and *right*. I wrapped my arms around his shoulders and buried my head in the crook between his neck and shoulder as if by muscle memory, breathing in his familiar scent, the slight smell of sweat, and finally let myself cry.

The tears came from more than Sasha's secret. I cried for all lost things—the happy future I'd envisioned for my best friend and my brother. The easy threesome we'd been all our lives, which had morphed with their couplehood into my being a little bit on the periphery, and now might morph again. I cried for the little niece or nephew I might never know, and for the pain a decision like that would cause all of us.

I cried for me and Ben, and the past we'd lost, and the future we'd never have.

He held me all through it, not talking, not doing anything except offering me the warmth and comfort of a human embrace, while Jake—big, goofy Jake, somehow sensing that something was wrong—sat quietly beside him and pressed his head into my armpit.

Ben didn't let go until my sobs finally slowed, and then he only pulled back, not away. "Come inside," he said gently, wiping at my cheeks with his thumbs. "Come inside and talk."

I didn't even try to resist, just followed him as obediently as Jake into the kitchen, where he poured me a glass of ice water and we sat at his breakfast table, across from each other.

"What happened?" he asked.

I shook my head, mute. I wanted so badly to let out all the things I'd been tamping down—my fears for Sasha and how she'd feel years from now if she made a choice she couldn't live with. About whether she and Stu could weather it. No, I realized...I wanted to tell *Ben*. But I was silenced by my loyalty to my best friend, and to my brother.

Yet Ben was sitting across from me with his eyes on mine—steady, strong, sure, the way he used to look at me when we were together that made me feel as if I were the most important thing happening at that moment. The most important thing in his world, period. And I couldn't help unburdening at least part of it.

"I...I have a client who's going through something right now," I said hesitantly. If I said "a friend," Ben would immediately guess who I was talking about.

He said nothing, just held my gaze as intimately as if he were touching me.

"My...client," I said at last, "has a big decision to make. And she's really scared, and that's making it hard for her to see what she really wants." More tears crested the bottom of my eyes and I roughly swiped them away. "And I think she's about to make the wrong choice, one that might hurt someone I...someone she really cares about. She might hurt her*self.*"

"What do you mean, the wrong choice?"

I looked up, confused that he'd asked a question with such an obvious answer. "The one that won't make her happy," I explained. "The one she'll regret."

Ben's eyebrows drew together. "How do you know which one that is?"

I blinked, momentarily stymied. I couldn't tell him how I knew, because then I'd have to reveal that I was talking about Sasha, who I knew as well as I knew myself. I knew that she'd always dreamed of commitment and love and security, and of being part of a family of her own. I knew she loved my brother like no one else she'd ever been with, and that if something happened to the two of them, it might break her in a way she'd never be able to repair herself from.

Except...I thought of the way Stu had been with her ever since this had started. Supportive. Loving. Yes, my brother was totally on board for marriage and kids in a way I'd never imagined. But I remembered how he'd reacted at Sticks and Stones, even when she was expressing deep-seated doubts that I'd thought would tear out his heart. He'd moved *toward* her, not away. Wrapped his arm around her to support her, literally and figuratively. Stu, I realized in a flash of insight, was totally on board with Sasha no matter *what* she decided—because he loved her, and all he wanted was for her to be happy.

It was me who was trying so hard to get her to do what *I* thought was best for her.

Ben was right: How could I possibly presume to know what that was?

Suddenly I saw it: Sasha already *had* everything she'd dreamed of. The kind of unconditional love she'd always wanted from Stu, who would clearly stand beside her no matter what came. Being part of a family she could call her own—me and my parents and my brother. She didn't need a ring or a baby to make those dreams come true. Those were *my* dreams for her.

Hot shame flooded over me in a wave so strong I felt sick with it. I leaned forward onto propped elbows, sinking my head into my palms, covering my face.

That was exactly what I'd done with Ben, too. I'd been so caught up in what I wanted, in my dreams for our future, I hadn't even considered what he wanted. What was best for him.

That wasn't love. That was just selfish need.

Maybe he was happier with Pamela than he'd ever been with me.

I breathed heavily into my cupped palms, my eyes closed, wishing I could sink into the ground and have it close back over me.

"Brook..." Ben said quietly after a long time, and I knew the universe hadn't answered my prayer to be swallowed up and vanish.

"I just wanted to fix this," I said brokenly into my hands, talking about Sasha. Talking about Ben and me.

"That's one of the nicest things about you, Brook. You always want to help the people you care about."

I looked up, meeting his dark hazel eyes that were still focused on me with warmth and concern, no trace of the contempt I deserved, and I fought a wave of fresh tears.

He smiled gently, reaching across the table. "And you care about everyone."

I yanked my hand out of reach, rejecting the comfort I didn't deserve. "If that were true then I wouldn't try to push people into what I think is best," I said thickly.

Ben pulled his arm back, watching me with a shadow in his eyes I couldn't read. "Sometimes that's the hardest part about loving someone. Doing nothing. Just standing back and letting things take their course."

It was so easy for me to know that in therapy—that I could do what I could to help clarify things, but then I had let a client find the way to his or her own personal truth. And yet in my own life I did the exact opposite.

As Ben had just said, I had to stop trying to control things I had no power over, no right to control, and stand back and let things take their course.

My heart like a brick in my chest, I slumped backward, and Jake arrowed under the table and plopped his head in my suddenly available lap. I stroked his ears, comforting myself as much as him. I took a deep breath in, let it out. And then once more.

"Thanks for listening, Ben," I finally said when I could trust my voice. "You've always been a good friend to me. Even after..." I stopped, avoiding our past by instinct, until I realized that I needed to face up to that too. "Even after I hurt you. I never meant to do that, and I'm so sorry for it."

Something passed over his face that I couldn't read. "I know that, Brook. You told me."

"I know I said it at the time. I just want you to know...I've done a lot of thinking about it since then."

"You don't have to keep apologizing. I've spent time thinking about it too. You were right—technically we weren't together at the time, and—"

I slashed a hand through the air as if to cut his words, needing to say this to him. "Technically doesn't matter. I was so messed-up then, and I don't even think I realized how much. I...I broke a trust between us. It was stupid, and I regret it...so much."

"You were honest with me, Brook. You told me you weren't ready for anything serious."

"That didn't mean I had to..." I hated saying it out loud, bringing up the specter of Chip Santana and my stupid hookup with him. For so long I wished I could undo it, pretend it had never happened, but the reason I was sitting across a table from this man having this awkward conversation, instead of happily in a committed relationship with him, as he'd wanted at the time, as I desperately wanted now, was because it had. I couldn't keep overlooking my own shortcomings and mistakes.

"It didn't mean I had to betray you," I forced out. "What we were to each other."

Heat flooded my face and it was hard to meet Ben's gaze. But I owed him that. I owed him the knowledge that I had finally accepted responsibility for the choices I'd made, realized that, whether we were technically together at the time or not, I'd broken faith with something important between us.

"I've already forgiven it, Brook. You've got to do the same thing."

It was exactly what I'd told Michael.

"Ben," I began. "The other night...downtown. When you saw me with...with Michael—"

He waved off my words. "You don't owe me any explanation about that, Brook."

"No, but I want to...He came back to town. Unexpectedly. And we talked. And I..." I looked down at the table. "I forgave him," I said quietly. "Surprisingly." I glanced up to where Ben was watching me with absolutely no expression.

"And he works in promotion now," I went on, wanting desperately to make him understand—but what, I didn't know. I didn't understand myself what was going on between us. "He asked about trying to promote me—I mean, my business. The Breakup Doctor stuff. So we're sort of working together at the moment."

"Okay."

"Okay," I said lamely. "I just...didn't want you to be upset."

"Is it any of my business, Brook?" he asked. "Who you date?"

I felt foolish. Of course it didn't bother him. Why would it?

I looked away, afraid that the expression I couldn't read in his eyes might be pity.

"Brook?" he asked.

"No," I said, and the effort it took to push my lips into a smile actually hurt. "I guess it isn't." I scooted away from the table and stood, a forlorn Jake gazing up at me disappointedly at the removal of my lap. "I'm going to..." I eked past the immovable object that was Jake, and Ben stood as I came around the table, making no move to stop me.

"Can I ask you a question?" I blurted before I could change my mind.

"Sure."

In the months since the awful morning after we broke up, when Ben had walked in on me and a shirtless Chip Santana in a horrible mute testimony of what we'd done, I'd wanted to know why he'd come to my house. The night before he'd been crystal-clear—he was ready for a serious relationship, and if I wasn't then there was nothing more to say between us. His certainty about that was most of the reason I'd ended up with Chip that night in the first place—I'd been heartbroken to lose Ben, but given all the emotional upheaval I'd had in my life after Michael dumped me, and then Kendall, I hadn't been ready to commit to something serious yet, no matter how much I loved Ben.

And yet not twelve hours later he'd come back, strolling into my backyard with Jake because I hadn't answered the front door, that warm, pleased smile on his face that he'd always worn whenever he'd seen me. At least, until he caught sight of a half-naked, tattooed Chip sitting beside me on the sofa on my back porch. In the terrible scene that had ensued, there was certainly no way to ask Ben why he'd come.

But what did I have to lose now?

"That day," I began hesitantly, my face heating. "That morning on my porch...Why were you coming over?"

Something flickered over his face—a shadow of remembered pain, maybe, or anger. Maybe something softer—but that was probably wishful thinking on my part.

"I was coming to apologize," he said, watching Jake scramble under the table to get closer to us. "I was wrong the night before. I forced you into a corner, and that wasn't fair." He cleared his throat and met my eye again. "The truth was, Brook, I would have taken you on any level you were ready for, and I was coming to make sure I didn't lose you over some stupid ultimatum I gave in a knee-jerk moment of insecurity."

Pain flooded over me in a wave so strong I physically felt the knife of it in my chest.

If I hadn't called Chip that night in a blinding moment of rejection...If I hadn't opened the door when he showed up in the middle of the night...If I'd been able to sit with my emotions for a change, instead of pushing them down, distracting myself from them the way I always had...If I'd waited out the anguish of losing Ben until the rational light of morning...

If.

I would have been standing here at his side, instead of across a vast uncrossable divide.

And Ben would be with *me*, instead of Pamela.

But love didn't always mean things went exactly the way you wanted them to. I finally saw that now. It meant that even when it didn't, you loved that person anyway, and supported what they wanted for *themselves*.

Even if it broke your heart.

"Thanks for telling me," I murmured, emotion threatening to choke me. "I'd really better go." I leaned over to give Jake's silky head a few strokes.

"I'll see you later," I said softly, wondering, after everything, if I would.

Chapter Twenty-four

When my doorbell rang later that night, I wasn't surprised to see Sasha.

She looked wrecked, with tired circles beneath her eyes—atypically makeup-free—and pinched lines at the corners of her mouth. "Can I come in?" she asked hesitantly.

"Since when do you have to ask?"

I could see her biting the inside of her lip. "I wasn't sure you'd want to see me…considering."

"Don't be an idiot." I left her standing at the door and went to sit on the sofa along the front wall, and after a moment Sasha stepped inside and shut the door.

She stopped just inside the entryway, staring at my cocktail table, where I'd set out a tray with cheese and crackers, fruit, water, and a bottle of red wine. "Are you expecting company?"

"You," I said, leaning forward to open the wine. "Come on in."

The expression on her face would have been hilarious if the situation were different: Sasha looked confused, hopeful, and wary, like a wild mustang facing a cowboy with an apple in one hand and a lasso in the other.

"Lisa told me she talked to you," she began, making no move to sit.

"She did. She offered me a raise."

Sasha's mouth dropped open in outrage. "Are you shitting me? She told me there was no money in the budget for raises!"

I gave a one-shouldered shrug. "I can't help it if I'm indispensable."

She narrowed her eyes at me. "You realize they also give *me* a full benefits package and paid time off, right?"

I let a half-smile leak out. "I'm just teasing you. Lisa actually said you were her best reporter, and if she could find the money in the budget to keep you, she would."

"*Lisa* said that? Holy shit. That's like being knighted from anyone else."

For a moment we were just us again, nothing between us but years of friendship, and we shared a grin across the room. Then Sash seemed to remember, and hers disappeared.

"She told me she told you," she said. "Why aren't you yelling at me?"

"Why aren't you sitting?" I asked, holding out one of the two glasses of cabernet I'd poured.

One hand fluttered to her belly. "Wine? I don't—"

"If you've made your decision, is it really going to matter anymore?" I asked as gently as I could.

Sasha blinked several times, and I saw her lips tremble. But finally she stepped forward, took the glass, and sat beside me. "I'm sorry I didn't tell you," she whispered. "About the job offer, I mean. I just...I needed time to think things out on my own. And I knew how you'd feel...what you'd say," she went on. She broke my gaze and stared down into her wineglass, then finally raised it to her lips and took a sip.

Sasha didn't know how clearly I could understand that; wasn't that why I hadn't told her about what happened with Michael, with Ben?

"I think you should take it."

Wine went everywhere as she choked. "What?" she managed.

I calmly pulled a napkin from the tray and dabbed at the purple spatters all over my sofa and the white denim of my skinny jeans. "I know how important your career is to you, Sash. It's a great opportunity. A much bigger paper in a much bigger market—" My voice had started to wobble, and I stopped to swallow a mouthful of my own wine, trying to steady it. "There's no chance for advancement like that in this town. We both know that."

Once again she narrowed a suspicious gaze on me. "What is this? Reverse psychology? Some kind of desensitization? What?"

I sighed and leaned forward to set my glass down on the tray. "This is me saying what I should have said all along. That you are the only one who knows the right thing for you. That I love you and want whatever you feel is best for you. That I will be standing right there beside you no matter what you choose."

Her eyes filled with tears as I spoke. "How can you say that?" she asked, almost angrily. "I am *ruining* your family's life!"

"Well, *someone* has a healthy sense of self-importance," I said dryly.

"Stop it! Stop being so funny and nice to me! I don't deserve it!"

"Hey!" I barked. "Get your shit together, Patterson." My sharp tone stunned her tears dry, and she stared at me.

"Why are you yelling at me?"

"I thought that's what you wanted!" I yelled. I torqued back my volume, but pushed ahead with what I'd been trying for hours to find the right words for. "Look…we all do the best we can with wherever we are at the moment. That didn't used to be all that great for either one of us. But we're not kids anymore. We're getting better at this life crap—but sometimes there's just no right answer, and all you can do is make the *rightest* choice." I felt my own eyes growing hot with tears, and I resisted the urge to medicate them away with a distracting gulp of wine. "I don't know the rightest choice for you, Sash. No one does but you. But I know *my* rightest choice, and that's to support you—no matter what. No matter what you need to do for *you*, in every way that counts you're my sister, and that's never going to change."

Sasha let out a sudden sob, more wine sloshing over the sides of her glass onto the floor and my table as she blindly reached to set it down. I ignored the spill as she collapsed forward into my arms, and I held her while she cried.

"This is all I do anymore," she sobbed into my shoulder. "I cry. I cry at everything. I cried at a Cialis commercial last night. Hormones!" she wailed. "I'm all mixed-up, Brook. I don't know what to do. Please just tell me what to do!"

I let go, brushing away her tears with my thumbs the way Ben had done with me only hours ago. "I can't, Sash. No one can. But if you need someone to talk it out with, objectively...well, I'll try." I offered her an apologetic smile. "Or I can make some professional referrals."

She gave a shaky laugh.

"Does Stu know about the job offer?" I asked carefully.

"I already told you, I tell him everything."

She'd told Stu about this even when she couldn't tell me. Stu and Sasha, I realized, despite their constant oversexed grab-assing and childish exploits, had one of the healthiest relationships I'd ever seen. I couldn't help believing that no matter what happened, they'd make it through this together.

The days of my being the axis of our world of three were over, I knew in a rush, and from now on I'd always be just a little outside of their twosome.

But maybe that was the way it should be. As I'd said to Sasha, we weren't children anymore, and it was time for all of us to grow up a little.

"I'm glad," I told her genuinely. "You guys will figure things out together. And Sash, if you need me—for *anything*." I nudged her with my shoulder. "I'm here."

Sasha nodded tearfully, but I could already see her gathering herself back together. "Thanks, Brookie. That means everything."

When she rose to leave, she seemed to take in the splotches of wine scattered all over my furniture and my person.

"Oh, crap...I'm sorry about the mess all over your house."

I shrugged. "I sort of deserved it, after what I did to yours."

"Agreed," she said a little too vehemently.

I walked her to the door and we hugged before she let herself out into the cool orange blossom–scented evening.

Yes, it was time to grow up, I thought as I noticed her mostly untouched glass of wine still sitting on my cocktail table.

I finally knew better than to let it raise a childish flicker of hope.

Chapter Twenty-five

Michael rang my doorbell sharply at six thirty on Friday. I wasn't quite ready—he'd always operated on "band time," which could mean anything from fifteen minutes after he'd promised to be somewhere, to an hour, to forgetting it entirely—and I answered in bare feet and a ridiculous terry cloth robe that my mom had given me one Christmas.

"Whoa!" I said as I took in his outfit: gray pants with a lavender button-down and a boldly colored Jerry Garcia tie that told me the old Michael wasn't completely extinguished. I was glad of that. "You look nice."

He eyed the appliqued cartoon flamingos dotting my robe. "You look...unusual."

"I am so close to ready, you have no idea. Give me three minutes."

Michael's outfit told me loud and clear what I'd been trying not to think about all week: This was a Real Live Date.

I'd planned to downplay that with jeans and a silk top, but there was no way I could do that now. I reached for a faux-wraparound knit dress and a pair of heels, swiped on lip gloss, and then stood at the bathroom counter leaning my weight on my hands till I calmed my racing heart.

Michael was still standing in the entryway when I came out.

"You're allowed to sit," I said, putting on earrings.

"Yeah, I know, I was...Wow."

I gave a nervous bubble of laughter. "Thanks."

For a moment we stood at the door, looking at each other, till I had to break the intensity of his stare by reaching for my purse on the entry table.

Outside, Michael followed me to the passenger side of his older-model Lexus—it was still hard to believe he'd traded his funky old Jeep for something so sedate. I shot him a glance as he flanked me. "What are you doing?"

"I'm opening your door."

"You're...?" I couldn't help it—I laughed. It felt like the first time in days, and I relished the feeling. "Seriously, Michael, did you go on like a makeover show or something? You're weirding me out. You're too good to be true."

He just grinned, and held the door while I got in.

"Where are we headed?"

"The Plantation," he said, rather proudly.

I froze. Ben had taken me there to celebrate my first group session last fall. It had been a turning point for us—that night, after hours of a perfect meal and giggling over our hilariously serious waiter, when we got back to my house I'd finally opened myself up to him, warts and all, showing him my mortifying drunken tattoo, confessing pretty much the lowest point I'd hit after Kendall dumped me...and ironically, telling him about Michael—the first time I'd ever let myself even say his name since our broken engagement. It had been our first real intimacy—before the sex, before we'd even admitted we'd fallen in love. It was the most naked and vulnerable I'd ever been with anyone.

I'd been through too much this week—I didn't have it in me to face going to the same restaurant with Michael.

But he looked so pleased with himself; he was trying so hard to abide by everything I'd asked of him, to prove that he was an adult now, a professional, and that my business was in good hands—and that I was. I swallowed. "That's a bit fancy," I said in a small voice, hoping he'd reconsider.

"Didn't see that coming, did you?"

"Nope. I sure didn't." I made myself return his smile, but it felt more like a labial contraction as I swung my other leg inside and Michael shut the door.

...

It actually turned out to be a great night.

By the time we were seated—in a different room of the restored old manor house from the one Ben and I had been in, with a different waiter—Michael and I had fallen back into our old easy rhythms. We ordered scads of food, stuffing ourselves from each other's plates, and a bottle of wine, which lubricated any residual awkwardness and made it easy for us to laugh, to tell each other stories, to reminisce.

When the bill came I reached for it, but he grabbed it away, insisting that he wanted to treat. "The least I can do after everything is buy you a nice dinner," he said with a crooked grin, and I let him.

I never thought I'd ever see Michael again, let alone have a conversation with him—and certainly not that we'd be able to reclaim our friendship after everything that had happened. And yet it seemed we'd done it. A thorn I hadn't even realized had been pricking me had been removed, and it felt so good not only not to hate him anymore, but to be reminded why I had liked him in the first place. And for a few hours I almost forgot about Sasha, about Stu...about Ben—or at least the sharp pain of it all faded into a dull ache.

Maybe this was how things had to happen all along. We'd both admitted we'd been different people back then, that we'd changed. Maybe our paths were always meant to run together after all—just not that soon.

By the time we got back to my house I was feeling a little bit tipsy—I'd suggested a cab, but Michael rightly pointed out that three-fourths of the wine bottle had gone into my gullet, not his. He got out and walked me to the door.

"You're like a real gentleman," I said, giggling as I rummaged for my keys.

"Almost just like one," he said wryly, with a smile I termed avuncular.

Avuncular. I turned the word over in my head, and liked it so much I said it aloud.

"A *vun*cular."

"What?"

I just grinned, waving a hand in the air. "Pay me no mind. I'm loopy. You're fun. I forgot."

And then suddenly stucco was pressing into my back—I could feel the rough nubs of its texture through the knit of my dress—and hands were on my shoulders...and then lips were on my mouth.

Michael's lips.

On my mouth.

They were soft but insistent, warm and exactly the right amount of wet—the way they always were. And I knew before he did it that he'd bring his hands to my face, cupping my head and pulling me closer. Michael had always been a nearly perfect kisser.

And he still was.

I shoved him backward as I pushed myself away from the wall and faced off with him, legs and arms akimbo like an Ultimate Cage Fighting champ on the defense.

"What are you doing?" I blurted, all my giddiness evaporated.

He raised an eyebrow. "Well, if you have to ask I didn't really do it right."

"Stop it. I'm serious. What was that?"

"It was a *kiss*, Brook! For God's sake!"

"Why?" I sputtered.

"Why?!" He moved a step away from me, shoving a hand into his hair that left it wild and sticking up, the way I remembered it. "Why do you think?"

"I don't know!" I shouted, then glanced to my nearest neighbor's house, dark and quiet.

He sighed and stepped back, giving me space, but kept his eyes on mine. "What's going on, Brook?"

"I don't know," I repeated, my voice lower.

"Tell me what you're thinking."

"I don't know." It was like I was stuck on a loop.

"Oh, come on, Brook!" he said, aggravated.

"Shhh!"

"No, not 'shhh,'" he fired back. "Talk to me! For once, would you please talk to me instead of shutting down?"

That sobered me up.

"Fine," I said in a harsh whisper after a long, charged moment. "Come inside."

I snatched the keys from the bottom of my bag so hard one bounced back and bit into my skin as they popped out of the detritus of my purse, but I welcomed the pain as something to focus on. I threw open the door and gave a staccato gesture for him to go in.

I slapped on all the overhead lights in the living room, and we both blinked in the sudden glare.

"Sit," I said shortly.

He did, with a heavy sigh. "Why are you mad?"

It was a genuine question, not rhetorical or angry, asked in a reasonable voice. He truly didn't understand.

Which made two of us.

I took a calming breath and sank into the chair opposite the sofa he'd sat on. He'd called me on my old instinct to retreat behind my stone walls, and that wasn't who I wanted to be anymore. He'd asked me to be genuine with him, and I would.

"You kissed me," I said simply.

"Agreed."

He still looked blank, and I raised my hands palms up. "You *kissed* me, Michael," I said, as if clarifying. "We were taking things slow."

"Aren't we?"

"I *thought* so," I retorted.

"And you didn't want me to overwhelm you—to take you over. And I'm not, Brook. I've done everything you asked of me. I'll keep doing it if you want. However long you want—I told you that. But I also told you how I felt, and it's not like that's going to change."

Something shifted uncomfortably in my belly.

He leaned forward, and then immediately back, as if he were conscious of trying not to crowd me. "This isn't a game where you can set the rules and we have to strictly play by them. People can change—you have. And God knows I'm trying to show you I have."

"I can see that," I conceded, but my tone was still sharp. "But why are you backing me into a corner?"

He shot me a bewildered look. "I didn't think I..." He blew out a sigh and leaned forward, elbows propped on his knees, looking down at his clasped hands as if thinking.

"Look..." he finally went on quietly. "If there's someone else...Ben"—his name on Michael's lips knifed through me, and I looked away—"I'll get out of the way. If you don't feel anything for me anymore...I'll get out of the way. But if neither of those things is true...are you really willing to walk away from this without ever knowing if it could have been something?"

I couldn't look at him—didn't want to meet his gaze and see the truth reflected in them: that he wasn't wrong. That I'd been sending mixed signals.

Now he was forcing me to make a definitive decision...and that was what was making me angry.

Which wasn't fair, and it wasn't rational. But I wasn't feeling particularly rational at the moment.

"I think you should go," I said quietly.

He slapped his hands on his thighs hard, and in the silence the sound echoed like a gunshot, making me jump. "Dammit, Brook, don't do this! Don't shut down and shut me out!"

"I'm not! I just...It's too much!" I felt as if I were suffocating, and I couldn't seem to think straight with him sitting here in my house, across from me, asking me for something I wasn't sure if I still wanted or could give. When you're out of ammunition, you get out of the foxhole. "I can't think, Michael. You just have to give me some time to *think*. Okay?"

He looked at me for a long moment, and finally nodded. "Okay." He stood up. "Okay. I get that. I said I'd wait as long as you need, and I will. But..." One hand lifted toward me, and he looked as if he wanted to move closer, but the cocktail table blocked his way. I didn't know if

I was grateful for that or disappointed. He dropped his arm back to his side. "Brook…" He shook his head, as if the words he wanted wouldn't come. "I know I don't have any right to ask this, after the way I…what I did to you, but I'm asking anyway. Just…let me hear from you. Okay?"

Woodenly I nodded. "You will. I won't leave you hanging."

Chapter Twenty-six

I hardly slept that night. When I did drift off it was light and unsatisfying, ill-formed thoughts of Michael and Ben, Sasha and Stu chasing themselves through my dreams, keeping me unsettled and half-awake, roiling with indecision and confusion and pain.

I was grateful to have my group therapy session to drag my thoughts out of my own head—but they all came crashing back the minute I stepped outside into the bright Saturday-afternoon sunshine. When my phone rang as I climbed into my car I was almost afraid to answer it—but it was only my dad.

"Hey, doll, I was hoping to bring something by tomorrow morning, if you're free."

All week I'd desperately been wishing I could cancel my beach day tomorrow with Ben and Jake. I didn't think I could keep up the farce of a friendship now that I'd extinguished my secret hope of more. Daddy's visit gave me the excuse I needed and I said yes, then took the coward's way out and texted Ben that I wouldn't be able to make it tomorrow.

He didn't reply.

For a while my dad used to stop by all the time with various tools and supplies for our ongoing rehab of my extreme fixer-upper. But over the last months, neck-deep in Breakup Doctor business, I'd lost impetus, and my father had taken to spending most weekends fishing with Stu on Dad's boat sort-of named after my mom, the *Joie de Viv*. The house had been in a half-before, half-after state for some time now: My office area and front living room were in decent shape, but the kitchen, den, and master bedroom not so much.

If Daddy was in a renovation mood again this weekend, that might be perfect—nothing sounded better to me right now than some heavy demolition.

But when the doorbell rang a little after nine a.m. on Sunday, it wasn't sledgehammers and circular saws my father had brought, but a bag of doughnuts and the rocking chair he'd been working on in the garage for months. He'd set it down on my front walk and was sitting in it, slowly rocking forward and backward, a waxed-paper bag from Merritt's Bakery on his lap as he chewed a bite of the chocolate-frosted in his hand.

"Morning, doll," he said, grinning.

"Daddy? I thought this was for Mom?"

"Your mother has her own chair, sweetheart. I thought my girl needed one for herself."

He handed me the bag and his doughnut, and I followed him through my house with them as he carried the chair onto my lanai. Together we moved the furniture so the chair had room to rock, facing out toward my overgrown backyard.

The wood gleamed in the morning sunlight angling onto the porch, glowing a rich warm caramel from every meticulously smoothed surface. A paprika-colored outdoor cushion covered the seat and part of the back. It was beautiful workmanship—everything my father made was—but the old-fashioned chair wasn't exactly me. Still, I was touched by the gesture and the months of effort that had gone into it, so I lowered myself into it and pushed myself into a rocking motion. Of course the chair moved like it was on casters.

I smiled up at him. "It's gorgeous, Daddy. I love it. Thank you."

He settled onto the sofa across from me, reaching for his doughnut I'd set on top of the bag. He tossed the rest of the pastries to me and I pulled out a Bavarian crème—my favorite—and we munched quietly together. My father always brought a wonderful sense of peace to our silences, and for a long time the only sound was my own chewing, the gentle crunch of unswept dirt under the chair's runners, and the guttural croaking of egrets outside the screened porch.

"I moved the chairs I made for your mom and me down to the dock," he said after a while, as if continuing our conversation. "I don't know if you noticed?"

I hadn't.

"We've been sitting down there a lot lately. Just taking some time to relax at the end of a day, make some space in our heads, enjoy the evening. We get so busy sometimes we forget how lucky we are down here that we can do that—sit out by the water—in winter, when the rest of the country's all bundled up against the cold. We forget how beautiful that canal is, especially at sunset; the sun sinks right over the Caloosahatchee, turns the whole thing orange. Just about the color of those cushions there on your chair."

I was bemused by the idea of my always-in-motion mother and my ever-tinkering dad sitting out in their rocking chairs out on the dock, like the most clichéd of old people. By the fact that my dad, never much of a talker even when I tried to engage him, was rambling on, waxing poetic about Florida and the river and the sunset.

"Your mother picked those cushions out for you," he went on, oblivious. "She's got such an eye for that kind of thing, and I don't know which end is up with anything but woodworking."

"It's perfect," I said honestly. The deep orange was a needed pop of color on my neutral porch, and tied in with the warm earth tones I'd selected inside the house. It pleased me that my mother had paid such attention to my preferences in décor—and to me. But even more, the fact that my mom and dad were doing things together, enjoying each other's company, felt as if my world were resettling on its axis once again. It had been a long year since her defection from their marriage.

Dad's voice rumbled out over the breeze. "It's nice. Sometimes you have to remember to do that, you know?"

I'd lost the thread of our conversation. "Do what, Daddy?"

My father was looking at me strangely, an unreadable smile on his face as he watched me rocking and eating (my second doughnut, but who was counting?).

"Nothing."

...

I'd taken my dad's response to my question as a dismissal—he'd changed his mind about trying to explain what he'd been getting at, reverted to his usual taciturn self, and we'd finished the doughnuts in companionable silence as I rocked in the chair he'd made me until at last he'd stood and patted himself down for his keys, kissed me on the cheek, and said he had to go.

When I got to family dinner that night, I was bewildered to discover the kitchen deserted, my dad's workshop empty. A frisson of concern tickling my belly, I searched the house, calling their names, until finally, when I opened the sliding glass doors to their lanai, I heard my parents' distant voices coming from down at the dock.

I picked my way down the stone walkway from their back screen door toward the water and found the two of them in the rocking chairs just as Dad had said, each of them holding a cocktail, facing out to where the orange ball of the sun was just sinking into the river. True to my dad's description, it laid a glowing path of fire along the canal.

"Is everything okay?" I heard the thread of uncertainty in my own voice.

"Hey, there, doll! Couldn't be better," my dad said.

"Hi, honey," Mom said, angling her head back toward me.

"Did you cancel dinner?" I asked, confused. "There's nothing cooking in the kitchen."

"No, dinner's still on. We lost track of time and so your dad suggested we order pizza tonight for a change."

What was going on? They knew all of us were coming over for dinner, but they'd just been sitting here—and Mom forgot to *cook*? There was no such thing as a non-home-cooked Sunday dinner. And she'd called me "honey."

Was my mother dying?

"What's going on?" I voiced my thoughts anxiously, coming around to face my parents head-on.

"What do you mean?" Mom said.

I fisted hands on my hips, eyeing them both with a hard stare. "What are you *doing*?"

Dad shrugged, and he and my mom exchanged a look.

My mother actually smiled as she answered, "Nothing."

That was when I understood that my father's "Nothing" that morning had, in fact, been the answer to my question—what he wanted me to remember to do.

When Stu and Sasha arrived, I gave them each a hug, holding them a little longer than usual. Stu squeezed me so tight the breath whooshed out of me, but I said nothing, just returned the pressure. My baby brother was dealing with some real-world shit he'd never counted on. All I could do was let him know I had his back if he needed me. Sasha was slow to meet my eyes, an apology swimming in hers, but I tried to bolster her with my smile, and kept my arm around her waist as we went into the kitchen.

Dinner was quieter than usual, Stu and Sasha barely offering a few words in the weekly roundup, but if Mom noticed she didn't point it out. Instead, after we'd all gone around the table, she surprised us by taking a turn of her own. "Well, your father and I have a little bit of news. We'll be away for ten days as soon as *Glass Menagerie* closes, and need you kids to keep an eye on things at the house."

Stu, Sasha, and I exchanged glances. "Away where?" I asked.

Dad was grinning at my mom, his eyes alight. "Wherever your mom wants to go," he said. "I think we're thinking a driving tour out west, maybe the Grand Canyon."

I raised my eyebrows. That seemed a little cornpone for my mom. "Seriously?" I said to her.

She raised her shoulders. "Your father's never seen it. I want him to."

They were looking only at each other, and for a moment we kids weren't even there.

"I can grab the mail and rotate the lights," I said, and then in a fit of magnanimity borne of the warmth blooming in my chest, I added, "And I can even check on your Naples apartment if you want."

"I don't have that anymore," Mom said lightly, reaching for the salad.

Again Stu, Sasha, and I bounced glances off one another.

"You don't?" Stu asked cautiously.

"I released it." She said it as casually as if she were announcing the side dishes for the evening, rather than telling all of us kids that she and my dad were back together—full-time.

I blinked, and looked across the table to see Sasha and Stu wearing matching grins that probably reflected the one growing across my own face. For just that moment everything was wonderful, and I let myself simply enjoy it.

As we cleaned up afterward, I noticed the glass phoenix I'd given my mother in the windowsill above the sink, glittering even in the harsh overhead light. It was the only knickknack out—Mom didn't like clutter—and the sight of it chased away a little bit more of the sadness that sat on my shoulders like a shroud.

...

Monday morning, when I snapped awake at four thirty a.m. from muscle memory, unable to get back to sleep, instead of torturing myself listening to Jim Veneer carrying on with my old radio show without me, I took my coffee out onto the porch and settled into Daddy's chair. I pushed off with my feet experimentally, swaying forward and back with the chair's movement.

After work, in the gap left by Jake's absence, I took a glass of lemonade out and rocked.

As the week went on, sitting in Dad's chair on my porch looking out over my backyard became a routine. At first I was antsy, rocking fast, my mind buzzing over my to-do list, a thorny issue with a client, or topics for my newspaper column.

I worried over Sasha and Stu like the most devout of Catholics on well-worn rosary beads. Would they make it through this challenge together? Would Sasha resent him forever if she turned down this job—took on the new job of motherhood she seemed increasingly certain she didn't want? Would he ever truly get over it if she didn't?

I thought about Ben—drove myself crazy with pictures of him and Pamela getting ready for their adventure, or stationed together in an isolated village, working toward common goals by day, sharing a common grass hut by night, removed from the world and the petty desires and problems of someone like me.

I wrestled—endlessly—with my feelings for Michael. So much of my resistance to him had been related to Ben. With that option finally closed off, would I always regret it, as Michael had said, if I didn't give him—give us—one more chance now that we'd both grown up a little?

Gradually my busy thoughts uncoiled a little as I rocked on my patio with my coffee in the mornings, or a glass of juice or wine at the end of the day, and instead of the constant stream of rumination I began to actually see my surroundings—the chipped and peeling areas on my porch that needed to be scraped and repainted, the lawn that was overdue for mowing, the beds that hadn't been mulched since I moved in. A new to-do list took amorphous shape in my mind.

Little by little I found my imagination wandering off aimlessly, picturing the weedy areas cleared and flowers growing in their place, a miniature citrus grove I could plant in one sunny corner, a place for a vegetable garden in another. I made no specific plans, just looked and dreamed and listened to the sounds of tanagers chirping their bouncy melodies in the oak tree outside the porch door, a distant lawn mower somewhere in the neighborhood, the whoosh of cars speeding by on Winkler Avenue behind my house.

One evening I picked up Sasha and we went to Homegoods. Since Jake had savaged my bedding and curtains the first night I'd had him, I'd been using a cheap bare-bones comforter and had never bothered with new window treatments.

I'd spent so much time and energy on the "public" spaces of my house—the office area, the living room—but I'd let my own personal spaces stagnate. So that night we picked out a fluffy comforter in sunny shades of yellow and cream, with a cheery teal stripe that instantly lifted my mood. Sasha directed me toward crisp ecru sheets in a high thread count that she swore I'd love to feel against my skin, beachy off-white linen curtains, and a stack of new pillows. Afterward we stopped at Lowe's and she helped me pick out carpet—a thick pile the color of sand—for the bare concrete floor I'd never bothered to cover after I ripped up the previous owner's horrible ancient blue carpet, and bamboo blinds for the windows.

We never talked about her pregnancy.

As the chatter of my busy mind began to quiet, I realized that things became clearer all on their own, like the blue sky patiently waiting to be revealed when the billowing storm clouds dissipated.

I'd kept myself away from Ben, despite being in love with him, because I'd wanted to find out who I was on my own. Yet as soon as I'd seen him again, I'd defaulted into fix-it mode. Without realizing it, like Nina Edelburg, who'd left her boyfriend in St. Pete when he didn't accept her ultimatum, I'd put my own goals on hold while I tried to figure out ways to make things right, to make Ben once again want me back.

I saw that now for the mistake it had been. But it was an equal mistake, I was growing to believe, to have thought that I had to isolate myself until I finally became the person I wanted to be.

Human beings aren't solitary creatures. We aren't meant to be alone—and we don't have to be to figure out who we are and what we want. I'd been afraid to make a commitment until I finally had everything just perfect in my life, but I saw now that I'd be alone forever if that was my standard.

Sometimes you just had to jump, and trust that you'd figure things out on the way down.

Chapter Twenty-seven

I was nervous as I walked down the aisle, but I also couldn't wait to get there.

The black-and-brown dog was waiting in the same patient position when I got to his kennel, almost as if he'd known I was coming: sitting calmly facing the gate, tail gently wagging against the concrete. When he saw me walking down the row with Angela he stood and his tail sped up, but still he didn't leap up barking like all the other dogs were doing. He merely watched me expectantly, as if he knew I was here solely for him, and when Andrea reached for the gate to let him out he took a step back, as if politely waiting for her to come in, before I crouched down and held out an arm.

"Here, boy!" I said. "Come on, buddy. Let's go home."

He trotted out immediately, as though he'd only been waiting for my invitation.

I'd forgotten to bring a leash—Angela kindly gave me one of the donated ones the shelter kept on the wall for just this purpose. And on the way home I realized that I hadn't thought to buy him a dog bed, or toys, or a brush for the hair that was already longer than the last time I'd seen him, or even a bag of food.

But that was okay. We'd figure all that out.

I hadn't had a dog since I was a child, and I'd never borne the sole responsibility for one. But I thought I was finally ready for the commitment. And the risks.

On the way home we stopped at a pet-supply megastore on 41, and although I was concerned about trying to wrangle an unfamiliar creature in an unfamiliar environment, I brought the dog in with me.

I needn't have worried. He zigzagged down the aisles as I shopped, avidly exploring everything at his level, but he never even drew his leash taut, periodically turning to check that I was still behind him. Andrea had warned me that often shelter dogs—especially older ones—took a while to bond to their new owners, but already he seemed to feel the same deep draw to me that I'd felt to him from the get-go.

I got just the basics—a bag of food, some treats, and a brand-new collar and leash (purple, to suit his regal bearing). Once he settled in and we got to know each other, we could come back and pick out toys and a bed and whatever else I saw we needed as I learned about him.

Back at my house I let him off the leash just inside the garage door.

"Okay, buddy. This is your new home. Go check it out."

The dog made a wary circuit as I trailed behind him, investigating every single room, one after the next, as noncommittal as a potential home buyer on a showing. Finally he stood at the back door and glanced back at me. I obliged, letting him onto the porch, and after another thorough exploration of the lanai he stood at the screen door until I pushed it open too. Then he walked outside, went straight to the largest of my oak trees, and lifted his leg—right in Jake's favorite spot. He came trotting immediately back inside, curling up into a comma on the Saltillo tile and grinning up at me as if saying, Now *I'm interested in the place.*

I called Sasha and asked if she and Stu were free to drop by, and thirty minutes later I opened the door to see the two of them side by side.

"I have something to show you," I said, opening the door wider.

"You got a doggie!" my animal-crazy brother cried, and dropped to a crouch in front of the animal, who sat close at my side. Stu rubbed his ears and neck and shoulders, exclaiming over the dog, who grinned amiably enough at my brother, but otherwise sat calmly.

"He's the one from Andrea's shelter?" Sasha asked me over their heads.

I nodded. "I wanted you to meet him."

"What's his name?" Stu asked, dropping to a full sit. I joined him, and after a moment so did Sasha, the three of us ringing the dog on the concrete floor.

"Slick," Sasha answered, just as I said, "Winston." She glanced at me.

"Look at him." I indicated the dog, who was lying on his stomach in the center of our circle with his legs neatly tucked, stately as a New York library lion. "He's too dignified to be a Slick."

As if he agreed, Winston inched closer to me, pressing alongside my leg.

"I can't believe you got a dog," Stu said, watching enviously as Winston clearly made his human allegiance known.

"Yeah," Sasha said. "What happened to 'it's too much commitment' and 'it's guaranteed to eventually break your heart'?"

I grinned, lifting one shoulder as I stroked his soft crooked ears. "I don't know. I guess I decided the tradeoff is worth it."

We sat in amiable silence in our little circle for a while, all three of us watching Winston like a fascinating new toy. "I'm so glad you saved him," Sasha finally murmured.

"No." I looked back down to where my dog lay contentedly beside me, feeling loneliness trickle away and my heart flood with pure comfort and affection and warmth. "I think maybe he's saving me."

...

Sasha and Stu wound up staying for a late lunch, and for a few hours we were back to normal. If there was any tension between them about Sasha's job offer or the decision I suspected she was still wrestling with, I didn't see it, and I didn't ask about it. When they left I hugged them each goodbye at the door, and while Stu knelt to commune with Winston, I turned to Sasha.

"Want to go grab dinner one night this week?" I asked her. "Or go shopping?"

She searched my face as if looking for a hidden agenda, but I could tell when she realized there was none. I was through trying to "fix" things. Her forehead smoothed and she gave the beginnings of a smile. "Yeah. I'll call."

After they left I walked Winston, and took him into the backyard to walk the perimeter of his new domain with him, and fed him, realizing only as he finished the last of the bowl that five o'clock was probably too early; he'd be hungry again by bedtime.

He and I were still getting used to each other. But already I felt less alone. Happier. More able to face things I knew would be emotional.

Like seeing Michael.

I called and asked him to come over—I couldn't leave Winston on his first night in an unfamiliar place. After Jake had destroyed my bedroom the first time I'd left him alone at my house, I wasn't in a hurry to lose another set of nice textiles to freaked-out-dog teeth.

When Michael showed up the dog simply stood beside me in the doorway when I opened it, as if we were a couple welcoming a guest into our home.

After Michael fussed over Winston and we were settled in the living room, I didn't waste time working up to things. A quick, clean blow was kindest—I knew that firsthand—so I simply stated things, as kindly and gently—but directly—as I knew how.

Pain flitted through Michael's eyes at my words. "I had a feeling that's what you called me over here to tell me."

"How did you know?"

He was leaning forward in the armchair across from my sofa, elbows on his knees and hands dangling between his legs. "You used to look at me a certain way," he said slowly. "Like every day you'd hit the lottery and you couldn't quite believe it." A sad smile curved his lips. "I haven't seen that in your eyes since I came back. Except once."

"You did?" I said, surprised. The reason I'd finally called Michael over was because I'd realized that that feeling I'd once had for him had long since gone.

"The night we saw your ex downtown."

My throat ached, and I turned my gaze away. "I'm sorry, Michael."

He lifted his shoulders. "It's my own doing. I blew it. Thinking we could pick back up again was a long shot...but I had to try."

His words hung between us for a few moments. "Do you remember the day you proposed to me?" I asked him.

A sad grin crept across his mouth. "Underwater Jesus. Dropping the ring. God."

I smiled back, remembering. "It was such a unique way to ask me to marry you. So romantic."

"Yeah."

"But..." I shifted on the sofa, not sure whether I should say it. "A part of me was always afraid that the real reason you did it that way was so you didn't actually have to speak the words."

Michael looked as if he'd taken a plank in the face. "That wasn't why I did it!"

At his raised voice Winston sat up, moving closer to me and facing Michael in an alert position, as if warning him to be cool.

I shook my head, stroking the dog. "I don't think it was, consciously. But I always wondered if even then, a big part of you wasn't sure."

"I don't...I don't know," he said, as if the idea were only just dawning on him.

"It doesn't matter. The thing is...even though I thought that, I said yes anyway. I wanted it so badly, and I was afraid that if I asked you—if I said anything at all about it—you'd change your mind. So what I'm saying is, don't blame yourself for how things happened. I chose not to look too closely at what I knew was right in front of me."

The words lay heavy between us.

"I don't think I can stay here," Michael said finally.

I nodded. "I get it. Let's talk a little later, then, when we—"

"No," he interrupted me. "I mean here in Fort Myers."

Now it was my turn to fall silent. "But..." I said finally, "what about working together?" I swallowed, a pain I hadn't expected sliding between my ribs. "What about us...our friendship?"

His grass-green eyes clouded. "I can't be friends with you, Brook. Not now."

"So all that was BS, then?" I fired off angrily. "About just wanting to be back in my life on any level?"

"No! I meant that! I still mean it. But, Jesus, Brook..." He threw himself backward in the chair, rubbing his temple with a hand. "How am I supposed to be around you...with you...and know that no matter how strongly I'm feeling for you...you're not feeling the same things? Especially when I have to watch you feel them with someone else." Pain and regret ripped a jagged edge in his expression.

"That's...not happening. That ended a long time ago."

"But you still have feelings for him?"

I looked down at Winston, wanting to see anything else but the look in Michael's eyes. "I do. That doesn't just go away."

"No," he said quietly. "Not for everyone."

My gaze snapped back up to meet his. "It didn't just 'go away' for me with you, Michael. Why do you think I haven't been able to have a healthy relationship since we broke up? I couldn't get *over* you. You've been even more present with me since you left than you were when we were together."

"Then *why*? If it's not because of this...this other guy...why isn't it there anymore for us?"

"Something's still there, Michael. It always will be. How could it not? But"—I gentled my tone, but knew it wouldn't soften the words—"not like it was."

I saw him flinch.

"Maybe too much happened between us. Or maybe I've changed too much—we both have. I don't know why." I spread my hands helplessly. "But you still matter to me so much. How can you just leave again? How can we *not* be in each other's lives?"

He shook his head wearily. "I just can't. Not yet. Give me some time."

"How much time?" I knew it wasn't a fair question even as I asked it. Veruca Salt rearing her impatient head again.

"I don't know." He shrugged. "A while."

That hurt—a lot more than I'd expected. Michael had once felt like a limb—something I couldn't imagine ever living without. But then, after he left, I'd grown so used to *not* having him in my life—how could he feel so essential again, so quickly?

"I wish it were different," I said, hearing childish hurt in my voice.

"God, Brook, so do I," he said fervently. He stood up, as did Winston, as if ready to escort him out. "I have to go."

"Michael—"

"Don't, okay? Please. Just...Goodbye, Brook."

He didn't look at me as he let himself out the front door, and the sound of it closing behind him echoed in the silence of the room like a thunderclap.

...

I stayed up late, the aftermath of all the emotions Michael and I had stirred up again churning inside me. Regret was chief among them—for what might have been for us if things had gone differently...but mostly for what I knew Michael was feeling now. I'd felt it myself for so long after he'd left, and though there had been a time when I'd have wished that on him and so much more, now all I wanted was to ease his pain.

But I understood where he was coming from. After all, up until recently I was the queen of "You can't be friends with your ex." At least when one person's feelings still ran high—all that was was an exercise in self-torture, as Michael had said: watching someone you still fiercely loved *not* love you back the same way. I couldn't begin to blame him for wanting to spare himself that pain.

But I also viscerally understood the other side of that equation for the first time. Just because I didn't care about Michael that way anymore didn't mean I didn't care about him, period. I did—so much that losing him all over again felt like a fresh wound ripped into my chest. I hoped that one day, when the feelings weren't so raw, we could try again to be friends. Until then I'd have to learn all over again how to live without him—at least for a while. I had to respect his choice, even though it wasn't mine.

But what *was* my choice was my friendship with Ben, I'd realized in the darkest hours of the night. Winston lay stretched out on the floor beside my bed on an old blanket I'd folded into fourths, his eyes shining back up at mine in the filtered moonlight every time I angled my head over to look at him, as if worried that if he shut them, he'd wake to find himself back in his concrete kennel in the shelter, all of this a dream.

I could understand what Michael had to do because I felt the same way with Ben—I couldn't bear to watch him be so happy with Per...with Pamela when I still ached for him.

But the alternative was to cut him out of my life completely. And like Michael and me, at the core of what Ben and I had once had was a solid friendship. Now that I knew directly how much it could hurt for someone to rip that away, I couldn't make myself do it to Ben.

Yes, it might tear my heart out of my chest to see him and Pamela grow closer, to say goodbye when they left to travel across the world together and work side by side. It might feel like my guts were being eviscerated when they came back, maybe got married...had kids.

Or maybe by then my feelings would finally have faded enough to let me truly be happy for him—for the two of them—and be part of both their lives, the family friend who'd turn up now and then for parties and dinners and occasional holidays. Auntie Brook.

The idea made everything in me contract. But one day it wouldn't.

And until that day, I decided as the sky began to lighten outside my window, I could choose to still have Ben in my life on some level— even if it were so much less than I wanted. Even if it meant I had to figure out a way to cope with the hurt of it until it finally went away.

And that was when I called him.

My hand shook as I pressed "call" on my phone early that Sunday morning.

"Hi," came the familiar voice, curling around me like a fleece blanket on a cold night. Ben sounded surprised.

"Hi." The single syllable shook, and I cleared my throat. "I wanted to let you know I can't make it to Dog Beach today."

There was a long silence, and then: "Okay. I figured."

"But I wondered if you and Jake would come to Lakes Park instead? There's...someone I really want you to get to know."

This time the silence stretched so long, I thought he'd hung up. I knew when I'd called that there was a good chance he'd say no.

"Please, Ben," I added quietly. "It's important to me."

I heard him take in a breath, then let it out, and then: "Okay, Brook. What time?"

Chapter Twenty-eight

As early as I arrived to Lakes Park, when I pulled into the same parking area where, weeks ago, I'd picked up Jake, Ben's greenish-gray SUV was already snugged into an end spot closest to the grills and picnic tables.

The park was otherwise empty except for one lone figure out in an open grassy area to the left where the city often offered outdoor concerts and shows. A man was bent over something on the St. Augustine grass—a kite, I realized when I saw him start to run, facing backward, the old-fashioned diamond-shaped paper kite lofting up a dozen feet into the air before arcing around and diving back to the ground.

I heard the sound of a car door and yanked my gaze back to Ben's vehicle, where one long, jeans-clad leg was exiting the driver's-side door. I drove closer as he stood and turned, hearing my engine.

His face was tight, I saw through the windshield, but as he watched me park the harsh shadows bracketing his eyes and mouth softened; then he simply looked confused. By the time I stepped out on my side he was bending to look into the window, and I could see the smile that touched his mouth.

"Who's this?" he asked as I came around.

"This," I said, leaning close to open the passenger door, "is Winston." My new companion stepped gracefully out, already leashed, and sat regarding Ben. "We met a couple of weeks ago, but we just claimed each other yesterday."

He straightened, turning to me. "You got a dog?"

I angled a smile down at my new companion. "I did. I wasn't sure I was ready...but then I was."

Ben kept his gaze on me for a long moment, then looked back down at the dog. "It's nice to meet you, Winston," he said directly to him.

The dog raised one black-and-brown paw as if offering it to be kissed, and I laughed.

"Wow! You've already trained him?" Ben asked, leaning down to take his paw for a shake before releasing it.

"I can't take any credit. He came to me as a perfect gentleman."

As Ben scratched his ears, Winston leaned obligingly against his hand, but stayed planted where he was. "He's so well-behaved. Kind of the anti-Jake," he said with a slight laugh, but then he sobered, glancing up at me. "I guess that's why you picked him."

"No. He picked me." I glanced over to Ben's SUV. "I thought it might do him some good to meet Jake, actually. I think Winston's a little afraid to let go. Worried that if he isn't perfect I might not want him." Affection for this creature I'd known for such a short time flooded me. There was a reason we'd ended up together. "I thought Dog Beach might be a bit much till he's a little more used to his new life, but I hoped Jake could show him how to let loose a little."

Ben grinned. "That's sort of his forte. I'll let him out."

As soon as he did Jake went wild, nearly pulling Ben back around the vehicle to investigate this new friend, and then bunny-hopping in a semicircle around Winston as he barked excitedly in his face. Winston simply gazed off into the tree line, as if pretending none of it were happening.

"See what I mean?" I said. "I'm afraid he's a little *too* good. He doesn't let himself be a dog."

Ben shook his head. "Actually, I think this is how an adult dog trains a puppy—or a crazy dog," he said, glancing fondly at Jake. "Sort of how a parent ignores a child's tantrum. Want to walk them and see what happens?"

Ben's mom had taught me that packs integrated by migrating together, and that the surest way to introduce two dogs was by taking them for a long walk. At the thought of her sad expression the night she and Ben had seen me with Michael, regret panged my chest. There had been a pretty big part of me that had wanted to claim Adelaide forever, for all the warmth and easy affection she'd once lavished on me that my own more reserved mom didn't.

But that was okay, I reminded myself. Maybe I could be friends again with Adelaide too. One day.

We headed off toward the trail that ran through the melaleuca and oak and banyan trees ringing the park, Winston and I in the lead and Jake and Ben following close behind. As we walked, Jake kept his head pressed close to Winston's rear end, dipping it frequently to catch the other dog's back leg in his jaws and nibble like it was a chicken bone, trying to entice Winston to engage.

Which he finally did, rearing around with a growl and a show of teeth that made my heart stutter a beat before he turned blithely to trot on beside me.

"Whoa," I said, pulling him back to my side. "Sorry. I didn't think he was aggressive, but I can—"

"Doggie politics," Ben said behind me. "If he'd wanted to hurt Jake he would have. Let's see if they work it out."

When the path opened a bit wider Ben came up alongside me, and after a few moments Jake fell into step on his other side, so that both dogs flanked the two of us. We walked for a long time like that, the only sounds our feet and paws scraping against the dirt trail, the soft flutelike notes of a nearby mourning dove, and a chorus of random bird tweets as background.

Ben looked over at me and winked. "Maybe Winston's the best thing that ever happened to Jake. Look how calm he is."

Jake was walking alongside Ben, facing straight ahead, not pulling or yanking the leash for a change, executing a near-perfect "heel" I'd never seen any indication he had in his repertoire.

We walked until we reached a little bridge that crossed a small stream and led deeper into the park, a bench set in the clearing in front of it under a peeling red gumbo-limbo.

"Let's sit for minute and see how they do now," Ben suggested.

As soon as we stopped, Jake shot straight over to Winston, and this time my dog touched noses with him, then sat and let Jake thrust his nose into his ear, checking things out. After a moment Winston got up and moved away, coming closer to me, and Jake dropped his giant body to the ground with a sigh, his head on his paws, gazing at Winston with distant longing. But he stayed put.

"Not bad," I said to Ben, who had settled beside me on the bench. But my grin melted away as soon as I realized how close he was sitting. So close I could feel the warmth of his leg radiating against mine. So close that if I shifted just the tiniest bit, I'd be leaning against his shoulder as though we were lovers.

I turned my head back toward the dogs in front of us and closed my eyes for a moment. I could handle this.

Ben's voice rumbled up into the silence. "When you said you wanted me to meet someone, I thought you meant your ex-fiancé."

My eyes opened. "You...Oh," I said, realizing how my words must have sounded. "And you came anyway?"

He raised a shoulder, watching as Jake inched closer to a disinterested Winston. "You asked me to."

"Oh." My heart pinched again. Why would it be awkward for him? As far as Ben was concerned he and I were friends. It was only me who was still wrestling deeper feelings.

This was going to be harder than I thought. Did Michael have the right idea after all—to put some distance between us until he could be around me without this pull of longing that was threatening to choke me?

I took a breath and then swallowed away the tightness in my throat, determined to try. "He's leaving, actually," I said in an admirably steady voice.

"Leaving?"

I nodded. "Town. Turns out...well, he wanted to try again with the two of us."

"I see." Ben's voice was devoid of inflection, but I didn't trust myself to look at him. "And you?"

I shrugged, still facing forward. "That's why he's leaving. I didn't."

"Oh." The single syllable floated up toward the trees and was lost amid birdsong. "Why not?" he asked after a time.

I slid a quick glance toward him to try to read his expression, but he was looking at the dogs too, neither of us facing the other.

Here was where a friendship with Ben butted up against limitations. If this were Sasha I'd spill everything—how even if I'd wanted them not to, my feelings for Michael had died, at least in that way. And how, as desperately as I wanted them to, my feelings for Ben had not.

But I wasn't in love with Sasha. With Sasha I wouldn't be risking my dignity by telling her how I felt—and I wouldn't be risking her happiness by loading her up with guilt over all the things she didn't feel for me anymore when she was happily in love with someone else.

It wasn't fair to tell Ben all of that. Not when he had no idea that I was still mired in emotions for him that he'd long since left behind. Not when it was my decision and my actions that had set that ball rolling in the first place.

So all I said was, "He's not the person I want to be with."

I didn't wait for an answer to my comment—I only had so much willpower, and if we kept sitting here in the romantic, isolated cathedral of trees that surrounded us, I'd be lying across Ben's lap any second now, wailing out my feelings like a Hallmark special and begging him to love me back. Instead I stood, and Winston got to his feet as well. Jake scrambled up as he did, surging toward my dog, but Winston fixed him with a scaly eye, and Jake's butt plopped back down on the ground.

Ben was smiling. "I may have to borrow your dog now and then. I think he's good for mine."

"Sure," I said, rallying a buddy-buddy *Anytime, pal* grin. "Ready to go back?"

Ben stood, looking oddly at me. "I am."

We walked back the way we'd come, Jake's nose to Winston's tail like Hannibal's elephants, Ben and I walking in amiable silence through the sunlight-dappled forest—until he broke it.

"Pamela got the Doctors Without Borders job," he said conversationally.

I tried not to whoosh out air, but I heard it escaping me in a hiss. I'd known this was coming, and here it was.

"That's great!" I said, my voice sounding creaky and thin with no breath behind it. "You guys are going to have a...a life-changing experience together." It actually hurt to swallow past the lump in my throat, but I pushed it down and stretched a smile onto my face. "I really wish you the best, Ben. You deserve to be happy." My steps felt like the march of a wooden soldier.

"I told her no."

Again the air left me in a rush, and this time I stopped, bending over and grabbing my knees to catch my breath as if I'd taken a basketball in the stomach.

"Brook! Are you okay?" Ben was at my side in a second, a hand on my back. Winston's black nose came into my field of vision, popping his head around to make sure I was all right, while Jake thrust his face into my private regions as if trying to prop me up from behind.

"What?" I eked out.

His hand was warm on the small of my back, and I shivered as his fingers moved ever so slightly across the bare skin where my t-shirt rode up. "Africa. I'm not going."

My heart started to thud. I was misunderstanding him. I had to be. "Long-distance dating's going to be hard," I fished, unwilling to believe what I thought my ears were hearing and make a fool of myself yet again.

"Yes," he agreed, and my heart flopped limply to the bottom of my chest cavity. "Except that we're not dating anymore."

This time I sort of collapsed to the dirt into a cross-legged sit. Jake naturally took this as an invitation to lapdoggery, draping himself across my right thigh, while Winston lay pressed against my left.

Bolstered by doggie bookends. Ben looked down at me calmly as I sat on the forest floor, staring up at him. "What?" I croaked.

He was watching me like a scientist eyeballing a lab monkey. "We broke things off the night you surprised us in the kitchen."

"Two *weeks* ago?" I yelped. And then: "Because you wouldn't go to Africa with her?"

"That was part of it," he admitted. "But not all of it."

"Then...why?" My heart thudded, afraid to hope.

He lowered himself beside me on the mulched path, watching me steadily the whole time. "She wasn't the person I wanted to be with," he echoed my words.

Goose bumps took over every inch of my body as what he'd said sank in. Followed by an unexpected wave of affront. "Were you going to tell me that?" I demanded.

The skin bracketing his eyes crinkled in amusement. "Eventually. Not while you were dating your ex, probably."

"I wasn't dating him! It was *you* I wanted!"

"How was I supposed to know that? You never said."

"Because I was trying to respect *your* relationship! You were happy, and I didn't want to screw things up for you or make you feel guilty by telling you that I didn't want to move on with anyone else because I'm still in love with *you*," I accused.

His eyebrows shot upward. "You are?" he said.

"And anyway, I thought it wasn't any of your business," I plowed on, feeling my cheeks catch fire. "I thought you didn't care."

A grin crept over his face. "I lied."

Slowly he reached one hand over and brushed the backs of his fingers against my cheek, my heart trip-hammering in my chest. Then he reached farther, into my hair and to the back of my neck, and pulled me in toward him, over Jake's oblivious prone body between us, angling his own body closer.

His lips on mine were warm and soft and achingly, wondrously familiar.

...

The sun was high in the sky when we finally walked out of the woods, all of us together, my fingers linked through Ben's and the dogs walking side by side like well-trained little soldiers.

As we came back out to the edge of the field, I saw the solitary figure at the other end still working valiantly to launch his kite. He'd finally gotten it airborne, but it shuddered uncertainly twenty or thirty feet in the air behind his running form. This was the crucial part of flying a kite, I remembered from lessons with my mom and dad at the beach when Stu and I were kids. When it was fighting the air currents low to the ground it could go one of two ways: plunging back down to crash into the dirt, or lofting up and riding the gentler currents higher up.

We walked toward our vehicles, Ben and I both watching as the kite dipped, froze for a moment, and then launched high into the air, sailing smoothly into the sky overhead.

Chapter Twenty-nine

We all gathered for Sunday dinner at my parents' house—me, Sasha and Stu...and Ben.

"Of course he's welcome, Brook Lyn," my mom said when I'd called to make sure she was okay with one extra mouth at the table. Though I could tell she was trying to conceal it, I could hear the surprise in her tone. It had been a long time since I'd brought anyone to family dinner. "It'll be a pleasure to finally meet this boy."

Dad shook Ben's hand at the door, welcoming him inside, and Mom greeted him with a hug.

A *hug*. Once again I had to wonder whether my mother had some terminal illness she wasn't telling us about.

Ben pitched right in, asking what he could do to help, and Mom assigned him plate duty—bringing the dishes over while she filled them with meat loaf, potatoes, and Brussels sprouts, and taking them to the table while Sasha and I poured drinks, and Stu got out the cloth napkins at Mom's directive.

The good linens meant that Mom knew Ben was special.

One thing that hadn't changed was the weekly download routine—where Mom grilled each of us kids on our week as we sat to eat, this time starting with me.

I told everyone about losing the radio show, and even my mom expressed sympathy. "But that's okay," I said. "Maybe this will open up other opportunities."

"Good attitude, hon," my dad praised me.

Ben was to my left, and I expected Mom to skip over him. To my surprise, she nodded down the table at him and said, "So, Ben, I hear you're a builder. What's the latest in your business?"

Mom was never my confidante—for dating or anything else—and I couldn't remember when I might have mentioned Ben's business to her. Maybe I had, or maybe it was Sasha—the two of them often seemed far closer than Mom and I usually found a way to be. Either way, it warmed my heart that she remembered.

Ben leaped right into the swing of things, briefly telling my family about his thoughts on repurposing the abandoned Seaboard railroad tracks through town, and that he'd already started drawing up a proposal to submit to the city.

"That's a very civic-minded project to take on," Mom said. "It's good to leave the world a little better than you found it."

I smiled inwardly at the advice she'd drilled into me and Stu since we were kids, thinking about how Ben had found a way to change the world after all—just a little closer to home. Thank God.

As if reading my thoughts, he found my hand under the table and squeezed.

When it was Stu's turn, my brother was uncharacteristically brief—"Same old for now, Ma," he said with a wink.

Mom pursed her lips—glibness was not okay at Sunday dinners—but out of deference to our guest, I was sure, she simply moved on to Sasha. "What's going on at the paper these days?"

Sasha had stopped eating, her hands in her lap under the table. She looked nervous, and suddenly the breath froze in my throat. "Well, I got an offer from the *Tampa Trib* that would mean a big promotion for me," she said hesitantly.

My heart dropped to my feet.

That was it. She'd made her final decision.

I'd sworn to support her and I would, but it would have been so much easier to have some time to absorb her choice alone, without having to paste a false smile on my face in front of my parents...in front of Ben, who still didn't know anything about my brother and Sasha's situation.

"Sweetheart, that's fantastic!" Dad said.

Mom was frowning. "You're moving?"

"Not exactly," Sash said, resting her chin in one palm and drumming her fingers against her cheek.

"Oh, my lord," my mother said in a strangely hushed voice. Sasha knew better than to put elbows on the table, but Mom castigating her for it was the least of my concerns at the moment.

And then I saw what my mother had seen—the glittering stone on Sasha's fourth finger. My heart stuttered in my chest, then resumed its beating triple-time.

"I asked Sasha to get hitched," Stu said, a wide grin splitting his face. "And by some unknown miracle, she said yes."

The table exploded around me, but all I could do was sit motionless, cocooned in a bubble of shock.

Across the table Sasha met my eyes, never pulling her gaze from mine as she went on: "And there's one other thing. There's going to be a new Ogden in about seven months."

This time I covered my mouth with my hands as everyone once again exploded into chaos. Sasha caught my eye and gave the tiniest of nods.

Dad was congratulating the two of them, lit up like the Rockefeller tree, while Mom tried hard to come up with something about doing things in the proper order and not jumping the gun, but she couldn't suppress the smile—full teeth—that took over her face. Ben added his congratulations before sliding a glance to me, his expression suddenly turning concerned.

"Brook Lyn, what's the matter with you?" my mom asked, startling me.

Tears—one more thing on the list of many that I was learning I couldn't control—coursed down my cheeks, and I still sat with my hands over my trembling mouth like a speak-no-evil monkey. I lowered them, reminding myself that as far as anyone besides Sasha and Stu knew, this was the first I'd heard of any of this. "I'm just...happy for you guys. I'm so happy." My voice choked on the last word, and Mom's gaze on me narrowed.

"Since when are you so sentimental?" she said.

"Sometimes people can surprise you," Sasha answered for me, but her eyes stayed glued on mine.

I held her gaze, unable to do anything more than nod.

•••

After dinner, when the excitement of Sasha and Stu's announcement had finally ebbed to a throbbing hum, Dad invited Ben to see his woodworking shop in the garage, and Stu bailed on clearing the table with me and Sasha to join them.

"Daddy made me that rocking chair on my back porch," I told Ben as they filed toward the garage, and then looked over to my dad. "I use it all the time. Just to sit and relax," I told him.

My father winked at me, as if understanding all that I didn't say. "Looks like I gotta start a new chair now, so my daughter-in-law can rock my grandbaby," he said with a glance to my mom, and to my surprise she sidled over next to him and wrapped her arms around his waist. As I set two dishes I carried on the counter (because God forbid we stack them at Mom's house—"This isn't a diner!"), I saw him squeeze her close, and she shut her eyes and pressed her face into his chest for the barest moment.

I didn't know what had happened to bring them back together so tightly, but whatever it was, I was grateful.

He kissed the top of her head and let her go, and Mom dove into the dishes like a porpoise into a school of fish. As the boys trekked out toward the garage I grabbed a towel to dry, and Sasha stood ready to put everything away, but Mom made a shooing motion without looking up at us.

"That's enough—all these people in my kitchen. Go on, you two—give me some space here."

Being excused from cleanup duties was unprecedented, but Sasha and I weren't about to question it. We absconded out to my parents' lanai, settling onto adjacent chaises facing the pool. The canal leading out to the Caloosahatchee beyond it revealed itself in the purple evening only in the splashes of illumination from dock lights dotting its length, and the almost inaudible lapping of its calm waters.

"I'm sorry," Sasha said to me in the quiet darkness.

I angled a disbelieving glance at her. "Sorry? For what?"

"I know it hurt your feelings that I didn't tell you first."

I shrugged indifferently. "No, it didn't."

"Liar," she retorted, and I had to laugh.

"Yeah, okay. It did. But I get it."

"You do?"

"I know I made things harder on you while you were figuring all this out."

Sasha shook her head. "No. That's not it at all. It's just..." She glanced up toward the kitchen window, where we could see the top of my mom's head as she attacked the dishes with exceptional fervor. "I always thought that when the time came for something like this, I'd do some big wonderful announcement to you, just the two of us. But I kind of blew that," she said wryly. "And then I realized I wanted us to share it with the whole family."

A smile plucked at my lips at her words. We'd always seen Sasha as part of our family, but this was the first time she seemed to really believe that we were hers.

"Sash...are you sure about this?" I said, keeping my voice pitched low.

She looked at me with one skeptical eyebrow raised. "After spending weeks trying to convince me I'm ready, now you're trying to unconvince me?"

"Not at all. It's just...what changed?"

Sasha looked out toward the dark slash of my parents' yard where it dropped off to the canal. "Nothing," she said finally.

I puzzled over that for a moment—it was the same answer my dad had given me when I asked him what he expected me to do while I rocked in the chair he'd made me.

"You mean you just relaxed and leaned into it?" I ventured.

Sasha snorted. "Oh, hell, no. I'm still scared shit— witless." She rolled her eyes at me. "I guess I have to start cleaning up the language. Anyway, ever since the night I came over to your house...after Lisa...Stu and I have really *talked*. And it turns out he's terrified too."

I shook my head. "But how does that help?"

She shrugged. "I was so freaked out. But he seemed like this was no big deal. And that was freaking me out even more—like he didn't see what I was seeing: how huge this is, what a responsibility, how much can go wrong. But it turns out he has even more disaster scenarios than I do! I had no idea how many possible birth defects and disabilities are out there. And do you know how many women die in childbirth or experience serious complications? It's horrific!" she said, but her tone was upbeat.

"And this magically assuaged your fears how...?" I asked, frowning.

She beamed, spreading her hands, palms up. "In no way whatsoever! I'm completely terrified! We both are!"

"Of course you are," I said without thinking. "Any decent prospective parent in their right mind *would* be."

I wanted to chew off my own tongue. Sasha had finally come around to everything I'd hoped so desperately to convince her of, and I was saying the exact wrong thing.

"Exactly," she murmured, her smile softening to something almost beatific.

And I got it.

I reached over into the space between us, my hand extended, and Sasha took it. "You two are going to be more than decent parents."

"We'll see," she said. "We can't do worse than *my* mom and dad. And we've got an awfully good example in yours," she said, tipping her chin toward the house. She looked away again, out over the light-studded canal, then looked down at her lap. "You know, for all the things I worried I'd have to give up by having kids...the one thing I couldn't imagine losing was Stu." She shrugged again. "As long as we're doing this together, everything else will fall into place."

My heart swelled, even as it broke a little for what Sasha was having to let go of. "I'm sorry about Tampa," I said softly.

She looked up at me, and I was startled to see her still smiling. "Don't be. At Stu's suggestion I asked about work-sharing the position with another writer, and the *Trib* was open to it. Looks like I'll be working there part-time...and Stu's hiring a project manager for his company so he can stay home with the spawn on the days I'm in Tampa." She rested a hand on her flat belly.

My brother, a stay-at-home dad? I marveled. Part-time or not, I'd never imagined it.

Just a couple of years ago our lives had all been on predictable, steady paths I'd thought they'd continue on indefinitely: I was blithely content in my old therapy practice, heading toward marriage with a man I thought I wanted to spend my life with; Sasha had one disastrous date after another as she searched for someone worthy of giving her heart to; Stu was working through a string of girls quickly enough to guarantee he'd never give his to any of them.

None of us were anywhere we thought we'd end up.

And yet...

I heard the glass door sliding open, and Stu and Ben came outside.

Scooting over, I made room for Ben on the chaise next to me as Stu slung a leg behind Sasha and settled in behind her.

"What are you two doing out here?" Ben asked.

I glanced over at my brother and my best friend, nestled back-to-front with his arms cocooned around her, resting on her belly. The warmth of Ben's hand wrapped around mine seeped inside me as I leaned closer into him.

"Nothing," I said.

We sat silent in the comforting blanket of night, all of us listening to the steady nasal honking of a cane toad by the water, smelling the musky marine scent of the river, and feeling the mild tropical breeze against our skin.

...

It was strange that I'd never seen the monthly rental where Michael had been staying on San Carlos Island. It had never even occurred to me to come over.

Nestled in a tiny lot right on the back bay, the little cracker house was small, but charming, painted a sunny peach, with awnings in cheery stripes of green and white. A well-tended green lawn cocooned the house on all sides, leading back to the best part: a dock of weathered gray wood where a brand-new folding chair testified to Michael spending time sitting beside the water he loved.

I was glad to see that he'd been staying someplace nice. Even if he wasn't staying any longer.

I'd gotten his call earlier today—he was headed out, back to Portland, and if I had a minute to stop by he'd like to say goodbye.

Of course I said yes.

When he opened the glossy wooden front door at my knock, his face was slightly flushed and shiny in the bright sun, his hair tousled and hanging into his eyes, the way it used to at the end of a long gig when he'd been giving it up onstage for two hours. His gray t-shirt clung lightly against sweat-damp skin to a body I'd once known as well as my own. Two suitcases behind him in the entryway testified to his imminent departure, and a lump clogged my throat. I wished he didn't have to go, but I understood why he did.

"Hi," he said.

"Hi."

We stood there looking awkwardly at each other. Now, despite all that we'd been through together, with nowhere for us to go it seemed there was nothing left to say.

"You're all packed?" I said stupidly, gesturing to the luggage piled in the front hall, and he shrugged.

"Didn't have much." Again we stood there in an uncomfortable silence, Michael just inside the door, me standing on the porch, the grating shriek of a seagull high overhead plucking at my nerves.

Finally I let out a nervous chuckle. "I'm glad you called. I was hoping to see you one—" I stopped before uttering "one last time." "Well...to say goodbye in person."

He shoved his hands into the pockets of his faded jeans, staring at me. "Yeah. And also...I wanted to tell you something."

My heart seized for a beat before resuming its rhythm. Whatever it was he needed to say to me, I would hear it. I owed him that, no matter how hard it might be for me to listen. "Okay."

He met my gaze for another long, steady moment before turning abruptly and grabbing his two suitcases. Straightening, he stepped back toward me and the door, pausing on the threshold as I stepped back to allow him past and turning to face me fully.

"The radio station called. They want you back. Your own show this time."

It took a second for his words to sink in—I'd been braced for something totally different—and when they did, I couldn't quite believe them. "Are you serious?"

He dipped his head. "I heard this morning, but I was hoping to tell you in person. Congrats, Brook. You deserve it."

Propelled along on a bubble of excitement rising up in me, I'd have thrown myself forward and hugged him if his hands hadn't been full with the suitcases.

Which, I realized, was probably his intention.

Instead I just let the smile taking me over have its way with my face. "You really are great at this," I said. "I would never have pursued it without you."

He nodded once in acknowledgment, his lips still sagging downward, then walked on past me toward his car with the luggage in hand. "Keep it up," he said over his shoulder. "What you do for people...you need to get the word out there." I stepped off the porch and onto the walkway, semi-following him out toward the driveway. "A lot of us need it," I thought he said as he set the bags down behind his car, but wasn't sure amid the soft crunch of the suitcases on the crushed-shell drive and the sound of the trunk of his car clicking open.

As I watched him lift the bags into the back, I wanted to say something, to let him know how important he had been to me, and in some ways would always be. "I love you" seemed cruel, even though it was true.

"Michael," I called as he pushed the trunk shut.

He turned, arms at his sides, waiting.

"I just want you to know...I'm so grateful. For everything."

He lifted one eyebrow in a dear and familiar gesture, skepticism quirking one corner of his lips. "Everything?"

I thought of all that had happened in the last two years, good and bad. Thought about what I'd been through, and where I was, and nodded. "Yes. All of it. Thank you."

His eyes crinkled at the corners as a slow smile crept across his face, chasing away the sadness tugging at his features, and I felt an answering one stretch my own cheeks. We stood there like that, two survivors grinning at each other across the battlefield, until he stepped into his car, started the engine, and shut the door.

I waved him down the street until I couldn't see him anymore, and then I turned to get inside my own car, headed back to the mainland and the life that was waiting for me there.

[Sneak peek at *Out of Pratice*,
book #4 in the Breakup Doctor series]

Chapter One

"For god's sake, Ashley—we can't have side boob on daytime TV."

The pretty blond wardrobe girl crouching in front of me with her hand in my cleavage frowned at the comment barked over at us from behind one of the cameras. I worried she'd pierce a lip on the open safety pin clenched in her teeth.

"Forty years of *The Young and the Restless* begs to differ, Rob," Ashley muttered under her breath. She drew together the opening of my silk blouse that wouldn't stay up under the weight of the lavalier mic attached to it, retrieving the pin and glancing up at me. "I'm going behind the placket, but I can do it with toupee tape if you're worried about a hole."

I managed a smile as she held the fabric over my modest C-cups that had caused all this ruckus two minutes before we were going live. "The pin is fine." I was less afraid of a hole in my shirt than I was of the director calling "action" while Ashley was head-down in my chest. I was nervous enough about being on television—the last thing I needed was to look like a joke.

Ashley finished just as Melissa Overton, the host of *Wake Up, Southwest Florida!*, slid back into her chair on the soundstage from a quick huddle with Rob, the show's director, during the commercial break. She shot me a blinding Crest Whitestrips smile and a thumbs-up.

"You ready for this, Brook?" she asked.

I took a breath and worked a smile onto my face. "As I'm going to be. Hey, Melissa...thanks again," I said.

"Brook, believe me, this is totally going to be my pleasure."

A shard of wariness shot through me, like the tingling of a phantom limb.

Melissa and I had a history. Both lifelong Fort Myers natives and homeroom classmates all throughout school by virtue of our alphabetical proximity, we'd had a falling-out in high school when she slept with my tenth-grade boyfriend while I was busy trying to decide whether to go all the way with him.

As it turned out, she'd done me a favor—Jack Andrews dropped her like a hot rock, with a public snubbing at the football game the very next day and a series of nasty rumors that had haunted Melissa our junior and senior years. She was convinced I'd started them, though everyone else knew it was Jack who'd kissed and told in the most graphic ways. Yet she'd blamed me for the whole business, and she'd been Public Frenemy Number One when we were younger.

I took another deep breath and shook off the flare of nerves. High school was a long time ago, and Melissa had been nothing but helpful and excited since her phone call a few weeks ago inviting me onto the local morning show she now hosted, for a feature on my Breakup Doctor practice.

She leaned close, putting a reassuring hand on mine as if reading my mind. "Don't worry. I'm just going to lob a couple of softballs and then we'll get into the practice, et cetera. Relax—this is going to be fun."

I nodded gratefully as she leaned back at the director's voice: "In five, four..." As I'd watched him do after every commercial break, he broke off on "three" and counted the rest down with his fingers, pointing at Melissa on "one."

"Wake up, southwest Florida—we're back!" Melissa chirped into the camera, flashing that halogen smile again. "And hold on to your coffee cups; we've got a little something special for you this morning. You might've read her column in the *Tropic Times*; maybe you've heard her on the radio on her afternoon call-in program Fridays on KXAR. Brook Ogden calls herself the Breakup Doctor, a specialist in advice to the lovelorn, treating people when they're at their most vulnerable—fresh off of heartbreak. Brook, welcome to the show!"

I thought my weekly on-air advice show had prepared me for this, but radio, I found out when the red light lit up on the camera directly opposite me, was not nearly as stressful as TV. Hot lights shone down from every angle, two cameras trained their unblinking black eyes on me, and a dozen people stood around the soundstage staring directly at me as if I were about to do a trick. All the saliva fled my mouth like a retreating tide, and my smile shook at the edges.

"Morning, Melissa. It's actually a counseling practice; I'm a therapist, and I—"

"You help people 'shape up after a breakup'—isn't that your catchy tagline?" She was facing me, and winked with her upstage eye, out of range of the camera. I relaxed infinitesimally—she was the pro, and I could just follow her lead.

"That's right," I said. "I specialize in relationships."

Melissa nodded sagely. "Let's talk about that. What kind of training goes into that specialty?"

"Well, after my bachelor's degree I completed—"

Melissa held up one perfectly manicured hand with a smile. "No, no—I mean specifically for relationship counseling."

I stared at her. "All counseling is actually rela—"

"Brook," Melissa cut me off, "are you avoiding the question?"

"Of course not. It's just that—"

"Then can you just tell us where you received your official training specifically in counseling people through breakups?"

I spread my hands, palms up. "Melissa, there *is* no certified training specifically for that, as far as I know."

Her eyebrows lifted. "Are you saying you've never even looked into it? Or that you're just sort of making it up as you go along? Or both?"

I tried not to laugh. "Neither. I mean, that's not exactly—"

"Okay, well, let's leave that for now. I understand you've gone through some difficult breakups yourself?" Her face was full of sympathy.

I squelched a flare of annoyance. Melissa wasn't half the interviewer I knew Sasha to be. My best friend would have made this interview flow like silk if this were one of her articles.

But Melissa was just trying to dig for a juicy story, like any TV interviewer would. I mustered up a smile.

"That's right, Melissa. Like pretty much all of us, I've had my share of heartbreak. That's actually what led me to this line of work, and I think it's a big part of what makes me successful at what I do."

She leaned forward, looking fascinated. "Tell me about that—how so?"

"Well, for starters, it certainly creates a lot of empathy." I laughed, but Melissa didn't join in. "You know...I think it makes me more able to understand what my clients are going through," I clarified. "And how it feels. How hard it can be to climb out of that pain on your own. How you sometimes can turn into someone you don't recognize, do things you would never imagine doing."

She nodded thoughtfully, hanging on my every word. "Right. Let's talk about that. You got left at the altar yourself, didn't you?"

Melissa had said we'd talk a little about my own relationship background, but I hadn't realized she'd go into specifics. "Not at the altar, no. But you're right, my former fiancé did end things fairly abruptly a month before our wedding. But that was a long time ago, and since then he and I have—"

"You got right back in the saddle, though, didn't you?"

Was she talking about Kendall? Kendall was a blip, a nothing, merely the final block that unbalanced my precarious Jenga psyche at the time. I wasn't going into that on television.

"If you mean that I recovered eventually and started dating again, yes, I did," I said, forcing myself to smile calmly at her. "In fact, at the moment I'm—"

Melissa turned away from me and smiled brightly into the camera. "We've actually got a picture of how that worked out...Rob?"

The red light on my camera winked out and I spun to look behind me, trying to see what photo Melissa had dug up, but the curtained background was just as it had been when I sat down. I darted my gaze around the soundstage, and when I saw the group of people standing off-camera with their eyes trained in the same direction, I followed their line of sight to a monitor.

I remembered that night with a horrific clarity even without the awful picture of me now emblazoned on the screen. After my spectacular breakup breakdown when my rebound ex, Kendall, dumped me via text message, I finally chased him down and demanded answers. The picture showed the culmination of that ill-advised night: me flat on my ass on the bricked patio of a busy downtown bar, sitting where I'd fallen in a puddle of spilled drinks and broken glass after Kendall had literally pushed me away, my face contorted as I screamed at him in the middle of a crowd at the Bar Belle, who looked on with varying expressions of pity, horror, and amusement.

I looked insane.

I'd seen Melissa downtown that Friday night as I tore from bar to bar in my frenzied hunt. She'd thrown her usual barbs my way, and in my precarious state of mind I'd lashed out with something cutting about the DUI that had lost her her last TV job. And then I didn't think another moment about her as I ran Kendall to ground.

But now I remembered seeing a glimpse of her hot-pink knit dress in the crowd at the Bar Belle as I was escorted off the premises. I remembered the smirk on her face. The way she'd held up her phone and waggled it at me with a smile as I scowled at her, uncomprehending.

She'd taken this photo.

I frantically searched the soundstage, wishing I'd brought someone with me so I'd have at least one friendly face amid the sea of eyes now staring flatly at me. Even Ashley the nice wardrobe girl had turned away.

Melissa was making a comically exaggerated "uh-oh" expression into the camera. "Whoopsie! I guess you weren't kidding about doing things you wouldn't usually do! At least, I hope not!" She tinkled a merry laugh.

I shook my head, reaching blindly to the lavalier mike clipped at the vee of my blouse. "This isn't what you—"

"Hang on now, Brook—don't run out on us just yet!" She smiled guilelessly in my direction, and when the red light flashed on I dropped my hand. Storming off the set was only going to make this worse. I was trapped, and Melissa knew it.

She swiveled and gave a plucky look to the camera, as if soldiering on despite grave setbacks. "Let's talk about your treatment with some of your patients."

I stared at her, hoping she could read the homicide in my eyes. "I call them clients," I said icily.

"Oh, like a call girl!" she said brightly, and tittered. "I understand you actually do little makeovers for them? Are you also a cosmetologist? An 'image consultant'?" She made air quotes around the term in a way that made it clear she thought such a thing was a joke.

"I don't do makeovers," I said tightly. "I have contacts who sometimes assist clients in looking and feeling their best. It can be a big help when people are at their lowest, and—"

"You really go *well* above and beyond, it sounds like." Melissa made sure that came out sounding nothing like a compliment. "We were actually able to find one of these 'clients'"—again with the mocking bunny fingers—"who's worked with you before—twice, actually, and in *two* different capacities, he says."

A sick, horrible feeling filled my belly.

"He came to you for 'Breakup Doctoring,' and also was a patient in your former *legitimate* counseling practice. Welcome, Chip Santana—thanks for joining us on air this morning."

"My pleasure, Melissa."

At the familiar rumble of that gravelly voice, I wished I'd listened to Sasha this morning when she advised me to eat a light breakfast, as my bacon and eggs flipped over with a nauseating lurch.

Chip Santana was the worst mistake I'd ever made, a walking hormone who'd plucked a primal animalistic chord in me the first time he'd walked into my old counseling practice for desperately needed anger management therapy, until I'd terminated his treatment. There was nothing good that he could possibly have to say.

"So, Chip, I understand that you've gone through counseling with Dr. Ogden?" Melissa asked the air with a rapacious grin.

"She's not a doctor," Chip's disembodied voice said, his voice overlapping mine as I automatically said the exact same thing.

Melissa made wide doe eyes. "She's *not*? Goodness."

"I'm a mental health counselor," I bit out. "As you already know. Fully licensed and trained and qualified to provide professional counseling."

I sounded defensive, and I heard it in the ringing silence that Melissa let fall as she looked at me with the kind of tragically disappointed expression I was used to receiving only from my mother.

"Tell us a little about your experiences, Chip. Was Brook able to help you?"

There was a long, slow inhalation that I knew from experience meant he'd taken a drag on a cigarette. "Well, at first, yeah—she's a great counselor, and I was making some progress with some, well, issues I was having."

Melissa frowned as if concerned. "I hate to pry or be insensitive"—*really?*—"but will you share with us what those were?"

"I don't mind, Melissa." Chip's tone implied something far more intimate, but then again, that was how he talked to almost every woman. I'd made the mistake of realizing that a little too late. "I had some temper issues. And like I said, the doc's great."

Melissa held up a hand. "She asked you to call her 'doc'?"

A chuckle, and then, "Nah, that's my nickname for her. Anyhow, it was going well till she cut off my treatment."

"Before you were ready?"

"Oh, yeah."

"And did she tell you why?"

I cringed as the heat of the dozen pairs of eyes on the soundstage crawled into me—along with those of however many viewers at home.

"Not at that time, no."

"But later?"

I couldn't let this go on. "Melissa, this is hardly on topic, and it's frankly a breach of privacy—both mine and my client's."

Melissa turned her sugar-sweet smile on me. "Now, Brook, Chip's talking to us of his own free will. And we're not discussing any of your other 'clients' specifically. And you're certainly free to end the interview if you're uncomfortable with some of these facts coming to light."

"There are no 'facts' here, Melissa," I said, my jaw tight. "This is pure sensationalism. The only *fact* is that you misled me as to the thrust of your interview and have tried to blindside me with what appears to be a premeditated smear campaign. That's bad journalism and bad ethics, and I trust your viewers, at least, are above it."

For one second I thought I'd gotten the better of her: Melissa's smug expression faltered. But just as quickly it reappeared with her catlike grin.

"So, Chip," she said, never breaking eye contact with me. "I understand you worked with the Breakup Doctor once more after your abruptly terminated treatment the first time?"

"Yep. We ran into each other at a club."

Oh, no.

"A 'club'?" Melissa asked brightly. "You mean like a book club?"

No. Nonono.

"Sort of a nightclub. An adult club, if you know what I mean."

Melissa's eyebrows rose in a parody of shock. "You mean a *sex* club?"

"Well, that's not exactly what they call it." Chip's gravelly laugh echoed around the soundstage.

"I was there with a client," I clarified tightly—then realized what I'd said just as soon as Melissa turned her wide O of a mouth on me. "I *followed* her there. To stop her from...to help her..." I trailed off miserably as Chip went on.

Of *course* he told her about my helping him make amends to the exes he'd wronged. Of course he said it "turned personal." Of course Melissa widened her eyes and turned a horrified gaze to me.

"You dated a *patient*, Brook?"

I gripped the arms of the chair. This was TV; the inquisition couldn't last forever—just till the next commercial break. All I had to do was get through the next few minutes.

"I did not. I never formally took Mr. Santana on as a client the second time—simply agreed to help as a friend. And when his..." I had to tread carefully here. Very specific others were watching too, and this was a charged area of my past. "When he stated that his feelings had grown beyond the client/therapist relationship, I took that into consideration on a personal level, yes." I concentrated on trying to will away the memory of that one disastrous night with Chip—and the horrible morning after—but my hot face told me it was telltale red. "Which was a mistake that I freely admit now, for personal reasons. But *not* an ethical violation."

"Well, that's one opinion," she said with a blithe shrug.

"That's a *fact*," I gritted out.

But morning television—at least on Melissa Overton's show, I was fast finding out—wasn't overly concerned with facts.

Too bad I hadn't realized that sooner.

...

When I checked my phone after the interview, I couldn't believe only eleven minutes had elapsed since I'd looked at it last. It felt as if I'd lost hours.

As if I'd lost a lot more than that.

Despite my best efforts to stay calm during her ambush, to rationally counter every false allegation Melissa made, I'd been fighting a losing battle. I'd seen enough election cycles to know that the truth didn't matter so much as the conviction and frequency with which a person asserted her version of it. And Melissa had been relentless with both.

I felt sick by the time she'd teased in the next segment—something about a dog and a bike that I barely heard through the blood pounding in my ears—and she held that artificial white smile till the director finally announced we were off the air. I wasted no time yanking off my mic and thrusting it blindly at Ashley, then rising to leave the set as the bustle carried on around me as though I were invisible.

But as I walked past her chair, Melissa finally turned to look at me. "Mmmm," she said, never breaking eye contact as she licked three fingers one by one. "I just love a big ice-cold dish of revenge...don't you?" She smiled—no overwhitened teeth this time, just a contemptuous curl of her lying lips. "Sooner or later, Brook, *everyone* learns not to cross my path."

I stopped dead in my tracks. I had a half dozen scathing, nasty retorts on the tip of my tongue, but instead I slowly and deliberately leaned toward her, angling over her where she sat. I was gratified when she pulled back, her cocky grin morphing into something uneasy.

"Melissa," I said with a terrible calm, "sooner or later no one's going to want to. I hope you're prepared for a lonely life."

I didn't wait to see her reaction as I turned my back on her, the set, and the scurrying crew, and walked away.

Chapter Two

"How are you?"

The question wasn't casual chitchat.

"I'm okay," I told my fiancé shakily.

The word *fiancé* had once been charged with fury and pain after my first engagement ended abruptly and without warning. Ben Garrett had transformed it into something shiny and bright and happy.

He'd called the second I pushed out of the heavy metal doors from the darkness of the television studio to the blinding southwest Florida sunshine.

"You handled it really well," he said. In the background I could hear the muted roar of construction equipment that told me he'd stepped inside the mobile RV office he took to all his company's build sites.

"It was a train wreck."

"It was rough." Ben never lied or candycoated. One of many things I loved about him. "But it could have gone a lot worse if you hadn't kept your head."

A little of the tightness in my chest eased. "Thanks."

"I wish I'd been there. You should have let me come."

"You're already up against the wire on this build. It's okay. I'm really okay."

"I know you are. But I know it had to sting too."

The prickle in my eyes let me know the morning had caught up to me, and I reached my Honda just in time, swinging myself inside and shutting the door before I let out the shudder of breath I'd been holding in. "Yeah. It did." My voice quaked, and I made no attempt to blink back the tears that crested my bottom lashes.

Ben just stayed on the phone as I pulled out of the lot, waiting with me while the pent-up rage and embarrassment of the interview funneled through me. Finally, as I eased onto beautiful palm-lined McGregor Avenue, a street that never failed to soothe me, I took a deep inhale of the river-scented air streaming in through my open window.

"Sorry about Chip Santana," I said, my voice steadier.

Ben's devastated expression when he caught me on the mortifying morning after my close encounter with Chip was something I never wanted to see—or cause—again. We'd been officially broken up at the time, but only by a few hours. It was the lowest point I'd ever been at.

"You couldn't have known." There wasn't an ounce of censure in his tone.

I pressed the phone against my cheek as if it were his hand, closing my eyes briefly. "I love you, Ben."

"Don't worry about the show," came the comforting rumble of his voice. "This'll pass. I love you."

As soon as we hung up I dialed Sasha.

"Honey, I'm so sorry," she answered without saying hello. "I caught the last half of it. Melissa's the same hateful cow she was in high school."

"She hasn't changed," I agreed. "Last half?"

"Oh, yeah, sorry. I—" A demanding wail in the background drowned her out. "Someone's in a mood," she said when it finally wound down.

"Impressive," I said. "What are you doing home with L.J.? I thought you were working today."

My best friend gave a weary sigh. "Yeah, so did I. But your mom forgot it was her day to watch him, and your brother is in a meeting with a development company he's had on the books for weeks, so...here I am."

Normally Stu would drop everything for Sasha, or for their son, L.J.—short for Little James, to differentiate him from my dad, for whom he was named. If he hadn't, I knew his meeting must be with a pretty big client for his landscaping business.

"Oh, Sash, I'm so sorry. Is it too late for you to head up to Tampa? Maybe I can swing by and grab L.J. and bring him to my office for the day."

Sasha laughed as another angry howl welled up in the background. "Unless you're doing scream therapy with your clients, I don't think that's going to work. Thanks, though. I'm about to drive the little man down to the beach. The car always knocks him out, and when he wakes up he'll be in his favorite place. What can he have to rage about then?"

A piercing cry made me pull the phone away from my ear.

"Okay," I said. "Well, call if you need anything. I'm booked till six tonight, but if I need to reschedule a client I can."

"No worries," Sasha said, as I heard the distinctive rattle of the Graco playpen she toted everywhere as easily as the high-end purses she used to sling over her shoulder. "When I can hear you over Axl Rose here, I'll call back—I want to talk about the show."

"Whenever," I said, knowing that might be later today or a few days from now. For most of our lives my best friend and I talked so often Stu would joke we should just implant our Bluetooth devices into our heads, but things had changed a lot. For us both.

It wasn't until after we'd hung up that I worried about what she'd said—my mom had forgotten it was her day to watch L.J.?

That was the second time.

Since my nephew had been born nine months ago, Mom had eagerly jumped into helping out with child care—first with Dad, so he could spend as much time as possible with his first grandbaby, and then on her own, to keep herself busy. How on earth could my precise, practical mother have simply forgotten about her grandson?

I'd built a cushion into my morning for the show and had some time before my first appointment of the day, so I detoured off McGregor and pulled into my parents' driveway. Mom's car in the open garage told me I'd caught her just about to go out.

When no one answered my knock I let myself in the front door. "Mom! It's me....Mom!"

I wandered into the house and toward the kitchen, which used to be command central for my mother. No Mom—but on one counter sat two pieces of bread directly on the granite, spread with mayo from a jar that still sat open beside them with a knife sticking out of it. Crumbs littered the countertop.

"Ma?" I called again, louder.

No reply.

In her bedroom the bed was neatly made, as it always was, the bathroom empty. I made a circuit of the house, calling for her, a tendril of unease unfurling. The garage door was open, her car in it—where could she have gone?

As I came back into the living room, I saw the sliding glass doors cracked, and I released the breath I hadn't realized I was holding. The lanai—of course.

But Mom wasn't wading in the pool, nor anywhere in the screened patio surrounding it.

"Mom!" My shout echoed off the seawall down by the canal and bounced back to me, along with my mother's voice—finally.

"Brook Lyn, why are you screaming like a banshee? I have neighbors."

I looked around, still not seeing her. "Ma?"

"Down here."

Sitting on the dock in one of the rocking chairs my dad had painstakingly handmade for the two of them was my mom, calmly rocking and looking out over the canal toward the river as placidly as Ma Kettle.

I crunched down the crushed-shell steps of the terraced walkway and rounded the chairs to face her. "Ma?" I said uncertainly. "What are you doing?"

She shrugged absently, her gaze still trained out over the water. "Nothing."

The word sliced into me and I closed my eyes for a moment.

When my dad had delivered a chair just like these to me last year—one he'd been working on for months—I'd wondered what on earth he expected me to do in it. That one-word answer had been his response—

his way of encouraging me to slow my hectic work schedule and let myself learn to be present for all life's moments that could sneak right past you if you weren't paying attention. It was such a beautiful gift, so typical of my taciturn, wise dad, and such perfect timing—though of course he'd known that.

Dad. God, I missed him every day. I couldn't imagine how much worse it must be for my mom. He'd pulled through Hodgkin's lymphoma just fine, after a course of chemo and radiation he handled as if it were just a bump in the road. But the treatment had caused one of his heart valves to swell, and without warning, months after he was out of the woods with the cancer, one night he'd gone into cardiac arrest and died in his workshop in the garage while my mother made them dinner.

It was a bitterly funny irony that my generous, loving father died of an enlarged heart.

I opened my eyes. "Mom," I said cautiously, "are you okay?"

Mom frowned and finally looked up at me. "Don't be dense, Brook Lyn. You can see I'm fine." She pushed off the chair's arms to stand up, her gaze grazing past my father's empty chair beside it. "I just wanted to sit for a minute."

"You left a mess on the counter. That's not like you."

"I was hungry and wanted a sandwich. Then I remembered we had no turkey. I wanted turkey."

"You hate turkey, Ma. You stopped buying it after Dad..." I trailed off, hating to say the words still, six months after his death.

"Well, I forgot. People forget things, Brook Lyn." She pushed past me toward the house, and I dogged her steps.

"You also forgot it's your day to watch L.J., Mom. You forgot to shut the garage door—has it been open all night?" I was talking to her back.

"Don't worry about me."

"I can't help it." I was practically panting trying to keep up with her as she let herself into the house. "Jeez, Ma, are you training for a marathon?"

She stopped and turned to me. "Watch your tone, young lady."

"Sorry. I'm just…I know this is hard on you. It's hard on all of us." We'd always thought my mom was the trunk of our family tree, but when my dad passed away we realized he'd been the roots that anchored her. Since he'd been gone she'd seemed adrift, scattered and faraway, and looking at her now my heart stitched. She looked so small and lost.

We weren't a huggy family, we Ogdens, but things had shifted for me in the last few years, and I was a lot more touchy-feely than I used to be. I stepped toward her with my arms open.

Mom took a step back.

"Brook Lyn, please. Let's not make a scene."

There was literally no one to see us except the ibises grazing the lawn, but I dropped my arms to my sides with a sharp slap against my thighs. "Fine. I was just stopping by to see if you were okay."

"Thank you. I'm fine. Now go—I have things to do."

"Okay, Ma." I leaned forward and sneaked a kiss onto her cheek before she could stop me. "I love you."

"Okay, okay. Go on," she said, shooing me toward the door. "You'll be late for school."

I stopped dead, swinging around to face her. "What did you say?"

She waved a hand in the air. "You know what I mean. Work."

"Right," I said slowly, studying her face. "I'll talk to you later. Shut the garage, okay?"

Out in the driveway I let myself into my Honda, my fingers cold despite the heat of the Florida day.

Coming October 2021:

Out of Practice
The Breakup Doctor Series #4

There's no shortage of broken hearts in Breakup Doctor Brook Ogden's successful breakup counseling practice—if love is a battlefield, then Brook is the cavalry. Luckily her own love life is in full recovery: after a long, tortuous road, she and Ben Garrett are finally headed down the aisle.

But when a local TV personality—and former frenemy—invites Brook onto her show, she's blindsided live on the air when the interview turns into an act of long-delayed revenge meant to publicly humiliate her. Brook's an expert at getting back on your feet when life knocks you down, but as the blows keep piling on—with a betrayal she never saw coming and a family crisis that threatens to pull the foundation out from under her—her confidence starts slinking away. With her clients dropping her faster than a one-night stand, suddenly the Breakup Doctor's career is in critical care.

Bedside Manners
The Breakup Doctor Series #2

Brook Ogden has never encountered a broken heart she couldn't patch together... Her counseling practice as the Breakup Doctor—on call to help you shape up after a breakup—is so busy she's expanded to offer group sessions. (Turns out there are far more than fifty ways to leave your lover.) Her radio show and advice column have made her a local celebrity, and even her personal life, after some gruesome breakups of her own, is in recovery: Ben Garrett started out as a revenge date against an ex, but has turned into so much more.

But when sizzling-hot Chip Santana, an old client she once shared a rather unprofessional midnight roll in the sand with, comes back into her life asking for her help, Brook can't say no. Yet while she's busy stitching up his relationship troubles, Chip reveals much more than a therapeutic interest in her.

In the standoff between her heart and her hormones, Brook's cool, collected Wise Therapist persona begins to crack like thrown wedding china. She's yelling at recalcitrant cheating husbands. Offering crazy advice to radio callers. She's even hugging her clients. When the situation goes critical, Brook's forced into a decision she isn't ready to make—and the Breakup Doctor has to decide what kind of casualties she's willing to accept.

Available at booksellers nationwide and online

A Little Bit of Grace
(Berkley Publishing)

Family is everything—Grace McAdams's mom must have said it to her a thousand times before she died. Before Grace's dad ran off with an aspiring actress half his age. Before only-child Grace found out she was unable to have children of her own. Before Brian—her childhood best friend, business partner, and finally her husband—dropped a "bombshell" on her in the form of her stunning new replacement.

Which means Grace now has...nothing.

Until a letter from a woman claiming to be a relative Grace never knew she had sends her on a journey—from the childhood home she had to move back into (three doors down from the happy couple) to a tropical paradise island to meet a total stranger who claims to be family. And Grace starts to uncover answers about the eccentric woman her family never mentioned: an octogenarian who writes a viral relationship-advice blog, a compulsive (and highly successful) matchmaker...and the keeper of an unimaginable family secret held for more than fifty years.

A heartfelt, funny story about family and forgiveness, starting over when the happy ending ends, and handling it all with a little bit of grace.

The Way We Weren't

(Releasing November 2021 from Berkley Publishing)

An unlikely friendship between a septuagenarian and a younger woman becomes a story of broken trust, lost love, and the unexpected blooming of hope against the longest odds.

"You trying to kill yourself, or are you just stupid?"

Marcie Malone didn't think she was either, but when she drives from Georgia to the southwestern shore of Florida without a plan and wakes up in a stranger's home, she doesn't seem to know anymore. Despondent and heartbroken over an unexpected loss and the man she thought she could count on, Marcie leaves him behind, along with her job and her whole life, and finds she has nowhere to go.

Herman Flint has seen just about everything in his seventy years living in a fading, blue-collar Florida town, but the body collapsed on the beach outside his window is something new. The woman is clearly in some kind of trouble and Flint wants no part of it—he's learned to live on his own just fine, without the hassle of worrying about others. But against his better judgment he takes Marcie in and lets her stay until she's on her feet on the condition she keeps out of his way.

As the unlikely pair slowly copes with the damages life has wrought, Marcie and Flint form an unlikely alliance that forces both to face secrets and dark truths from their past—and to decide whether to stay lost in the pain of the past or fight for healing and hope with the people they care about most.

ACKNOWLEDGMENTS

When I was an actor I was always stunned at the talent and dedication of the crew on film and commercial shoots, in theater productions, etc. These unsung heroes get none of the glory of the folks onstage, yet they're there long before the actors arrive and long after we leave, making everything possible. I feel the same way about all the people who generously help push me to create the best story I can:

My critique partners, John J. Asher, Kelly Harrell, and Amber Novak—the Penheads—all talented authors in their own right who graced me with their insight and abilities.

My agent, the indefatigable Courtney Miller-Callihan of Handspun Lit, who tirelessly championed this series into publication.

Erin George, who edited the first edition of this book with insight and grace.

Cover designer and formatter Camille Lemoine, also a brilliant author under the pen name Camilla Monk, brings a talent and vision to all my design needs that makes me look better than I have a right to.

Special thank-you to the book bloggers, reviewers, and kind fans who help get books into readers' hands; and always to readers, without whom books never come to life.

And of course, last and never least, my husband, Joel, whose faith, love, and support are safe harbor and home base. None of this means anything without you.